BROWSING COLLECTION
14-DAY CHECKOUT
No Holds • No Renewals

MARY

and the

BIRTH

of

FRANKENSTEIN

MARY

and the

BIRTH

of

FRANKENSTEIN

a novel

ANNE EEKHOUT

Translated from the Dutch by Laura Watkinson

HarperVia

An Imprint of HarperCollinsPublishers

Excerpt on page vii: Shelley, Mary. Introduction. *Frankenstein; or The Modern Prometheus*, by Shelley, Colburn and Bentley, London 1831.

Page ix: Vasalis, M. "Sprookje." *De vogel Phoenix*, A.A.M. Stols, 1947, English translation © Laura Watkinson, 2023. Reproduced by permission of Uitgeverij Van Oorschot.

HarperCollins books may be purchased for educational, business, or sales promotional use. For information, please email the Special Markets Department at SPsales@harpercollins.com.

Originally published as *Mary* in the Netherlands by De Bezige Bij in 2021.

FIRST EDITION

Designed by Yvonne Chan

Chapter-opening ornament © iku4/Shutterstock

Library of Congress Cataloging-in-Publication Data has been applied for.

ISBN 978-0-06-325674-3

23 24 25 26 27 LBC 5 4 3 2 1

For Bertram Koeleman,
a great storyteller, my great love

It was beneath the trees of the grounds belonging to our house, or on the bleak sides of the woodless mountains near, that my true compositions, the airy flights of my imagination, were born and fostered.

—MARY SHELLEY

Everything you can imagine is real.

—PABLO PICASSO

FAIRY STORY

For my mother and my little daughter

They both listen to her old tale,
wondrous things come flying by,
visible in their dilated eyes,
like flowers floating in a bowl.

There is a gentle tension in their being,
they are lost and sunk within each other,
—the white and the blond hair—
believe it, believe it,
everything she tells is true
and you'll never read anything more beautiful.

M. VASALIS

Contents

List of Characters

GENEVA

Mary Shelley—née Wollstonecraft Godwin (b. 1797)
Daughter of the philosopher and writer Mary Wollstonecraft and the philosopher and writer William Godwin, lover of Percy Shelley, mother of William.

Percy Shelley (b. 1792)
Mary's lover, poet. Although not officially married at this point, they present themselves as husband and wife.

William Shelley (b. 1816)
Willmouse. Mary and Percy's infant son.

Claire Clairmont (b. 1798)
Mary's stepsister, daughter of Mary Jane, Mary's father's second wife.

Lord Byron / Albe (b. 1788)
Notorious writer and poet. Occasional lover of Claire.

John Polidori (b. 1795)
Doctor and writer. Friend of Albe.

SCOTLAND

Isabella Baxter (b. 1795)
Daughter of William Baxter, sister of Margaret, Robert, and Johnny.

David Booth (b. 1776)
Margaret's husband. Runs a brewery.

Margaret Booth (b. 1789)
David's wife, Isabella's sister.

Johnny Baxter (b. 1805)
Isabella's younger brother.

Robert Baxter (b. 1796)
Isabella's older brother.

William Baxter (date uncertain)
Father of Isabella, Margaret, Robert, and Johnny.

May 1816
Cologny

Witching hour

This is the hour. Every night she dies, her daughter. She discovers it only in the morning, though she saw her lying there in the night, so quiet, head full of sleep. But she knows it must have happened at this hour, the witching hour, because that is when she always wakes up. Usually it is not for long; she wraps the slipped-off sheet around herself, presses her nose against Percy's warm back; he sighs in his sleep, she drowses off. But sometimes, sometimes it draws her out of bed. She does not know exactly what it is. She does not want to, and she is tired, she wants to go on sleeping, go on into this night, beyond this hour, but she already knows, she has to feel it. Every minute of this hour must burn against her skin. Because this is what she brought into the world. And this is what disappeared so swiftly.

The veranda keeps her dry, her overcoat keeps her warm, but not too far away from here the world is in the process of destroying itself. They have been here two weeks now, in Geneva, and ever since they arrived, storms and thunder have performed a frenzied ritual almost every day. Mary loves it when the sheet lightning persists, stretching like a cat and lighting up the skies for seconds at a time, painting it a pale purple, as if it were a canvas, a tent canopy above the earth, making the objects below seem unreal, a story, and yet lending them more meaning; her bare feet on the veranda, the weeds among the grass, the willow by the water, the Jura, rising on the other side of the lake, the boat, rocking in a basin of light.

In the other direction, up the hill, a faint light is shining at Albe and John's. She finds it reassuring. She might wake every night at three, but at least then Albe is not yet asleep. He is keeping watch. Undoubtedly with his gaze on the paper, where his quill dances chaotically, writing into the world what already exists within himself.

She turns and rocks on her toes. In the darkness she could not find her boots. Little William wakes easily—although the thunder does not bother him—and her stepsister, Claire, is finally asleep. And in her own bed too. She looks like a small child, and Percy takes her by the hand like a father. No, not like a father. Definitely not like a father.

Lightning cracks through the sky, humming upon the surface of the water, among the treetops, on her skin. Storms are different here than in England. More awake. More alive. More real. As if she might touch the light, hold it, as if it were holding her. The roar, the deep rumbling has something physical about it, as if it might join the living. As if it might gain access to her chest, her heart, her blood. There seems to be no end to the series of days in which the night lights up, the sun rarely shows itself, the garden becomes a swamp, nature falls silent—and sometimes they say to one another: maybe this is the end of the world. The Last Judgment. But then they laugh. Because each of them knows: God exists only in dreams and children's rhymes. Mary rubs her hands. The chill bites into her toes. And sometimes, she thinks, when one is very, very afraid.

But back in bed she cannot sleep again. The cold has taken up residence in her body and nothing—not a blanket, not the thought of a fire in the hearth, not the heat of Percy's back—can make her warm again.

That is because of Claire. She is barely any younger than Mary, and sometimes Mary thinks it would do Claire good if she saw her more as her real sister. But every day it becomes more difficult to accept Claire, let alone to help her, to comfort her, to entertain her. The men seem to find her less irritating. Albe even describes it as "a woman's way," whatever that is supposed to mean. Mary never stands up in the middle of a conversation and throws herself, weeping, onto the sofa, while saying that nothing, no, really, nothing is wrong, does she? It is not a woman's way. It is Claire's way. It flatters Percy, she knows that. It flatters him when Claire throws her arms around him, asks him to read poetry to her until she falls asleep, when she laughs at his jokes, her head thrown right back, pale skin from her chin to far, far below, her breasts asking for looks, for touch, for attention. Claire cannot exist without attention. She would probably die if she were ignored for three days. She has it from her mother, from Mary Jane, that need for attention. Mary believes her father had no idea how hysterical, how vain, how bossy Mary Jane was—until he married her and she and her daughter, Claire, came to live with them. Ever since Mary became aware, rationally aware, that she has no mother, that fact has been the very definition of sadness. All sadness fell into precisely that shape, was viewed in that mirror. But from the moment her father remarried, this became the scale upon which she weighed everything: this mother or no mother?

And her thoughts always came down to the same: no mother. Or at least, having to live with only the stories about her own, dead mother, with the image above her father's desk, of the woman who mattered to so many people: so clever and courageous, so unconventional in her life and her convictions. She was no longer alive, Mary had never known her, but she was everywhere. And above all: she was perfect. She would never become angry with Mary. She would never disapprove of her decisions. Mary would never be ashamed of her mother. And she would never have to be afraid of losing her love. Her mother would always love her, as she had on her deathbed: Mary as her little doll in her arms, the pure, complete, uninhibited love would never have the chance to fade or to be soiled by the quotidian. And that was what Mary's mother was like inside her head. The perfect mother, in fact. Both in spite of and thanks to the fact that she no longer existed.

A CLAP OF THUNDER, Percy turns over with a groan. His knee jabs Mary's side. In the moonlight shining through the crack of the shutters, she can see his face. Her tempestuously beautiful elf. She knows no other man who, with such fine features and translucent skin, like a satin moth, almost like a girl, holds such a strong attraction for her. And she is his great love. She does know that, but it is not easy. The fact that his philosophy is not quite hers—maybe in theory, yet not in practice—puts their love to the test again and again. Perhaps it is tolerable that, now and then, he loves another woman. Perhaps. But that it does not bother him, that he actually encourages her to share her bed with another man—that tortures her soul. At the same time, she sees how he looks when she talks to Albe about his poems, or about her father. Those are the moments when jealousy strikes him, she thinks, a cold fear in his eyes. The jealousy he feels then has nothing to do with her. Percy is not afraid that she will choose Albe over him. He is afraid that Albe will choose *her* over him. That the great, wild poet Lord Byron finds her more interesting than Percy Shelley, who still has so much to learn. Does he have enough talent? Eloquence? Percy has pinned his hopes on Albe. Could he show him the light? Could Albe give him advice, become his mentor, maybe even his friend? Very occasionally, when Percy is so insecure—oh, he does not say so, but she can see it, the faint hope in his eyes, the childish impatience in his movements—then she fears for a moment that she does not love him.

She kisses him softly on the cheek. He groans again. Turns over. The knee in her side disappears. And slumber, finally, approaches. She feels the arms of sleep unfolding like wings, wrapping her tightly, protectively, not unpleasantly, and taking her consciousness away.

◆ ◆ ◆

After the journey, which he did not appear to enjoy very much—after all, children are not made for traveling—William seems to feel at home at Maison Chapuis. The rooms are large and light, high windows with a view of the big garden, the lake, the Jura beyond. And of the rain, of course. Of the slate-gray sky. He is still too young to crawl around. Or she would no doubt have spent the whole day running after him through all the rooms, keeping him away from the fireplace, from the bookshelves, from the corners of the tables. But he has just learned to turn from his back onto his stomach, and he will come no farther than that for a while. Her Willmouse is five months old, and she enjoys every one of his days. And yet she cannot let go of the thought of her, of her firstborn. If she had lived, she would have been toddling around this place. Short, chubby legs, little bare feet step-stepping from the rug in front of the fireplace onto the shiny wooden floorboards, step-stepping through the doorway, into the hall, to the stairs, no, that's not allowed, come on, hold my hand, let's go back, that's right. Look, there's your brother, give him a cuddle.

"Is everything all right?" Claire drops down beside Mary on the sofa. William, who just closed his eyes, opens them again. Claire tickles him under the chin. "You're just staring into space."

Mary nods. Claire does not understand, even after all these years, that Mary sometimes slips away from the world. But Claire is not the same as her, not in blood, not in temperament, and not in empathy. Only, now and then, in a shared moment, in an uncontrollable fit of laughter as Claire's mother and Mary's father anxiously prepare the house for guests. It is only adults who can be like that, or so they think, so they see in each other's eyes, we will never be like that. But that was long ago. She has not seen them in a long time, her father and Mary Jane. It is so difficult now, since she has been with Percy, since her little girl.

"I am a little tired," says Mary. "How was it with Albe?"

"Oh, good," says Claire, winding a lock of hair around her finger. "He's invited us to dinner. Crackers and beans, no doubt."

Albe's eating habits do not appeal to Claire. Neither do Mary and Percy's, though. She misses the meat.

"Well, you don't have to go," says Mary. She immediately regrets it.

"Of course I do." Claire's eyes widen with shock. "Albe wanted me to come. He said so."

Mary stands up. William has dozed off again. His beautiful, pale face. But don't become too pale, Willmouse, she whispers in her mind. Without another word, she leaves the room to put William in his cradle. Sleep well. Soon you'll be awake again.

◆ ◆ ◆

"Mary." Albe embraces her. He smells of chamomile and something sweet, his stubble brushing her cheek. "I'm glad you came. There's something I'd like to show you."

Mary sees Percy's inability to join them and Albe's annoyance at this inability in his brief smile. He follows Claire to the drawing room. Albe takes a candlestick from the dresser and leads Mary by the hand down the hall and to a dark room at the back of the house. Villa Diodati is considerably larger than their house, but Chapuis is better situated, she thinks. Albe's house is darker, surrounded by trees with dense foliage, like stern and eternal guards. Inside, even in the daytime, you need candles or a lamp. The doorposts, the window frames and paneling, the many bookshelves are made of mahogany, the carpets run from wall to wall, in red or blue, with equally dark patterns. Brown is also the prevailing color in Albe's study. The evening light falls through the strands of ivy that creep across the windows. Albe places the candlestick on his desk and gathers up some loose papers.

"Come here." He beckons Mary from behind his desk. "I'm working on a new part of *Childe Harold*. I think it's going to be good. I'd like you to read it and tell me what you think."

Something in the way Albe asks her makes her sense that there is no need for her to feel flattered; he simply views her as his equal. At least, as a critic.

So she says, "I'd be happy to. I'd like to read it."

Albe rolls up the papers. "They're copies. Feel free to make notes." He hands them to her. "Shelley may read them too. If he wishes to."

Percy will say—to her—that he does not wish to read them. But he will read them.

"Mary." The candlelight falls into the light brown of his eyes, making them deeper. "I should like to read more of your work. Something that originated inside your head, not outside of it. A real story, a poem."

"Perhaps I'm a writer like my parents," she says. "Perhaps I can only write about real things."

"I am fairly certain that is not the case." Albe smiles. "Is the difference between real and not real truly that great?"

◆ ◆ ◆

Percy is sitting beside her at the table. John, Albe's friend and personal physician, is on her other side. Claire—of course—is next to Percy *and* next to Albe, who ignores her most of the time. Sometimes, when he has had a good deal of wine, has smoked something, or is simply in a good mood, Albe really talks to Claire. Sometimes he kisses her and they disappear for a time. At such moments, Mary tries not to pay attention to Percy, because even though he acts no differently than usual, she sees in all his movements the agitation of a complex sort of loss. She does not know exactly what he fears losing. Maybe it is similar to what she fears.

Since Percy saw her enter the drawing room with Albe and with the roll of papers in her hand, he has been doing his best not to look at her and to concentrate on Claire. That is tricky, because if you give Claire your attention, she does not let go and you can easily become caught up in gossip about London acquaintances and about her heartfelt fear of all manner of things that she was terrified of as a child and has never got over: the devil, witches, patterns in the fire, patterns in the clouds, whispers carried by the wind. Now and then she thinks Claire enjoys it. That the consolation is the reward. That the fear is worth it all.

"Adeline found asparagus at the market," says Albe in a terribly cheerful voice.

The asparagus is well seasoned but stringy. They cannot help but laugh a little. John grimaces at Mary. Adeline is mainly good at preparing meat, as she told Albe when he hired her as a cook and housekeeper. Luckily, she can also bake bread and there is more than enough wine. Albe tops them up every time a glass is half-empty.

"How is William?" Mary does not know if John really cares, but he asks her almost every day.

"Oh," Claire exclaims, "William is such a little treasure. He smiled at me today."

"What man would not smile at you?"

She does not believe that he means it, nor that he intends it in jest. From any other man Mary would have found such a remark irritating, but not from John. John has a way of putting people at ease. He knows exactly what to say, and what tone to use.

"He went to sleep on time today, thank God," says Mary. "We've found a nurse for him, Elise."

"That's good," says Albe.

"We don't really have the money, but so be it." Percy takes a swig of wine, does not look at her.

"Consider it an investment in Mary's future," says John. "How can she write if the baby requires constant attention?"

Claire nods enthusiastically.

"Don't whine, Shelley. You're sitting there like some grumpy old man. We're in Switzerland. Look around you!" Albe throws his arms in the air. "You're here with your wife, with your child. With me." They all laugh, including Percy, but Mary doubts that Albe meant it as a joke.

"I gave your wife something to read. It would be an honor if you would take a look at it, too."

The difference in Percy's eyes, his face, his whole demeanor is unimaginable. Within a fraction of a second, everything within him has brightened up. He has transformed from a sullen man into an eager, grateful little boy. Mary feels relieved and, at the same time, disappointed. In Albe, in Percy, or in herself.

AFTER DINNER, they retire to the drawing room, where the fire has to be stoked up high. There is another storm tonight. The first clap of thunder feels like someone grasping Mary's heart.

"That doesn't look good," says John, peering outside.

Through the window, the sky swirls from gray to dark blue to black and back again. The last of the daylight will soon have gone completely. The rain lashes against the windowpanes. Elise will stay with William until they return. The thought of him lying in his cradle, screaming with no one hearing him, his cries stolen by the wind, makes her chest clench. It will never again be like it was that time, she has to tell herself. There is always someone with him. To stop him from suddenly and silently slipping away.

More wine is poured, but this time, as John warns them, it is mixed with laudanum. He is a doctor, so they trust him to prepare the drink. Mary knows that Sam Coleridge, a good friend of her father's, often uses it, that he swears by the drug when he is writing, so she is rather curious. She cannot remember ever having been given it, although she often used to be ill. The bitter taste summons a vague memory within her. More like a feeling, like a dream; a hand sliding towards her over silk sheets. Percy and Albe have become involved in a conversation about electricity. Percy is sitting beside her, absentmindedly stroking her arm, as he listens to Albe, who is telling a story about frogs brought back to life by the power of galvanism.

"Life force," says Percy, staring at the fire. "That's the proof, isn't it?"

"Proof of what?" asks John.

"That there can be no God. If there is some vital force that man can control, it is illogical—if not impossible—that there is a God."

"What nonsense," says John. "That's not proof."

"If God exists, that force and the ability to bestow it would be solely his preserve, wouldn't it?" Percy is given his second glass of laudanum-laced wine.

"It's still not proof," says John. "What you believe belongs to God does not constitute a fact."

"Listen to my doctor," says Albe. "Dr. Polidori knows everything."

"I don't know everything at all," John continues, far too seriously, "but I do know what proof is. Wine?" he asks Mary and she nods, because she can feel the effect of the laudanum, and that makes her forget the taste. She sinks deeper into the cushions on the sofa.

Claire is lounging in a chair by the fireplace, half lying down, eyes wide open. It is not clear if she is listening. Now and then, lightning flashes behind her and she is startled, as if she has received a shock.

"No more for Claire," says John.

He sits down on the rug at Mary's feet, leaning half against her legs, and it seems almost like a gesture, a friendly, companionable gesture, and that suddenly moves her.

"But . . ." Albe leans forward. "The fact that there is no evidence that no god exists does not mean that a god does exist. So, for the record, let us assume for a moment that there is no god."

"Which is the case," mumbles Percy. He undoes the buckles of his boots and takes them off. He rests his legs on Mary's lap, his head on the armrest.

When did we all start feeling so at home? wonders Mary. She suddenly feels old—and old-fashioned. She wants to do something strange as well.

"Anyway," Albe continues, as he takes a small pipe from his jacket pocket, "the idea that people can use electricity to generate vital force themselves is very interesting. Being able to bring dead matter back to life. Just imagine—your dead grandmother alive once more." He smiles broadly.

But Mary is not thinking about grandmothers. Whether the subject is death, war, wine, or nature, Mary's brain always finds a path that leads to her little girl, to her first child. And when she asks herself if she ever wants that to end, she has no answer.

They go on talking, the men, but she is no longer listening. She cannot listen anymore. She has rested her hand in John's hair.

Thoughts no longer have logical order, no beginning, no end, no cause or necessity. They exist simply as they are: random and nonsensical, yet nevertheless overwhelming. The breaking of glass, the pitiful cry of something unimaginable, a fish the size of a ship, moonlight creeping in through cracks, an unspeakably terrifying head, a snake, as slippery as jelly, sliding through her fingers. In the end, everything slips through her fingers. Because that is how it goes.

AT SOME POINT that evening Percy kisses her, in the midst of the others. The reason is unclear, or maybe her mind was elsewhere for a moment. Claire is sitting on Albe's lap, kissing his neck, as he absentmindedly slides one hand over her hip, holding his glass with his other hand, almost continuously taking little sips. John is at the window, looking outside. The lightning flashes between the silhouettes of the trees, sometimes for seconds at once, so that the world once again takes on that silent strangeness, as if the veil of reality has been lifted and she can briefly see the world beneath it: a world in which nothing can be kept at bay by the intellect; no memory, no threat, no spirit.

Percy kisses her cheek, her temple, her forehead, her nose. Then, long and slowly, he kisses her mouth. Mary thinks somehow she was angry with him, but she cannot quite remember why, and she smells his scent, his scent of oranges, but spicy, and she kisses him back, her dear elf, her insecure, cantankerous, wonderful poet. And what happens next is not clear. They make love, or they fall asleep together and she dreams that they make love. The sky is black, the storm is over. Someone is standing under the window, he calls her name, but it does not sound like her name. And then she knows she is dreaming, because the one who is calling her does not exist.

AT NIGHT MARY thinks she can hear her little girl. She is crying. She is wailing. She knows her. She is so certain that she has made a mistake: she is alive! Of course she is alive. All that time, months and months. What a bad mother she was to think her child dead! But that time is over now, she has to go to her, to her little Clara. She has to nurse her, look deep into her blue eyes, hug her to her breast forever, so firmly that neither of them can breathe. Otherwise she will slip away from her, she knows, no, she is already slipping away from her. Between the cracks of awakening, she knows: oh God. This world. Oh God. And she loses her again. The sound that woke her in this witching hour is alarming enough. She has shaken off the dream, the half dream. She is still at Diodati. A single candle is lighting the room, the embers in the fireplace are still glowing slightly. Mary gets up off the sofa, where she was lying half under a blanket, her neck crooked, and tries to understand what is going on. The sound is coming from upstairs. Someone is crying, screaming hoarsely. She takes the candle, heads up the wide staircase. Is it Claire? Once again she thinks what she so often thinks when she is woken by a Claire who seems to be possessed by some evil spirit: we should never have let her come. But it had in fact been Claire's idea for them to spend the summer here, close to Albe, and it was Percy who had seen it as an opportunity to get to know the writer. When she reaches the landing, she follows the sound. There is a faint light in one of the bedrooms: an oil lamp with a low flame. Claire is sitting on the bed, leaning against the wall, legs pulled up, hair tousled, eyes fluttering, and hands plucking at her dress. Percy is lying on his side next to her, his hand on her stomach, as he looks up at her and whispers things that are not meant for Mary's ears or which Mary's ears simply do not hear. She stands there, in the doorway. Percy has not yet seen her, and who knows what Claire is seeing. If you were to ask Mary if Claire does this a little bit on purpose, her answer would differ from one day to the next. Sometimes Mary feels sorry for her, she really does, and believes that Claire is a victim of herself. And sometimes she believes that she herself is Claire's prime victim.

"I don't want to see this!" shouts Claire. She is staring at the window, where there is nothing to see; the shutters are closed. Her hands are clawing at the air now. "Everything is dripping," she rasps, "nothing is as it was, Perce. This is real! I can't do this." She sobs with a high-pitched snarl. A hyena, thinks Mary.

Percy sits upright and takes hold of her. Claire dangles like a doll in his arms, her eyes fixed on the window. Percy strokes her back, kisses her tangled hair, his eyes closed.

"I don't want this," Claire cries. "I don't want this anymore."

Mary turns around. She does not mind. This is fine. He is only comforting her and what man wants a morbidly anxious woman, but still it makes her stomach ache, a hard, stone stomach cramp, which is not only pain but also anger. She knows it is not Percy's fault. It is Claire's. Back on the sofa, at the point when her thoughts are barely coherent, she feels that she needs to pee. In the hallway, on the way to the lavatory, a shadow presses her to the wall. It is Albe. She lets him, as she knows it does not mean anything. He is drunk and wants to say something to her. Albe does whatever makes him feel good. Albe is her friend.

"You know why I gave it to you, don't you?"

His breath feels foul in her face, smells of animal fat or sheep shit. She tries a gentle push.

Albe gently pushes back.

She nods. Something is starting to dawn on her, but it seems far away, unimportant. Now he nods too, closes his eyes. He starts singing. Very softly. Mary cannot make out the words, but it sounds like a lullaby. He stands there, with his arms against the wall, his shoulder against hers, his breath in her ear. And suddenly she feels something loosening inside her head. With a small crack, it comes free, tumbles down, through her throat, through her stomach to her gut. And there it lies: warm and insistent. She should know what it is.

June 1812
Dundee

June 12, 1812

Almost my entire life in London and then: a week on a boat, just the waves, the waves, the waves. I had so longed to see the sea, but on that rough and rugged boat, she became an accursed beloved. The gift she gave me was sickness, robbing me of my vitality and my hope. But those times when I felt good enough to go on deck, to look out over the rail on the bow and across the white-crested waves, as she drove her salty splashes into my face and the wind, the wind blew into me, blasting everything clean and bright with constantly renewed vigor, I found her the most beautiful, the most insane, the most awesome of all and I knew that my adventure, my life with her had begun.

At the exact moment I descended the gangplank—one small step at a time—I felt that this was where I would find what I was looking for, although I did not yet know what I was seeking. There were not many people standing on the quay. A man with fair side-burns, younger than my father, but with a calm smile, nodded at me.

"Miss Godwin, welcome. I am William Baxter." Fortunately, I found his accent easy enough to understand. Mr. Baxter took my case from my hand. "How was your journey?"

The sailing had been a horror. During the daytime it was bearable, when I could clasp my hands to the railing, a firm and narrow strip to hold on to above the depths of the North Sea, to which I could fasten my thoughts: those quick handclapping games with Claire, Fanny's breath on my back when we lay in bed, listening to Papa playing the piano downstairs, a baby crying in the street, carts passing on the cobblestones outside, horses' hooves pounding to the rhythm of the ship's pitching. It was the nights on the boat that were unimaginably awful. A no-man's-land of blackness, in which the words "above" and "below" no longer had any significance, in which every swell swirled in my stomach, in which I sometimes doubted my own existence. And I was alone, so terribly alone.

I was uncertain whether to tell him all that, but he had already started talking again. "This is my son Robert. The others are waiting at home. It's not far."

In the carriage, I looked at Robert, who was sitting opposite me. I thought he was around my age, and he had an earnest air about him. Still, he smiled at me. He had a nice smile, without any ulterior motives, I thought.

"Our house is in the center of Dundee, not far from the harbor, in fact. It's known as 'the Cottage,'" said Mr. Baxter.

"Our little cottage," Robert said with a grin.

The harbor slowly disappeared from view, giving way to small houses, a church, shops. We passed a pharmacy, a draper's shop, a tailor's, and a bookshop.

"How many bookshops do you have in Dundee?" I asked.

"Four or so," said Robert. "That one over there is excellent. And so is Rumpton's, down the road. I'll take you there one day."

"Let her recover from the journey first," said Mr. Baxter. "I promised your father that, in addition to all your adventures as a young lady far from home, you will also have plenty of rest. We all want you to be healthy again as soon as possible, don't we?"

I nodded. Although the weather was actually too warm for it, I was wearing a gown with long sleeves. It was not that I was ashamed of my skin condition. It was more that I was not in the mood for questions, for looks. It had started the year before: flaking skin, red and irritated patches, itching, such terrible itching, and only on my arms. The doctor had prescribed an ointment, but it made no difference. Mary Jane forbade me to scratch, and I knew she was right, but I never want to admit that Mary Jane is right. And besides, it is impossible not to scratch. I can stop myself during the daytime but at night, when I am in bed, my arms free from those tight sleeves, I yearn for the relief of my fingernails. When it heals, if it heals, there will be scars, Mary Jane warned me. But that might be true even without the scratching. My father did not concern himself with it. He has never had much interest in appearance. Perhaps he does not know how much beauty matters in the life of girls, of women. No, I am sure he is aware. But it will be something he disapproves of. And although I understand it, his arrogance annoys me. No woman alive can allow herself the luxury of not caring about her appearance. The sheer fact that only a man may say beauty does not matter because it should not matter only goes to show the extent to which—unfortunately—he is wrong.

Mr. Baxter smiled at me. "We are very happy to welcome you as our guest, Miss Godwin."

"Please call me Mary," I said.

He nodded and smiled as if he had a secret. I saw now that his hair was already graying, particularly his sideburns, which stretched far along his jawbone.

"My mother was a great admirer of yours, Mary," said Robert. "As is Isabella, by the way. Perhaps you could talk to her about your mother's books. Isabella has been so glum lately. It's as if . . ."

"Robert." It was not loud. Not the way my father can raise his voice. When I was younger, that used to make my stomach ache. But it was effective. Robert immediately stopped talking. He looked at his father. I could not quite interpret his expression; he looked reproachful, but also seemed distracted, as though his father had set him thinking. Silently—I had barely noticed it—a dull sadness crept into me.

"Here we are!" cried Mr. Baxter and the heaviness left my body. The carriage stopped in front of a house that was at least three times the size of our home in London.

A young girl opened the door for us—it was Grace, the maid, and she took my case from Robert.

Mr. Baxter walked ahead of me into the drawing room. The sun streamed in through the large windows, onto the thick rugs on the gleaming dark wooden floor and various sofas and armchairs around the fireplace. Everywhere I looked, there were books. On the bookshelves that climbed the walls to the ceiling, of course, but also stacked on tables, windowsills, even on the backs of some of the chairs. In the corner of the room stood a shiny black grand piano with such a powerful presence that I thought for a moment it was breathing.

IN THE KITCHEN I was introduced to Elsie, the cook. Then Robert led me upstairs so I could rest for a while. The four large windows on the south-facing side of my room looked out on the houses in the street, the street behind that, and the River Tay beyond. The windows to the west were narrower and from there I could look out over the landscape. The hills that must stretch inland for many miles. They were covered with bushes, grass, heather in shades of green, yellow, and, more distant, brown. There was a path, and a few houses up the hill. This was a country of the past. Of the stories in my books. Of water spirits, mermen, and monsters, hidden deep among the hills. Of streams with slippery moss-covered stones that served as crossing places. A land where fear and love, imagination and truth coexisted on the riverside, in the undergrowth, under ancient trees. There was nothing that could not grow here. There was nothing that might not exist here.

I pulled my case up onto the bed, hung my gowns and corsets in the closet. Undergarments, stockings, and bonnets went on the shelf. I had brought nine books with me. They included Horace Walpole, Samuel Coleridge, and the published letters of Abigail Adams, in addition to works my father had given me, mostly philosophy and a recent analysis of the French Revolution. It is not that I am uninterested in the world outside, God knows that I am. But I have become aware of an ever-increasing interest in my own world. The dreams I have, the nightmares, my daydreams. I notice that the writers in my books have brains that work just like mine. A brain that connects what has never been connected, what perhaps is not supposed to be connected.

THAT NIGHT WE ate together. In addition to Mr. Baxter and Robert, there was also little Johnny. Only Isabella was not there. My father had told me about the family, and I knew there were two daughters:

Margaret, who was married, and Isabella, who was a little older than I. Their mother had died a year ago. My father said Isabella would be glad of my coming. No one spoke about her, and I did not dare to ask about her. Her brothers and her father were in high spirits. The food was good, and the conversation flowed naturally. I kept myself somewhat to myself, feeling shy with a family I did not know, who did not know me. But before long it felt familiar and they began to ask me questions, to make little jokes, and I thought about home, in London, what it was like at the dinner table there, how I had to watch Mary Jane sitting and chewing away opposite me, how my father, if he came to the table at all, left his mind in his study; Claire chattering away, about her new boots, the play she wanted to see, how wonderful Thomas Moore actually was; how quietly Fanny ate, or did not eat, softly skimming her cutlery over her plate. I looked around and felt so happy that it frightened me.

AFTER THE MEAL, Mr. Baxter read a story to little Johnny, and I could see the wild adventures taking shape in the boy's eyes. I looked at the fire, from the reading chair I sat in, Coleridge on my lap, and I listened to Mr. Baxter's voice. Less than a year ago, Johnny's mother must have sat with him like that in front of the fire, and she would have been the one telling the story. I tried to imagine what that must be like, a mother close to you, a mother's voice just for you, and how it must feel to miss her, when you knew—when you knew *exactly*—what her voice had sounded like.

I LAY IN BED, my new bed, in the home of the family who were going to be my family for the time being. The sheets smelled of starch and vaguely of flowers. The shutters were not quite closed, and a strip of light crossed the floor to my bed. My first day with the Baxters had exceeded my hopes and expectations, and I was already looking forward to the next day, to the weeks ahead. I fell asleep with a feeling of lightness, and my first dream began while I was still playing out my upcoming adventures for myself on the ceiling of the bedroom. The sound of a bear or a wolf marked the beginning of the dream, which was realistic, but which I can no longer remember. I can only recall the feeling that came with it: a wretched trepidation, a sense of a vivid evil that had not yet been shown to me.

June 14, 1812

They are very kind and welcoming, the Baxters. Far more than I had imagined when I was on my way to these strangers. My father knew Mr. Baxter only from their correspondence. They include me in everything, and I feel like a sister returning home to a troubled family. I still have not met Isabella. I know she is there, as her brothers take her food up to her room. I do not quite dare to ask about her. Is she ill? How long has it been since she last left her room? And what does she do in there all day long?

This morning Johnny sat me down at the piano and played a piece with me. We had the greatest enjoyment when he asked me to play something—anything!—while he practiced his scales. It was a cacophony, of course, and Robert came into the drawing room with his hands over his ears and a grimace on his face.

"Stop it," he said, "you'll wake the spirits," but Johnny laughed and shooed him away with a stack of sheet music.

"That's not true," said Johnny. He put on a serious expression and started to play a piece I recognized, but whose title I did not know. The slow, deep notes filled the room, seemed to soak into the red damask curtains, to stick to the mahogany furniture. "The spirits never sleep."

AFTER TEATIME, Robert emerged from behind my book. I was sitting in the large armchair by the fireplace. Blackened remains of the fire from the night before lay waiting in the grate for someone to come and turn them into ashes with the poker. Usually that someone is Johnny, who likes to pretend the poker is a sword, or a lance, which continues until Grace realizes what is going on, takes the poker from him, and wipes the blackness from his hands and cheeks.

"Do you like scary stories?" Robert asked, giving Walpole a tap. I had just started reading *The Castle of Otranto* and the book had already captured my complete attention. There was something about the way the castle and the atmosphere were described that fascinated me. I could not wait to discover what foul deeds would be done, how the dark corridors and the turret rooms would fulfil their dark functions, and what terrible fate awaited Manfred.

Robert sat on the arm of the chair. "If you like this, you should read Radcliffe, too. Very scary."

I had heard of it: Ann Radcliffe, *The Mysteries of Udolpho*. My father sold it in the bookshop—and it sold well. It was why Claire had given me this copy of Walpole. She told me her mother had said we were not allowed to read such exciting stories, but that she had brought the Otranto story from the shop because, unlike Ann Radcliffe's book, few copies of it were sold these days, so no one would miss it. The book had terrified her and so now it was my turn to read it so that I could recognize the ghosts that lived in her head at night and render them harmless. When we said our farewells on the pier in London, she whispered that she expected me to read it quickly and to send her a letter to relieve her of her fears.

"If you want to read it, you'll have to ask Isabella. She has it," Robert said. He gave my shoulder a playful nudge and left the room. How on earth was I expected to get hold of the book if Isabella, who never showed her face, had it? It occurred to me that she was not leaving her room because of me. Because I was there. Had she shut herself away when I arrived in Dundee? Because—yes, why exactly?—because I had come to disrupt the normal order of things? Her brothers were very kind and seemed genuinely delighted that I was staying with them for a time. So, why wasn't Isabella?

THIS AFTERNOON, when I was about to go out for a walk, Johnny asked me to go and look for ladybirds with him. It was such a sweet request that I could not turn him down. We walked around the garden, which was still wet with this morning's rain, I holding up my skirt, Johnny skipping like a foal, chattering all the time, and it felt so wonderfully natural. As if I were walking with my little brother, and this were my house, as if I had always lived here. They proved hard to find, the ladybirds. In fact, we did not find a single one, and Johnny suggested that they might be hiding because of the rain. I know nothing about insects, but I could well imagine that he was right. At the bottom of the garden, as we stood leaning against the fence looking at the hills beyond, where I had wanted to walk, he gave my arm a tug.

"What's that?" he asked.

I was wearing my pale pink gown, the sleeves of which do not reach all the way to my wrists, and I realized he was looking at my skin, at the red bumps, the cracks and flakes and the raised patches that almost shone because the skin was stretched so tightly. I told Johnny that I have a sickness on my arms that damages the skin, making it bleed at times, and itch. And Johnny, dear Johnny, he went on looking at my arms, and then gently touched the skin. He did not find it ugly, or dirty, or frightening. I even believe he thought it beautiful, in an intriguing way.

And that was when I decided to ask him.

"How is Isabella?" I tried to sound nonchalant, but it did not seem to matter either way.

"Oh," he said, "she's been very sad since Mama died."

It was as if I had been hit by something, a blunt, hard object. Of course, they had lost their mother. And I, like an idiot, had assumed they had all recovered from their loss by now because I never heard anyone mention it. But just because the others seemed to be getting on with their lives did not mean that Isabella was able to do the same.

"Has she been alone in her room all this time?" I asked. I could not imagine that was the case. For a whole year? And no one had said anything about it?

We slowly walked back to the house. Johnny pulled a leaf off the hedge and tore it to pieces. "She sometimes comes out. But that's usually where she is. I miss her." Johnny looked up at me. His big eyes were blue and gleaming.

"What happens when you knock on her door?"

He shrugged. "She usually tells me to go away. But I don't try very often anymore."

At the back door, we kicked the wall to knock the mud off our shoes. I could finally lower my skirt again. We went into the kitchen, where Grace was making cocoa. The smell made my nose sting, and I almost started crying.

June 19, 1812

Last night I met her in the hallway. I was startled, felt tingling all over my body. She was shocked too, eyes like wild patches of white in the darkness. I was the only one with a candle. We stood there, barefoot on the floorboards, a couple of yards away from each other, and maybe she was a ghost, maybe she was an apparition or a witch, but then she said something. She said: "Hello."

I chuckled. "Hello," I replied.

Isabella did not laugh. Her eyes were just as big as before, but now I saw that the irises were green, very bright green. "I heard something," she said.

"I'm Mary," I said.

"I know."

We stood in silence. There was no sound inside the house, but outside the wind took a run-up and tried to push the windows from their frames.

"Well, then," I said, "I'm going back to bed. I just came to see if any windows were open."

"Papa never leaves the windows open at night." A brief hint of a smile. "Scared something will come flying in."

"A bird?"

She shrugged. "Or something else."

Something unpleasant slithered through my stomach.

"I'll see you tomorrow," I said. "Maybe."

Isabella nodded. "All right. Tomorrow."

When I was lying in my bed again, I wondered if she would finally show herself downstairs at breakfast. I could hardly imagine her among the others, chatting and laughing and playing jokes on one another. It was as if she did not belong. As if no one knew her.

SHE KEPT HER promise. This morning, the family was sitting at the breakfast table, Elsie was pouring tea, and Grace was slicing bread at the counter when Isabella came in. We fell silent, looked up. Then Mr. Baxter shook his head almost imperceptibly and we went on talking. Isabella sat down in the chair opposite mine, the only one that was empty. A place had been laid for her, as it was every morning and evening, but this time her cutlery would not be returned to the drawer unused. I tried not to look at her: she was a beautiful dark haze on the edge of my vision. I attempted to resume my conversation with Robert, but he was now talking to Mr. Baxter. Isabella did not seem to make any effort at all to begin a conversation. She spread bramble jelly on a piece of bread, had tea poured for her.

"It's story night this evening," said Robert, nudging me with his elbow.

"Story night?"

He took a sip of tea. "Family tradition. Every second Friday of the month. Each of us, everyone who wants to, tells a story. It can be true or made up. Funny, scary, or pleasant. We have soup, drink a glass of wine or two. All of us together around the fireplace. Mr. Booth is coming too."

Out of the corner of my eye, I saw Isabella look up, and I dared to glance at her. Her eyes looked a little flat and empty, I thought.

"Who is Mr. Booth?" I asked.

"He's Margaret's husband. They live not too far away, in New-burgh. Booth is a character." Robert grinned.

"You can say that again." It was muffled, as Isabella was talking with her mouth full.

"There is something uncommon about him," said Robert. "You'll see for yourself."

I looked at Isabella. A liveliness had now leaped into her eyes, as if she were finally present. She had dark curls and very fair, almost transparent skin. There was a dimple in her chin, full, dark pink lips. I was curious if she would be coming tonight, if she would tell a story, but I said nothing, and then I remained silent for so long that the moment passed. Robert and Johnny were now talking about a story Mr. Booth had told the last time, about a sea witch with golden eyes that glowed so brightly they blinded men for good.

"Of course it only worked on men," I said and giggled. Isabella smiled faintly, which filled me with an idiotic joy.

I SPENT THE rest of the day trying to come up with a good story for that evening. It was not that I necessarily wished to tell a story, I thought in fact that it would be nice just to listen to the others, to be among them, to drift off, but I believed that, as a guest, I should contribute. I imagined they might expect it of me, even though they would probably never say as much. And I knew some good stories, didn't I? Stories they would not know? Stories I had read, or ones that Claire and I told each other. Sometimes I even exchange stories with Fanny, but she is not much of a storyteller, too shy, or her imagination is more demure than mine or Claire's. But I was finding it difficult. Robert had said it could be anything, but there was sure to be a tradition, in terms of length, of themes. Did they want something to make them laugh? Did they want something scary? And if so, what did they find amusing or frightening? I walked a little way towards the harbor. It was dry and overcast, warm, even a little muggy, but I was enjoying being alone for a while, exploring my surroundings, breathing in the unfamiliar air.

Seeing it now, it looked very different, almost as if I lived here, as if I had walked here so many times that it had become *my* harbor. I saw the fishermen emptying their nets onto the quayside, young men throwing fish after fish after fish into wooden crates. The fish thrashed around on top of one another, all snapping mouths and flapping gills. Their eyes were as dark as the night sky, or maybe as the depths of the sea. Barrels were unloaded, boats were moored and tethered to the quay with thick ropes. Seagulls circled, eyeing the mountain of fish; remarkably, they did not dive down to snatch a bite. Perhaps they had been chased away with such force that they had learned not to do it. Sometimes they let out cries, shrill and full of frustration—at least that was how it sounded to me.

"You're not from around here." A woman's voice, firm. Maybe reproachful.

On top of a barrel in front of a green building with STORE-HOUSE 2 written on the side, a woman of around sixty was sitting. Her face gave me the impression that she had had a hard life. Her hair was tucked up into a dirty cap, and there were dried-on brown stains on her apron. Her hands were busily moving, but she was holding nothing.

"Fishing work, fishing work, fishing work," she said.

I was not in the mood for a nonsensical conversation with someone who was clearly not in her right mind, so I decided to ignore her, but as I walked past her, she grabbed my hand. Hers felt rough and warm.

"Child," she said, a lot more friendly now, "everything is just fish all the time."

She looked at me so sadly; her eyes big and watery, the sort of blue that is almost white, as if the color had slowly been worn out over time, by all that she had had to see.

I wanted to say something in reply, something reassuring, but I could not quite think what. I thought it seemed most unpleasant to spend one's entire life surrounded by dead fish, too. I smiled at her, gave her hand a gentle squeeze.

"You know too, don't you?" she said. "About the stories. You have them too."

"The stories?" I had had enough now. Her hand was holding mine too tightly, her eyes staring too hard into mine. The day was becoming warm, oppressive, as the sun tried to press its heat through the thick layer of clouds.

"The one with the head of a man, the body of a fish, the witch from the sea. No one who knows him can tell the tale or flee."

"Sorry," I said, pulling my hand from hers with some difficulty. She looked startled, and a little angry.

"Ach, you don't know anything," she said and looked away from me.

I waited for a moment, but she continued doing whatever it was that she was doing with her empty hands and did not say another word. Folktales, I thought as I took a different route back to the Baxters' house. She must have been thinking about old folktales. And she was confused, the way old people have knots in their thoughts that they keep getting entangled in.

As I walked down the garden path, Johnny came to meet me. "Would you like to hear my story?"

I said I certainly would, but would he not prefer to save it for this evening? He shook his head and pulled me to a bench in the garden, where he began a story about flies and ladybirds going to war with the snails. It was a funny story, but I was distracted. I kept thinking about those fish looking up at the sky with their fathomlessly deep ocean eyes, crying out wordlessly for help.

IT WAS CLEARLY a special occasion for the Baxters. We all sat around the hearth. Johnny, Robert, and I on the sofa, close together, Mr. Baxter in an armchair, Isabella on the rug in front of the fire. Elsie had put out a couple of small tables with glasses of wine, cocoa for Johnny, soup, bread, and cake. Mr. Baxter wondered if we should start without Mr. Booth. He arrived just as Johnny was about to go first and tell his story. I do not believe that I had tried to picture Mr. Booth, but he had such an uncommon countenance that I struggle to find the right words. He made a friendly impression, was handsome and charming, but the longer you looked at him, the more his face took on something grotesque, as if something about him changed when you allowed your gaze to rest on him for too long. His hair was dark, with strands of light gray. He appeared to be around forty, a good deal older than Margaret, who was unable to come with him. When Mr. Booth entered the room, he was introduced to me. He took my hand and something unnatural happened. I was reminded of the fishwife's hand that I had held that afternoon, although Mr. Booth's hand was smooth, cool, and much firmer. And separately from that thought, it felt as if he were not only holding my hand, but also touching my head in some nonphysical manner. The top of my skull began to gently tingle, as when a person very lightly rests their hand on your hair. I withdrew my hand and the sensation on my head ceased. Nothing about Mr. Booth's face had changed. His expression as he looked at me was still just as warm and friendly as before.

"What an honor to meet you, young Miss Godwin," he said. "You are probably aware that I am a good friend of your father's and that I have very much been looking forward to your arrival here, as have, no doubt, the Baxters."

I felt myself blushing.

"Thank you," I said. "You may call me Mary."

He was offered the armchair closest to the fire, and then we could begin. Robert gave me a bowl of soup. Johnny started telling his story, and everyone fell silent. He had expanded his story about the war of the animals. Now the dragonflies had joined in too, but it was unclear which side they were on and what they were fighting for. Even so, it was a good tale.

Bread was passed around and Robert started to tell me something. I was only half listening. I had the impression that Isabella wanted to talk to me. Sometimes she looked at me, and when I looked back and saw her inquisitive eyes on me, her gaze moved on, as if it had been a coincidence.

Mr. Booth sat quietly listening. He drank a lot of wine, ate no soup. He smiled when Robert told a funny story and although he did not appear distracted, he was not entirely there in the way that the rest of us were. It felt as if he were present on two levels: on one level with us, with wine and bread and stories by the fireside, and on another level somewhere far above the mundanity of this scene. I looked often at him and Isabella this evening. When it was my turn to tell a story, I finally saw their attention fixed on me.

I took a sip of wine to calm my nerves.

"I went for a walk towards the harbor this morning," I began. "The weather was close, but dry, and I was thinking about home, about my sisters, Claire and Fanny, about my father. I wasn't homesick, that wasn't it. I was wondering, though, what they were doing and if they were thinking about me, too, and thinking I should write to them again. So, nothing out of the ordinary. It was busy at the harbor, as it probably is most of the time. I smelled the scent of the sea, of fish and salt, even sweat as I walked past the fishermen who were unloading their catch. At the end of the quayside, in front of a shed, I saw a woman who seemed somewhat out of place. She looked like a fishwife, but she was not working. Her empty hands were busy doing something, as if she were skinning invisible fish. She muttered some words that I could not make out. I felt no need to converse with her, but I wanted to walk past her, as a country road begins beyond the harbor that passes meadows full of the most beautiful flowers. As I came closer, I could understand what she was saying. She spoke in a lilting voice, as if it were a song:

> *Oh the fair Marie Fish's-Eye,*
> *drank from the water and didn't stay dry,*
> *on her throat she grew gills, two legs were one tail,*
> *she leaped into the sea, her skin made of scale.*
> *Skippers now sailing far out at sea*
> *are the only companions of the fair Marie.*
> *The waves so calm, the sky so blue,*
> *as the fair Marie circles the crew,*
> *a dead man's bride, her grooms forever asleep,*
> *pulling ship and sailors into the deep.*

"I wanted to walk away. I had heard enough. The woman was quite clearly not right in the head. Then she grabbed my hand tightly. As she looked at me, my breath caught in my throat. Her eyes were so very, very black, like a fish's eyes. Her mouth had fallen open; toothless, just like a fish's mouth. Then her cap slipped off, and a chill ran down my spine when I saw she had not hair, but scales. I tried to pull my arm away, but she was holding me with an uncanny strength. 'Do not drink the water,' she said. 'Do not drink it.' I had absolutely no intention of drinking any seawater, so I did not really need her warning, but I thanked her and she finally let me go. I was shocked, of course. She was strange and terrifying, although I did not have the impression that she was dangerous.

"By the time I reached the road, I had largely forgotten my shock. The sun had broken through the thick layer of clouds and was burning my bare arms. I had not thought to bring a parasol, and my hat could not protect me from so much sun, so before long I was craving some refreshment. At the edge of a meadow full of glorious poppies, there was a well. I brought up some water with the bucket, and the exertion made me even thirstier. The tin bucket, full of cool, sparkling water, felt cold on my palms as I raised its rim to my lips. The first gulp was divine, and so was the second, but after that I lost consciousness. When I came around, beside the well, the bucket lying toppled in the grass, the sun was already setting. I stood up, feeling remarkably well, and walked back home with a firm stride, as I needed to be back in time for our story night. Just before I opened the door and heard the laughter and noise from the kitchen, where Elsie was making soup, I noticed a small itchy spot on my neck. I suspected this afternoon's sunshine had caused my skin to burn. But when I went to my room and studied my neck in the mirror, I saw a small, silvery scale. Nonsense, I thought, that's impossible. I wanted to give myself a stern talking-to, so I looked in the mirror—and I found two fathomless night-black eyes looking back at me."

It was fantastic. The family clapped enthusiastically, and I could feel myself blushing. Robert pretended he wanted to check my neck, which made me laugh, but a stern look from his father called him to order. I was proud of myself for inventing something that gave people pleasure. I had taken something from real life and twisted it and spun it out until there was more to it than had really happened. Until it was more than the truth.

June 23, 1812

Now that I know where Isabella's room is, I often walk past it. My fingers stroke the doorknob. If you were to ask me what I find so unimaginably intriguing about her, I should not be able to give you an answer. But since I met her, suspicions have been swirling around inside me. I thought I was coming to Dundee to recover (and to get away from Mary Jane); but I was wrong. I believe I am here because of Isabella.

I OFTEN SIT in a corner by the window in the drawing room, reading or writing a little and listening to the conversations between Johnny and Robert, or between Robert and Mr. Baxter. In London I sometimes thought I simply did not love people. I could really dislike Fanny at times because she was so sweet, even when she should be angry; Claire, because she was incapable of sweetness, unless it suited her, which meant her love was not really love. Mary Jane, I do not even wish to speak of her. My father is the only one I love profoundly, but even that is complicated. But now, now that I am looking at this family, I think perhaps I was wrong. Maybe I do love people. And that idea makes me feel so light inside. As if I might just float away. Maybe it is all yet to begin. Maybe this is where it begins.

ISABELLA CAME TO sit beside me—it was beautiful weather, the sky as blue as if it were painted, the warmth of the sun caressing my skin under the parasol—as I was sitting in one of the sun chairs at the bottom of the garden. She took me by surprise, but perhaps that was because I was in the middle of Walpole and my nerves were afire as I was drawn into the world of that book. So, once again, she startled me. Apparently, she found that amusing. She asked what I was reading, and I showed her the book. I also told her that Claire was waiting at home for me to finish it so that I could write her a reassuring letter. Isabella gave me a brief smile. I did not know what else to say. Her smile, the way she tilted her head, her mouth curled up at the corner, made me forget all good sense. She tucked a loose lock of hair into a pin above her ear. She was not wearing a hat and the parasol was shading only me, so I foolishly asked if she was not going to be bothered by the sun.

"Yes," she said, "most probably." She did not smile, just looked at me almost in amazement.

I moved aside a little in the sun chair, but it was fairly obvious that there was not enough room for two.

Isabella shook her head. "I'm going to visit Margaret and Mr. Booth tomorrow. They live in Newburgh, in Fife. I wanted to ask if you would come with me. We can go in the carriage."

I was surprised that she asked me. Until that moment I had

believed she stayed in her room because of me, but now I was ashamed of that thought. As if the world revolved around me!

"Yes," I said. "I should like to come."

Isabella nodded and walked back to the house. As I thought about the next day, equal parts of agitation and joy fought for attention inside me.

June 24, 1812

The carriage was waiting for us early the next morning. It was not too far but Isabella had not seen her sister for some time, so we would spend the whole day with her and Mr. Booth and not be driven back home until after dinner. The carriage belonged to him. When Mr. Baxter needs a carriage, he hires one, but Mr. Booth is wealthier, or maybe he wishes to appear more distinguished. When we were inside the carriage, Isabella told me he has twelve people working for him, six of whom are engaged solely with running the estate. In addition to that, he has a number of employees at his brewery, mainly for the heavy work. Isabella and I sat side by side, looking out the windows at the tall elm trees along the road, at the carts carrying crates of fruit and fish and churns of milk, the houses we drove past, where clothes fluttered on washing lines, children crawled through the grass, and chickens fluttered up on the other side of the fence. I had the urge to ask her why she had at first shut herself away in her room and why, without anything having changed (at least as far as I could see), she was now spending time with her family again, why she wanted to take me to see her sister and brother-in-law, but I did not dare start to bring it up. I knew by now that she was seventeen, and that made it even more unnatural for me to talk to her on an equal level. The strange thing was that I could talk to Robert, who was not only older than me but also a boy. In fact, I got along well and naturally with the whole family, but I did not quite know how to behave around Isabella. So, instead of asking her the questions that were on my mind, I followed her lead, answering the questions she asked, even though she asked only few. And meanwhile I racked my brains to come up with some way to have such a natural connection with her as I did with her father and brothers.

The carriage stopped in front of a large country house surrounded by an expanse of gardens and meadows, all of which, Isabella told me, were part of the estate. As we climbed out of the carriage, we saw the figure of Mr. Booth standing between the columns on the porch. There appeared to be no expression on his face, which puzzled me. His face showed no happiness, no expectation, not even impatience. It was almost as if he had not seen us coming, but that could not possibly be the case: the coach had stopped less than twenty yards from him and he was looking straight at us.

Isabella walked towards him and extended her hand, greeting him with a gaiety in her voice that I did not think suited her. He took her hand and kissed it. Then he looked at me. I came up the short flight of stairs to the porch and gave him my hand too, which he also kissed and held for a moment. It was foolish, and I felt ashamed afterwards, but I wanted to pull my hand away. The way he held on to it for a moment, after that light yet definitely not inappropriate kiss, gave me an inexplicable feeling of impropriety, although it was not improper. He glanced at me, and his gray eyes seemed to reassure me. Oh, what a fuss I was making!

Mr. Booth let Isabella and me lead the way inside. In the hall, a young woman in an iridescent blue gown was sitting in a wheeled chair. Isabella hugged her and introduced me to Margaret. She had not told me her sister was an invalid and suddenly I resented her for that. Is it not right to warn a person, so that one may react as naturally as possible when one meets someone for the first time? I do not know for certain, but I fear that I looked a little shocked. I shook her hand and she smiled and said it was nice to make my acquaintance. The four of us went into the drawing room.

"David will give you a tour of the place later if you would like," Margaret said. She made an expansive gesture with her arms. I was indeed rather curious. The house was about four times the size of the Baxters' home, even though the only residents were Mr. Booth, Margaret, and a few servants.

Isabella and I were invited to sit on the sofa, Margaret wheeled her chair to sit across from us, and Mr. Booth sent for tea and sandwiches.

"Ladies, I am sorry, but I need to take care of a few things. Excuse me. I shall join you again at around noon." He smiled. "Enjoy yourselves."

Margaret seemed ill at ease. She smiled at me, at us, but it did not seem entirely sincere. At least not very warmhearted. She offered us sandwiches and while we ate she told us about the house, which was built two centuries ago using stones from the old abbey of Lindores. It was also where Mr. Booth ran his brewery, which was at the rear of the building. She spoke in a matter-of-fact way, as if she were not talking to her sister and a guest of the family, but to a business caller, as if fulfilling a duty.

"He brews the most popular beer for miles around. People drink it far and wide, in Fife, and even all the way to Perth and Dunkeld."

There was a brief sparkle in her eyes, and it made her appear a number of years younger.

Then she asked about me. She said she was curious about my father, even though she knew none of his works, and she wanted to know about our lives in London, and what I thought of the bookshop and if I liked reading.

"Very much," I answered. "Reading is what I enjoy most of all." That was, in fact, not entirely true. What I love doing most of all is daydreaming, fantasizing. But of course I could not say as much.

Meanwhile Isabella sat quietly drinking her tea. We had already finished the sandwiches, and the conversation had come to a natural end.

"Mary, Isabella, I shall withdraw to my room. I am fatigued. Feel free to explore the area, the house, the library, whatever you like. Make yourselves at home." Margaret did indeed look tired. She was pale and there was a dullness about her eyes, as if a gossamer-thin tissue had grown over them.

After she left the drawing room, neither of us spoke for a time. Then I put my teacup on the table and decided simply to ask.

"Why is Margaret in an invalid chair?"

It seemed almost as if Isabella had been expecting me to ask that question. She sighed. "She fell down the stairs," she said. "Come on."

She stood up and reached out her hand to me.

I wanted to ask many more questions. I wanted her to tell me what had happened, what the doctor had said, if she would ever be able to walk again. But Isabella pulled me along into the hallway, to the ebony staircase in the middle, which led upwards, dark and stately, and then through a door into the library. The shutters were closed, with only thin streaks of daylight coming through the cracks. Isabella walked, as if it were all she ever did, across the room and opened the shutters. Only then did the full extent of the library become clear. Two stories, with ceiling-height shelves along all the walls. Fireplaces on two sides, one framed by two large sofas and the other with a desk in front of it. Several richly colored carpets lay on the floor in the middle of the room, and there were small tables with flowers and candlesticks arranged on them. At one end of the room was a narrow spiral staircase to the upper floor, where you could walk between the balustrade and the bookcases that lined the walls.

"Mr. Booth has three thousand books," said Isabella. There was no admiration in her voice, although I could not imagine that she would not be impressed by that number. "Mainly academic works, but also novels and political writings."

We wandered past the bookshelves, climbed the spiral staircase, and looked down into the room below. At that moment, a cloud passed across the sun, strangely transforming the library from a warm and sacred place into a pale, cold imitation.

"I'm often allowed to borrow a book or two when I come to visit," said Isabella, mumbling in such a way that she seemed merely to be voicing a thought. I ran my fingertips along the spines. The tapping was a wonderfully familiar sound. How many times had I walked past the shelves in our bookshop, strumming my fingers over all those different books, over all those worlds, all those realities at my fingertips? As I paused at the letter G, I saw a number of books written by my father, which made me vicariously proud. Isabella had stopped at a bookcase full of Scottish myths and pulled out a book called *The Sacred Deep*. It was beautifully illustrated with curious depictions of octopuses the size of whaling ships, swordfish with human features, such as a beard or a faint, unfathomable smile, and sea creatures that seemed to be half male, half female, with breasts and beards, elegant, long hair, tough, muscular arms, and a fish's tail.

"Witches," Isabella said, pointing at a picture of a creature that, in addition to male and female characteristics was, on closer examination, also endowed with a peculiarity that exceeded all human bounds: a slight yet definite expression of gleeful malice.

Isabella looked up at me. And at that moment I knew that in some way we had found the explanation for our unexpected attraction to each other.

She carried the book down the spiral staircase, back to the drawing room, so that she could ask later if she might be allowed to take it to Dundee. I hoped she would read it with me or at least share with me the strange kinds of monsters she encountered within its pages.

There was still no one in the sitting room, but our tea had been cleared away. Isabella took me into the hall to put on our boots. "We're going outside," she said.

WOOL-WHITE CLOUDS CHASED across the blue sky at a dizzying pace. The sun was almost directly above our heads, and we felt the heat pressing down on our shoulders. We sought out the shady side of the house, as we had not brought parasols and there did not appear to be anyone around to ask for one. We walked around the outside of the house, which extended farther to the rear than I had imagined, and I noted a difference in architectural style towards the back. The windows began a number of yards above the ground here, so that we could not look inside, and the roof was higher and flat.

"This is the brewery," said Isabella.

And indeed we saw a tall set of double doors in the rear wall, through which a cart or carriage might be driven in and out. Barrels and wooden crates of various sizes were stacked in the yard. The smell was peculiar. A mixture of something spicy and something animal. Not entirely unpleasant, but certainly no scent I had ever smelled before.

"How often do you come here?" I asked.

Isabella turned around. I think she, too, felt as if we suddenly had something in common or in fact that we suddenly knew why we had something in common, because she smiled at me in a way I had never seen her smile before: happy, carefree. "Not that often. Once a month? Margaret married Mr. Booth five years ago, but I've only become a regular visitor since her accident. She can't get out as much these days, hardly ever in fact, and I want to keep her company."

"How did it happen?" I asked, but she did not hear, was already turning to leave the shade of the house and walk towards the flower garden.

I followed her. Among the poppies, the hibiscus, and the love-in-a-mist, which were not laid out neatly by variety, as one often sees, but mixed together in a glorious natural jumble, there must have been a couple of dozen butterflies fluttering around. I do not believe I have ever seen so many in one place. Isabella continued along the path to the back of the flower garden, where there was a well. We placed our hands on the cool edge. The water was so high that I could have touched it with my fingertips if I had leaned forward, but the mortar between the bricks of the well was green with moss and I did not want to dirty my clean gown when we were on a visit. Isabella pulled up the bucket and held it out to me. I laughed as I lifted the rim of the bucket to my mouth, and that made Isabella laugh too, and a splash of water fell down my neck and onto my gown. Startled, I stepped back, but in spite of the shock of the cold water I was still laughing, because I saw that Isabella was also laughing, with her hands over her mouth, apologetically, but still irrepressibly happy. I gave her a playful push and we decided to walk on a little farther, down the hill, and although the warmth was beating on our backs, we stayed in the sun, because we had tacitly decided that it did not matter. Because we were going for a walk. Two girls in the sunshine.

We lay in the grass at the foot of the hill, by the edge of the forest. Isabella could not tell me if this was all part of the estate, but there was no one around to chase us away. Besides, why would they? We lay on our backs, eyes closed. I thought of my gown from time to time, how the grass might leave stains on it that would be hard to get out, but we were lying so peacefully, the sun soothingly holding us down, like a warm, heavy blanket. I saw colors sparking in the reddish black of my eyelids and those movements stilled every thought that floated up within me. We did not say a word. Every now and then there was a breeze, cooling us just enough that we did not fall asleep. I could smell her. Sweat and soap mingled with the scent of warm grass and the wildflowers blooming between us. I could not explain it, but I felt the urge to lift my skirt a little, to undo my boots, to remove my stockings, and to lie there bare-legged in the grass, to feel the earth and grass against my skin, the hem of my gown on my knees, my foot against hers.

Startled, I gasped. I had fallen asleep after all. I had sat up so suddenly that Isabella opened her eyes too, and we decided to walk back, up the hill, past the well, through the flower garden, and into the house. It was probably already time for lunch.

LOOKING BACK, I wonder how it is possible that Mr. Booth was not shocked by our appearance. When Isabella and I entered the cool hallway, he was—or so it seemed—waiting there for us. He smiled.

"Nice walk, ladies? Martha has made gingerbread and vanilla custard, and there is soup and tea. She's laid the table in the dining room. Shall I lead the way?"

We passed a tall, richly decorated mirror and for a moment I thought the reflection I saw in it was not me. My hair was in all directions, with even a long stalk of grass sticking out of it. The sun had turned my face and neck a bold shade of red, and there were—indeed—a few green stains on my gown. Isabella, too, looked like some kind of vagabond, but I only saw that now. Perhaps because Isabella has a face that is both charming and resolute in all circumstances. There is a wisdom in her eyes and at the same time a gentle sort of mockery, as if all manners are only manners, all formality is simply for show, her own days merely waiting rooms for the big adventure.

I felt a little awkward when I discovered how terrible I looked, but Isabella did not seem to care too much.

Martha was pouring tea in the dining room. There were plates and bowls ready, with fruit, thick slices of gingerbread, butter, vanilla custard, and soup, and Mr. Booth assured us that there was more if we should wish. It seemed impossible that the three of us should finish all this food, but I was certainly hungry. Mary Jane had tried to teach Fanny, Claire, and me to eat less than we should actually like at each meal. According to her, it was healthy for a girl still to feel a little hunger after eating. This would stimulate the digestion and we would maintain a nice figure—not too thin and not too fat. But Mary Jane was not here, and besides, I did not believe she had any understanding of health matters.

Isabella and I were invited to sit opposite each other, and Mr. Booth was between us at the head of the table. We helped ourselves to food and he asked where we had been. Isabella told him we had not gone far, that it had been such lovely warm weather that we had sat in the grass.

"I thought as much," said Mr. Booth with a smile. It was the smile of a good friend, but not entirely. It was the smile of a father, but it was not quite that, either.

"Is Margaret still resting?" asked Isabella.

Mr. Booth looked up from his plate, where he was spreading butter onto a slice of gingerbread. He had long, thin fingers. His knuckles, though, were thick, which made his fingers appear even thinner. "Margaret is not feeling well. I think she will remain in her room for the rest of the day," he said.

Isabella's eyes grew wider. "The whole day?"

I could see she thought it a pity. It would probably be another month now before she could visit her sister again, and I believe she had been looking forward to it.

"Sadly, yes," said Mr. Booth. "She told me this morning that she was feeling unwell and she hoped that it would improve over the course of the day. She would have liked to spend more time with you today, I'm sure of that."

AFTER THE MEAL, Mr. Booth offered to give us a tour of the house. Isabella must have seen it countless times already, so she asked if

I would mind if she went and read in the drawing room instead. Although I would have preferred her to come with me, I did not tell her so, and Mr. Booth and I headed the other way down the hall. He first showed me the music room, where there was a shiny grand piano, much larger than the one at Isabella's, as well as a harp, a violoncello, and a clarionet.

"Do you play all these instruments yourself?" I asked.

Mr. Booth nodded. "When I married Margaret, I played only the violoncello and the piano. Margaret is a good harpist, and the clarionet was a wedding gift. Now I enjoy playing them all, and I do so relatively well, if I may say so myself."

There was a certain matter-of-factness in the way he spoke. I believed him at once. I thought he must have a special musical gift to be able to play four instruments well. And I suspected, in addition, that he was a man with little free time.

"If you like, I can play for you some time," he said, "but not now. I should like to show you the rest of the house, and I have an appointment soon."

We left the music room, passed the kitchen, which Mr. Booth skipped without a word, and headed upstairs to the first floor, where he showed me a number of large bedrooms before leading me into the library. I had, of course, been there only a few hours before with Isabella, but strangely, now that I entered with Mr. Booth, the room did not appear to be quite the same. It is hard to explain precisely, but it was not simply because of the sun, which by that point had turned away from the windows a little, making the wood of the bookshelves appear deep black rather than chocolate brown. It was more a change in the library's atmosphere: a slip in reality that had not occurred when Isabella and I had entered the room. Almost as if something were holding its breath. Mr. Booth led me along the shelves I had studied that morning, pointing out books that did not really interest me. He showed me that he had a first edition of Luigi Galvani's *Memorie sulla elettricità animale*, which he kept behind glass and took out to read only once a year. I nodded politely but I did not know any Italian, something that Mr. Booth did not take into account, so I was not entirely sure of the subject or why the book was so special. Judging by the title, it had something to do with memories, electricity, and animals, but that was all I could make of it. He asked if I wanted to climb the spiral staircase to the upper floor, but I shook my head.

"Let's go back to Isabella," I said.

As we left the room, I said I thought it a magnificent library, because I felt that I had said too little about his proud possession, and then he turned to look at me.

"Thank you, Mary," he said. "I thought you would find my book collection most interesting. When you visit again, I'll show you where my storybooks are in the gallery. There is a section up there of which I myself am particularly fond."

I wondered if he was talking about the shelves of myths. Of course, I barely knew Mr. Booth, but I did not have the impression that he was a man with much interest in the supernatural.

Downstairs in the drawing room, we found Isabella sitting in a window seat. The light was shining in so brightly that she had closed her eyes and for a moment it seemed as if she were sleeping. But then she opened her eyes and stood up. She had a curious expression on her face, as if she had been pondering something during our absence and now realized that we had brought the answer.

"Ladies," said Mr. Booth, "this evening we shall dine together and then the carriage will take you home. Unfortunately, I have an urgent appointment elsewhere, but it would sadden me if you were bored. I would wholeheartedly encourage you to take another pleasant walk, to Monk's Well perhaps, or to the fields down the road. Or you could of course spend some time in the library or the music room. I regret that I shall have to leave you on your own for a couple of hours. If there is anything you should need, Martha is in the kitchen." Then he turned around and left the drawing room. A little later, we heard the sound of the carriage driving up.

"Can you play an instrument?" I asked Isabella. She was standing at the window, with her back to me. I could not see any grass stains on her gown, but it was blue and considerably darker than mine, so perhaps they were not as noticeable.

"I can play a little piano, but not nearly as well as Margaret," she said.

As she spoke, her mind seemed elsewhere, as if a small part of her brain were reserved for speaking and acting, while most of it was for the thoughts she had and would, I was fairly certain, never share with me.

"I can only play the piano too," I said. "But I should really practice more. Mr. Booth said that Margaret plays the harp."

Isabella turned around, appeared to have been shaken awake. "And she plays it well, too. But Mr. Booth plays it better. He plays everything better."

"He's very intelligent, isn't he?" I asked, thinking how silly my question sounded.

"'Intelligent' isn't the right word." Isabella smiled slightly and ran her fingers over the skin of her other arm, which, I now noticed, was also burned quite red. "Mr. Booth is so intelligent that the word no longer suffices. He sometimes seems to know things he should have no way of knowing, do you understand?"

"What do you mean?"

At that moment, we heard a sound. It was like a sigh or a creaking floorboard, only there was no one there but us. Isabella's face froze.

"I once saw something so strange here." Her eyes narrowed and the color seemed to drain from her face.

I noticed my heart starting to beat faster. The thumping was like the ringing of a bell, like when you are high up in a church tower and feel the chimes going through your body.

"What do you mean?" I repeated.

"Hm," she said, and the part of her mind that had at first been elsewhere but had just been shaken awake appeared to drift back to sleep. "Let's go outside."

THIS IS A very special part of Scotland," said Isabella as we walked along the sandy path towards the grain fields, this time under a parasol that Martha had given us. "Such terrible things have happened here." She did not look at me. In the light filtering through the parasol, her skin appeared to be made of wax: smooth, immaculate, and pale as candle grease. Her entire appearance was so unlike Margaret's that it was hard to believe they were sisters. Perhaps Margaret moved differently before her accident, I thought. Perhaps then she had more grace, had eyes in which you could see even the night shining. Isabella's countenance is certainly not joyful, but she radiates an indefinable power, which Margaret lacks completely. Robert and Johnny also have that fire to a degree, but that intensity seems never to have been present within Margaret.

"What kind of things?" I thought the landscape was breathtaking. I could scarcely imagine what terrible things might have happened here. I knew London: its harshness and its glory, the spectacle, the sadness and poverty, the dirt and the noise, the people and the possibilities. But I did not know this place. It was so quiet here, so infinitely peaceful. Everything was nature—a pure world, as it had been for centuries. Here your feet walked on the earth instead of on cobblestones, here you touched trees instead of houses, here you could look all around and around and around instead of only ahead or behind. This place smelled of the world, rather than of people.

"Witches." Isabella stopped walking. She looked at me and started laughing. She laughed so loud, so shamelessly, that I could not help joining in.

"The Scottish witch is the worst of all," she said a little more calmly. "She does the most terrible things, much more terrible than you could imagine."

I began to wonder what the stories said about Scottish witches. What was the worst thing I could think of? Luring people? Tearing open their throats with a crooked yellow fingernail? Brewing potions from their victims' blood and hair?

"The Scottish witch eats babies. And she does not kill them first but eats them alive. Finger by finger, hand by hand, leg by leg. She drinks the blood from the veins, she uses the bones to mash up the eyes. She stands by the roadside awaiting lone travelers and then enchants them so that they jump into the sea, hang themselves at the nearest inn, or slash their wrists with a nail or a needle."

I looked at her. There was a dramatic gleam in her bright eyes. I will confess that I did not know how to react. Was she testing me? Did she want to find out if I was easily scared? Or did she believe this herself? Whatever the case, these were terrible fabrications, yes, but somewhere within me a space seemed to open up. A small place where these ghosts were allowed to exist and where I did not have to shy away from savagery. And that place, I thought, is a place that Isabella knows too.

We walked through the field, the heat subsiding. On the horizon, a bank of clouds was preparing to spread across the sky. Isabella walked ahead of me through the head-height stalks of grain. We said nothing and walked for a long time. At one point I began to wonder if the field would ever come to an end. The image of the rustling stalks as we passed through, Isabella's hair tied up, her narrow shoulders, her deep green eyes as she glanced back—it all engraved itself on my retinas, remaining with me even long after we had reached the end of the field. Even when we stopped to eat cake and share a bottle of water on a stone wall that was crawling with ants, and the dark gray clouds swept across the sky, and when we started on our way back, around the outside of the field this time, so that we could follow the path, and Isabella began to talk again, as if she had had to summon up the courage, or the inclination, or had woken from a trance.

About half a mile from the house, Isabella suddenly stopped. She looked at me, sighed, and a slight smile appeared on her face.

"I'm so glad you came with me today," she said. "I sometimes find it so terribly difficult to do things since Mama . . ." She turned away from me a little.

"I'm so very sorry," I said. I wanted to say something else, something nice and comforting, which would no doubt have come out clumsily and had no effect, but she turned around and hugged me. And in that embrace was everything: her silence, her inward gaze, her petulance and her uncontrollable laughter, her magnificent, terrible fabrications. The sun was shining in my eyes, so I closed them. She had her arms around my waist, my hands were gently stroking the hair that tumbled down her back, and there we stood.

"Ow!" Isabella jumped back and I saw a coal-black strand flash through the grass like a bolt of lightning.

"Oh no, no." Isabella sat down on the dusty path and looked at her ankle. Her stocking was torn. There was a bloody, ragged hole in it. Tears were rolling down her cheeks, but she looked angry.

"A filthy adder. It was an adder, wasn't it, Mary?"

I nodded. The wound did not seem to be bleeding badly, but that did not mean the bite was not serious, I thought. "Come, we must return to the house. Let us hope Mr. Booth has already returned."

ISABELLA LAY ON the sofa with her legs on Mr. Booth's lap. He had removed his jacket and rolled up the sleeves of his shirt. I stood there, holding her stained stocking: it was still warm. It lay in my hand like a small dying animal.

Mr. Booth pinched the wound with two fingers: two small holes, close together, with blood seeping out. It was very dark red, so gleaming, so real. He looked intently at the wound, as if his gaze might cause the blood to clot. Isabella lay with her head tipped back, turned to one side. He had given her laudanum. Three other small bottles with unclear labels stood on a small table beside the sofa. When the bleeding stopped, he would dab the wound with one of those ointments and bandage it with a piece of cotton to prevent infection. Sometimes she looked at me, or rather: she looked into me. Her eyes penetrated deeply into mine, as if she were looking inside me, through my eyes, seeing things that did not exist until the moment she saw them. And I felt them. They were horrifying, unimaginably large and true. She saw the things I sometimes suspected but did not truly believe in anymore. But she made the fleeting fear, the secret thoughts that sometimes flitted through me, coagulate within me. They became unyielding.

WE ARRIVED HOME hours ago. Isabella is sleeping, the Baxters are sleeping, I am the only one who is still awake. I and my candle at the table by the window, and I know it will never leave. I feel it in my heart, my guts, my toes. It is waiting.

"Help," I whisper now and then. But no one is there.

May 1816
Cologny

A storm, a stillness, a storm

The morning is so beautiful she could cry, as if she has never seen sunlight before. Finally, after more than three weeks, the sun has completely broken through the dense grayness. Every color now has more intensity, more life, as if a veil has lifted. Percy was too tired to accompany her, so Mary left him in bed with William beside him, making his morning noises. Throaty sounds, short cries, Percy sleeps through it, she does not sleep.

The garden is muddy and smells of everything mixed up together: lilies, arums, gladioli, lilacs, pear trees, grass, earth, life. Fortunately, her boots were by the door, so she can keep her feet dry. She has hitched up her gown with a belt so the hem will not get wet, but she takes the wrong paths, the ones with branches that want to touch her. Not too far away, over the hill, behind the hay barns, beyond the abandoned houses along the road, there is a meadow. She thinks there must be a cow there, maybe a few of them. Sometimes she hears them, early in the morning. A desolate calling.

"Mary!" Panting, John works his way up the hill. His boots are covered in mud. "I just saw you leave."

"You're up early," she says.

John looks as though he needs some sleep. His face is blotchy and red, he has stubble on his chin, and his eyes are deep in their sockets. Beneath his eyes, the skin is thick and gray.

"Did you get any sleep?" she asks.

He starts laughing softly, stumbles.

"Did you all spend the whole night drinking again?" She avoids a puddle on the path.

"Except for Percy, he was with . . ."

"Oh," says Mary. Oh. She was alone last night, alone with William. She assumed Percy and Claire were with Albe and John at Diodati. She feels her lips purse. She hates it when that happens. It makes her feel old.

Before they reach the top of the hill, the sky clouds over again. The sun disappears as suddenly as it came. The grayness of everything overwhelms her.

"Albe suggested you should all come for dinner this evening. He's acquired some French books of ghost stories from somewhere."

On top of the hill. The clouds are magnificent. It seems inconceivable that the sun she just saw is now shining behind that dense blanket of cloud.

"Mary?" John stands there, arms limp by his sides.

"Fine," she says. She would prefer not to look at him. If she looks at him, she feels that she will have to say things. John's gaze has such a depth and kindness that he always forces her to say more than she would like. Afterwards, it seems incomprehensible.

Then she sees them. Down the hill, behind a barn, there is a bare pasture. Three cows are standing there. They are bags of bones with scrawny hips and eyes that seem weary of life. She starts running. She hears John following her. He does not ask her where she is going. She runs down to the cows. Mary's hitched-up gown drops back down, she is panting. Her pinned-up hair is coming loose. She spreads her arms. Starts laughing, she cannot help it. At the bottom, she comes to a stop against the fence. Then John is standing beside her, also panting. A cow, just a couple of yards away from them, raises her head. Oh, those eyes. Those dark, sad eyes. In all dark eyes, she recognizes what has been lost. The oceans of memory that even—perhaps especially—for this cow span a lifetime. This is not simply an event in time, because it lasts, it continues to last and will never, never be over. And *that* is what she sees. That is what she recognizes. Every event creates itself over and over again in almost the same proportions, with almost the same impact, in almost the same way. The only difference is that the event comes from outside for the first time, works its way into the mind, and then remains, is retold, is imitated, is worked up into a story. Except with her. Her story is broken.

"What is it about cows?" John holds his open hand towards the cow. She does not react. "I never know if they are simply very calm or extremely unhappy."

Mary laughs a little.

"Shall I come over again this afternoon? *Per la lezione di italiano?*"

"Did you know I had another child?" She does not want to look at him. She never looks at him. "Before William?"

They are silent for a time.

"Is it no longer alive?" asks John.

"Percy prefers not to talk about it. He says it's too painful. Of course it's too painful. For the love of God, how could it *not* be too painful?"

On the other side of the meadow, the darkness in the air is becoming more compact. There is a deep rumbling that might come from the earth if one did not know better. She feels a splash on her neck.

"Percy is not as strong as you, Mary."

"That's not true. I don't know what it is, but he is certainly strong."

A drop on her nose, on her chin, on her hand. She looks to one side.

"He has been through less, I think."

John is the only man she knows who is never sure of himself, never. That is what she finds so wonderful about him. That eternal agony of doubt, which is so logical that every human should feel it, but no man does. Or at least there is no man who expresses his doubts. Except for John.

"Do you believe ghosts could exist?" In the distance, she hears a bird of prey screeching. It is a barbaric sound—she feels goose bumps on her arms.

John sighs pensively. Takes a deep breath. "I think that possibility is very small," he says.

"There are those who see them." They start to walk back. Farther on, a narrow gravel path winds up the hill. The sky turns gray, the rain is coming.

"There is no evidence whatsoever. It makes no sense from a physiological point of view either. Everything that lives withers and dies. You have to wonder why something would be left behind. Why something would return. And how?" John follows her up the path.

She does know that, of course. She is not stupid, or superstitious, like Claire. And yet she thinks about it, despite all logic, when her thoughts turn to her little girl.

"They're stories, Mary."

She turns around. Now she does look at him. "What do you mean?"

John gives a little shrug. Behind him, the sky turns ocher. "They're just stories. Made up. There's no need to be afraid of fabrications."

They walk on. Is she afraid? John knows a lot. Maybe he saw something in her eyes that she did not know existed. She hears John limping.

"What's wrong with your leg?"

He looks down, smiles. "I jumped off the balcony. It was somewhat higher than I thought. A little foolish."

"Off the balcony?"

She sees a glint in his eyes. Bravado? Pleasure?

John trips and almost falls flat on his face. Mary is just in time to grab his arm and save him from the fall.

"Lean on me."

Mary holds her arm at a right angle so that John can hook his arm around it and take the weight off his leg.

JUST AS THEY step across the threshold, it starts pouring. They take off their boots and hang up their coats. Percy is awake. He has lit the stove in the kitchen and made coffee. The room smells of warm autumn. He is at the table, immersed in Coleridge. With one hand, he is rocking William's cradle, which he has moved next to the table.

"Coffee!" says John, and the peace evaporates. Percy gets up to pour coffee, asks how her walk was. John pulls up a chair and sits with a thud and a sigh, tickles William, who was awake or is just waking up, on his stomach. Mary wraps her arms around Percy, by the stove. She kisses him on the back of his neck. And as always, his scent, his soft skin, his breathtaking wildness penetrates into her, into her lips and eyelids, into her fingertips, her breath, her blood. There are never words, but this is what she knows: he is inside her.

Percy puts coffee on the table for them. "Sorry, I have to write to Harriet. I keep putting it off. I'll be in the study."

Mary takes William out of his cradle. He feels warm, his cheeks have a red sheen.

"I'm just going to feed him," she says to John. "But do stay."

Mary takes William to the bedroom. On the bed, she makes a throne of pillows. She unbuttons her gown and takes out her breast. Since Elise has been there, her milk has come more easily, but it has also been more painful. Luckily, William still wants her breast. The moment she holds him to her nipple, his warm head in the crook of her elbow, a frown of concentration on his face, his tiny hands kneading the air, she feels a shock of joy and loss go through her body. Joy and loss, as if one cannot exist without the other, she thinks. As if everything, everything that there is, is already lost, because one day it will be lost. She ponders this, half-consciously, half-lost in a daydream; a fantasy about the beginning of things, about a shadow under the window, mermen and expanses of water and conjectures.

◆ ◆ ◆

Albe has lit the candles in the chandelier. Mary does not want to imagine how long it must have taken him. The effect is curious. The ceiling lights up brightly white, shadows growing along the walls.

Outside, one of the fiercest storms since they arrived here is raging. The candle flames flicker as if invisible fingers are pulling at them. They have gathered around the fireplace, pulled the sofa closer. Albe and Percy are sitting on the rug, Claire is lying on the sofa, her feet on John's lap. John's sore leg is up on a stool. He has examined himself and arrived at the diagnosis that he has bruised his ankle and should, for the time being, remain seated as much as possible. Mary is in the large reading armchair. The fire burns on her eyelids. Maybe she is exhausted. Maybe it is the wine with laudanum. A thunderclap of unreal proportions makes them all jump, except for Percy. He is reading Coleridge's collection. Mary brought it with her. The poet himself, a regular visitor to her father, gave it to her. Now Percy seems to be under its spell.

Albe fills the glasses again. How many have they had since dinner? Mary has no idea. Numbers mean nothing to her anymore.

"Mary, would you like to go first?"

Albe hands her a book with a gray cover, with *Fantasmagoriana* written on it. "Choose a story you like the look of."

It is a French translation of German ghost stories. She leafs through it. Stops at a story with the title *"Le Baiser."* Percy puts Coleridge down. Claire opens her eyes. Mary begins.

She knows she can read well. Her voice is warm, clear, her intonation pleasant. The story begins atmospherically: a country house, a family, a nursery. Twilight, a candle, a story, a lullaby. The mother comes for a kiss. The child is lying in her bed, the curtains are drawn. It is dark now. She should be sleeping, but she is not. Now and then the child hears something: the wind, a mouse, an owl? She is afraid she will not fall asleep. What if she is still awake later? What if, when the hour has begun, she is still not sleeping? Anyone who is awake at the witching hour sees everything. Anyone who sees everything will never sleep again. She thinks about Mother's kiss: firm, soft, just for her. She tries to think herself to sleep, but time keeps her awake. The more she wants it, the more sleep dances away from her. The night has forgotten to take her with it. The curtains around the bed are playing as if the wind is blowing. A splinter of moon makes objects visible (linen closet, closed doors, mirrors, dolls that are not themselves) that should be invisible now. Mother's kiss was full of confidence. It is only night. Could it be that grownups know nothing about the night? Have they forgotten? Can they dance at the witching hour because they no longer see anything? And yes, the closet is opening. A thin figure worms its way through the crack. The child thinks she has just died. There was so much fear that she almost became a believer, but now that she sees this (this thing without eyes, because it is night, with claws as long as its hair and a mouth that is big and gray), she knows she must have ended up in hell. The thing is standing beside her now, the child breathes very quietly, maybe then it will not notice her. But it leans forward, places its mouth, like a worm, so softly on hers and draws her slow breath away. In the morning, her mother knows as soon as she opens the door that something has gone wrong in the night. Her child has quietly departed, is lying breathless behind the half-closed curtain. She climbs in with her, arches her back, pulls up her legs, so that she fits beside her in the bed. She trembles as she strokes the cold body. No one warned her of the dangers of the night. She kisses that sweet form and goes back in time, to when the sun slipped into the horizon and she took her child into her own bed, where they fell asleep together.

For a moment, they are silent. Then Albe launches into a disjointed account of narrative reality and imagined reality in the story. No one appears to be listening. Percy tops up the glasses. John pokes the fire. Claire takes the book from Mary's hands and looks for a new story. Mary stares into the middle distance. The shutters are open, no one wants to go outside to close them. Branches scratch at the windows, there is an almost constant rumbling in the sky, and the rain falls and falls and falls. They drink.

Claire has found something and begins to read. A dead bride's head is brought to life, but the story barely catches Mary's attention. She had put her in bed with them, sent for the doctor, but it was far too late. Mary made a fortress of her body, curled around her child, her little girl, far too little, she had left her on her own, she had slept, unaware of the dangers of the night. They had not warned her. She should have kept her close, including at night. Especially at night. She had gone to check on her. An hour, perhaps two before she died. Why did she go and look? And why did she not go again? The fortress did not help at all. Her child lay dead within her walls. She could not say goodbye. No one had warned her. Her child was dead. Her soft, transparent body no longer served any purpose. Her miniature mouth, her ears like shells. Breathing hurt so much, Mary cursed every breath, but it did not stop. Everything went on working. Everything kept on going. No one had warned her.

"LET'S EACH WRITE a ghost story." Albe has desire in his eyes. Maybe the drink.

Percy nods. "Whoever writes the most frightening story wins."

Claire is not there. Gone to bed, driven by drink or because no one was paying her particular attention. Mary has curled up next to John on the sofa. She is leaning against his shoulder. She can feel how he is trembling, he loves her so much. Percy pays no heed to them; he knows how it is, knows he is the only one, knows she longs only for him.

"I'll do it if Mary does," says John with a big drunken smile.

The others look at him, at her.

"Yes," says Albe, "Mary can do it too. Surprise us, Mary."

She is unable to think clearly about it, but the remark annoys her. Why on earth should she let herself be persuaded to pit herself against these men? She does not need this. But something prevents her from voicing her thoughts. She thinks she wants to do it. She thinks something is there. Maybe. Maybe it is something terrible.

IN BED, AT DIODATI (because the storm is fiercer than usual, the storm is dangerous, the storm is a monster), sleep always seems about to begin, but something is in the way. It is as if her thoughts want to go somewhere she does not. They gallop ahead of her, she struggles to rein them in. But the harder she pulls, the harder they pull back. The carriage hurtles along the road. "Come on," she calls. "Easy now. Please, stop!" But the horses do not hear her, the storm rages, blowing her words away. Mud splashes against the wheels, the wind tugs at her hair and whips tears into her eyes. "We're taking you home," snorts one of the horses. "Where you belong."

When she looks around, the night has passed. The storm has blown itself out. She floats, sees hills, beautiful forests, a wide river. She sees the house she knows so well, the garden gate, the flowers. And across the river, the big house with the stately columns. A comforting lightness descends upon her. He is standing on the steps. He beckons and she thinks that it is fine, but as she floats closer, things become strange. Everything looks different, the trees have pointed, twisted branches, the sky has an orange-brown glow, and the house is taller, much taller than before. Something is not right. Something is not right at all. She wants to turn around, but she keeps floating closer. And then she sees it. No one warned her.

June–July 1812
Dundee

June 29, 1812

Isabella's ankle has still not healed completely. For a time, there was some doubt about whether she would be able to go to the fair in Fife, but she complained so persistently, sweetly, and dramatically that Mr. Baxter took another good look at her ankle, told Grace to bandage it as firmly as possible, and made Isabella promise that she would sit down often and not come home too late. All of us went, the whole family, in two carriages, and Isabella and I were to return with Johnny at the end of the day.

We sat beaming, side by side, she and I. We leaned out the window to see how far we still had to go. Eventually, the carriage could go no farther because there were too many vehicles on the road. So we walked the last part of the way, Isabella doing her best to disguise her slight limp. I had never experienced anything similar before, and I realized how much I was longing for things that had not belonged to my world until then. Unfamiliar events and mysterious scenes were calling, and my heart rang out happily within me. Screaming children, young men with bottles of beer, elegantly attired ladies, all mingling together. Johnny jumped up and down and around us. Robert tried to hold his hand so he would not get lost, but Johnny was in too high spirits. Robert grinned at me. He was about to say something to me, but Isabella pulled me along, into the crowd, away from the other Baxters. As well as the many stalls selling sweets, drinks, and other wares such as scarves, hats, parasols, jewelry, and paintings, there was a row of tents with people standing outside trying to lure passersby to enter. Bearded women, dwarfs, and fortune tellers awaited us, along with talking birds, a man who put his head inside a tiger's mouth, a young woman with two faces, and a cat circus.

"What is all of this?" I called out happily to Isabella.

She laughed. It was such a fine, uninhibited laugh—I had rarely seen her like that before.

"Would you like to see some strange sights?" she asked.

I looked around. It would be hard not to see strange sights here. I nodded.

"Come on." She pulled me with her to a big red tent at the end of the field with the word CURIOSITATIBUS painted on the wooden sign by the entrance in yellow and purple letters.

Isabella paid two halfpennies to a surly and bored-looking woman at the entrance and held aside the canvas door for me.

It was warm inside the tent. It was also rather dark and it smelled very strongly of flowers, so strongly that it was a little unpleasant. But there was also another scent hidden within that scent, one I could not place. A red glow was upon Isabella's face, and I believe she was looking at me, that was how it felt, but I could not see clearly. I felt her hand in mine, firmly, and I did not know if she needed my hand or if she thought I needed hers. I gradually began to make out the surroundings. Behind us were three stuffed owls on a high table. They had lost that typically stern look that owls have, seeming sad, almost fearful, as if locked away inside themselves. Nearby was a pillar with a Renaissance-style marble statue of a young woman standing on it, a cloth wrapped around her hips and bare breasts, but where her mouth should have been, a beak protruded, large and pointed. I could almost feel her as we walked past, as if her gaze were caressing my back. I gripped Isabella's hand more tightly, and she giggled. On the next table were a number of portraits, which were drawn very well. They were unmistakably children, but each had a strange, cunning expression on its face.

"Heavens above," I whispered.

Isabella rubbed her thumb over my palm. Then she pulled me to a table illuminated by two candles. There were glass jars of various sizes on the table, filled with cloudy water. In one jar, the water was very brown; in others it was greenish. There was something floating in there.

"My God!" Isabella clasped her hand over her mouth. She took a step back and let go of my hand. "That's repulsive."

I did not understand what she meant. I leaned forward to study the jar of brown water more closely and that was when I saw it: a little hand pressed against the side of the jar. I looked more closely and it was not only a hand: there was a little arm attached to it, a body, a head. All told, it was the size of my own hand, but it was completely whole. The head was comparatively large; eyes closed, bulging.

"Ah, poor child," I whispered. It had lived. Even if only inside its mother's belly. It had felt warmth, it had dreamed. It had been made, fed, had grown, it was going to live. But something happened.

Or, more likely, nothing happened. They did not want her mother to hold her, but the mother screamed, she screamed so loudly until they let her. And she lay there on the bed, in a tangle of red sheets, with pain that would never leave her. And they took her and carried her away and she would never, ever see her again, no matter how loudly she screamed: my baby, my baby, my baby!

"Mary, come on." Isabella had taken hold of me. She embraced me, encircled me, my cheeks making hers wet. She wiped us dry. And she kissed me on my dry cheek. A fluttering sought its way inside me, swirling wildly in my belly, wanting to be everywhere.

WE WANDERED AROUND the fair for hours. I bought some barley sugar and shared it with Johnny and Isabella. Johnny wanted to go on the merry-go-round, and we went with him. I became pleasantly dizzy from going up and down on the horse, from the people, from the tents that went around and around. Johnny sat on the horse to my left with a blissful grin on his face, Isabella to my right. I could feel her looking at me. I looked at her. I could not fathom her expression. It was as if she were looking for something deep inside me. Then she looked ahead again. She sat there on the horse, so stately, so serious, that there was something comical about it, and yet it was not. Her hands, her slender, pale hands, held the reins of the horse so firmly that they were trembling. I wanted to take hold of her hands. I wanted to comfort her, although I did not know what for, but I could not reach. We galloped on, in circles, up and down, and then it was over. Johnny went with Robert, and Isabella and I walked slowly on. The sun was already starting to set and when I looked at Isabella I saw an orange glow on her skin and in her hair. I thought I could smell her. She smelled of sun, of vanilla, and of a scent that I know only from Isabella and which is impossible to describe.

Suddenly she stood still. She held me back.

"What is it?"

"Ssh."

I tried to see what she could see, but there was so much, and no one thing seemed much stranger than any other.

"Mr. Booth," whispered Isabella.

And then I saw him. He was standing between two tents, talking to an old man with a graying ginger beard. Mr. Booth appeared collected and reasonable, but the man was gesturing angrily and at one point raised his voice. Mr. Booth moved closer to him and put his arm around his shoulders. That helped; the man grew calmer.

"Shall we go and say hello?" I asked.

Isabella quickly shook her head.

"What's wrong?"

"Mr. Booth doesn't come to the fair anymore."

"So?"

"You don't understand. These are not his kind of people."

"Maybe he had some business to take care of," I said. "Does he sell his beer here?"

Isabella looked hesitant. "He has people for that."

They had walked to the rear of the tent, so we could no longer see them.

"Young ladies!"

I was startled as, I believe, was Isabella. In front of the tent sat a stout, somewhat older lady. She was not dressed like most of the fair people: she was wearing a respectable gown, her boots were polished to a gleam, and a pearl necklace with a locket hung on her white throat. Her gray hair was pinned up tightly. She looked at us kindly, with narrowed eyes. The sun was low.

"You look like two adventurous young ladies. And you're not easily disturbed, are you?" She spoke very proper English, without a Scottish accent, and I wondered where she came from. "You like to be thrilled, but there is nothing that is too spine-chilling for you, is there?" The woman had a serious expression, but Isabella laughed.

"A thrill can only truly chill," she continued, "if what thrills and chills us is actually real, is that not true?" Now she was laughing too. Her teeth were a yellowish brown. "Real spine-chilling horrors— where can you find them these days?" She looked around with a sweeping gesture. "Not here, not in any of these tents—that much is clear! Deception. That's all it is, entertainment and deception. Except . . ." She turned and pointed at the tent she was sitting in front of. It seemed just like all the other tents. Isabella and I looked at each other, giggling skeptically.

"What is it?" asked Isabella.

"That, my dear, is a question I cannot answer. What can be seen inside this tent is not of this world. And so it cannot be described with words of this world."

I wanted to leave. I do not believe I was afraid, at least not of whatever was inside the tent, but I did not like the way the woman spoke. She did not appear to be inviting just any two people to enter her tent. It was almost as if she particularly wanted the two of us in there.

"Hm," nodded Isabella, as if she thought it profound. "Well, then we should take a look, don't you think, Mary?"

"Tuppence," the woman said quickly, holding out her hand.

Isabella placed the coins on her palm and, with a groan, the woman stood up from her stool. She pulled the canvas aside. There was a light inside the tent. As the woman dropped the canvas, a female voice began to sing. It sounded reedy, as if she had almost lost her voice. Isabella and I stopped. For some reason, the thought of walking any farther into the tent was terrible. Every step forward would feel like reliving your worst memory.

"Oh God," Isabella said quietly. It sounded as if she were crying.

It was so strange, as if I had suddenly been given more memories, as if I could now remember everything and I did not understand why I had forgotten those memories outside the tent, in my life. It made so much sense, they were so close to me. My mother dying, I could feel it, I could see it. Her eyes with futile hope floating in them, her lips feverishly hot on my skin. I could hear her speaking, her weak whispers, but I did not know what she said. And then I saw the child, my child, sleeping and dead, and the days she had lived seemed unreal; the longer she was dead, the more intensely she did not exist, as if only her death were real, only her non-life existed, because that would last an eternity, and in my stomach it grew dark, and the darkness said softly: the mother and the child had two things in common—guess what they were? It was cruel and it was true and who ever said that the truth must be good? The darkness decided: you cannot be the monster and the victim in one. It was as if my chest were wrapped around with the most vicious cord, carving into my heart, and then Isabella squeezed my hand so hard that the pain sparked through my arm. I looked at her in the semi-darkness, and her cheeks were wet, her eyes gleaming, her lashes thick and stuck together. The singing had stopped, some time ago, I thought. We turned around, I reached for the canvas, found the exit, and we fled. I do not believe the woman was outside any longer, but I am not certain, because we walked so fast, far away from the tent we had entered of our own volition, which did not bode well, but which did not cause our rashness to falter until the darkness revealed itself to us in its full glory, surrounding us and penetrating us with malevolent purity.

IN THE CARRIAGE on the way home, Johnny chattered away about the "two-faced woman," as he called her, the man without legs, all the sweets, the music, the picture book he had been given, the people, the cat circus. Isabella nodded now and then and smiled absently, but she said nothing. I tried to listen to Johnny's stories, but they drifted past me. I could hardly believe I had really seen and heard all those things inside that tent. If someone had told me we had fallen asleep, I would have believed it. Maybe I had imagined it. But had I also imagined Isabella's wet face? Her gleaming eyes? What had frightened us so much? It could only be that the woman in front of the tent had played upon our nerves with such skill that our minds had been fed with images, forces, and fears that came from depths we did not know.

◆ ◆ ◆

Johnny was in bed. We had given him milk and sung a few songs for him and by the third song he had fallen asleep. His sleeping head, his breathing, so delicate and wondrous, stung me, made my eyes burn. We went to my bedroom, Isabella and I. I lit a lamp with the fire from the hearth and placed it on the bedside table. Isabella lay beside me on my bed; I leaned against the headboard. She had her eyes open and was gazing at something that was floating between the fire and the ceiling.

"Mary?"

A spark.

She did not move, was still looking away from me.

"What did you see?"

The images returned, even though I had been quite successful at banishing them all evening. That child, the child I did not know, but which was mine all the same, had a strange and unique identity, tightly connected to the awareness of deep loss.

I looked at her, her eyes showed nothing, but maybe that was because she still was not looking at me. "I can't explain it," I said.

Then she looked at me, her lips pursing, her eyes growing bright. "I saw a man, but I do not know what he looked like. He was big, I knew him, but I can no longer remember who he was. I was afraid, Mary. He was too big. I mean, he was unreal, his spirit. It was not a human being."

A strand of blackness writhed inside my stomach.

"Now you." She was still looking at me.

For a while, I said nothing, but then I spoke: "I saw a child. A baby. It was my baby. But she was dead. And there was something else, but I'm not sure what. It was big. Black. Deep."

Isabella nodded.

"What kind of tent was that?" I asked.

Isabella turned towards me. "I don't know. It's as if I've seen something that doesn't exist, but which belongs with me even so. Do you understand?"

I thought back to the blackness. It surrounded her too. It penetrated her too. It was inside us.

I slid down, her arm around me, my back against her stomach, her breath tickling my neck. She started to sing very quietly. I had never heard Isabella sing and, although she did not reach some notes and her voice cracked a little on the low notes, I thought it was beautiful. I didn't understand the song entirely, as some of the words were Scots, but it was about the sea. About waves washing over one another, again and again, for centuries and centuries. About the sea knowing no time. No reason. No guilt. The sea knows only sorrow.

June 30, 1812

I woke early today, an hour earlier than usual. Something made me alert, as if a thought whispered that it was better to be awake. I washed and dressed myself and went downstairs. From behind Johnny's door came the sound of thumping and banging. It was cold and the morning light had not yet colored the house. Halfway down the stairs, I heard the piano. I did not know the tune. Notes high and low alternated in a fast, rhythmic tempo. I stood and listened. I suspected it was Robert. He usually played the piano in the morning before going to help his father at the factory. But I had never heard him play so beautifully before. He knew children's songs. Lullabies, tunes he made up himself, which were not bad, but had no depth, no emotion, no layers whatsoever.

Then, suddenly, the piece was over. I walked into the drawing room and saw Isabella at the piano. She turned on her stool and looked as if she had been expecting me.

"Mary," she said, standing up and coming towards me. "Did I wake you?"

That was not possible, as she knew. My room was on the other side of the house, a floor higher. I shook my head.

"You're up early," I said.

"You too." She looked at me with a pensive expression.

Were we thinking about the same thing? Were we thinking about what we had seen in the tent at the fair yesterday? Could she, like me, still feel that dark presence inside her? Had she, too, gone to sleep in the expectation, in the hope, that it was an evening feeling, an evening fear, which would seem ridiculous, absurd, during the daytime, and did she, too, feel, as soon as she awoke, that hideousness, the obvious presence of that something, that thing, that had seeped into us, through the cracks in our souls? That thing we could not name, which was at once sadness, fear, and indomitable fury and was holding fast with its barbs, bewitching us from within, making us heavier, more intense, hacking off our childhoods, at this point, now.

I looked up into her water-green eyes, which, I believed, had the courage to see what I had also seen: we had grown, but so had the ghosts and the monsters. They no longer waited under our beds, sharpening their claws, they were no longer hidden among the gowns in the closet, or in the shadows in the attic; no, they lived with us. They sat beside us as we read books, walked with us when we went for a stroll, lay beside us under the sheet of night.

"You play beautifully," I said. "What was that piece of music?"

Isabella smiled. "It's not a real piece. I came up with it myself."

"Really? You can compose?"

"She got that from Mama," Robert said from behind us. A silence fell, in which the entire house seemed to bathe. As if something had just been lost.

July 7, 1812

I had woken early again; there was something about the morning light that drove me out of bed, made me hastily pin up my hair in front of the mirror, so that I could snuggle into the big armchair in front of the fire in the drawing room with the cold gray pile of ashes, half reading, half dreaming with the last few pages of *Otranto*. Claire would undoubtedly be looking forward to my letter. Could I reassure her? I wondered about that. *The Castle of Otranto* was a very effective horror story; there had been moments in the evening and even during the daytime when the events in the story haunted me like a frightening and yet not entirely unpleasant daydream, but I had no doubts about the fictional nature of the narrative. It did not occur to me that it might contain an iota of truth. Yet I did not know how to put that into words. Even at home in London, such a thing would have been impossible. Claire was almost inconsolable when she allowed her fears to sink deep into her. Something inside her was convinced that an indescribable doom hung over her, perhaps over all of us. As a small child is afraid in the dark, is frightened of witches after a fairy tale, believes the existence of such things could be real, even likely—Claire still thought that way. In that respect, she had never advanced beyond the age of six and I somewhat resented her for that, although I also felt that it was not her fault. I thought about Mary Jane. If she had been my mother, there would have been a lot wrong with me as well. I was sure of that. Had Mary Jane never told her that ghosts do not really exist? When Claire crept into bed with her at night after a terrible dream, had she sent her back to her own bed without a word? Had something gone wrong with her even at such a tender age? I often thought that, and as always I felt sympathy for Claire. Strange little Claire.

AFTER BREAKFAST, the church service began, which took up most of Sunday. The Glasite Chapel, to which the Baxters belong, has a congregation of most pleasant people. Even the first time I went there with them, I was welcomed with kindness and interest. At lunch, a Mrs. Thomson wanted to know all about life in London, about my father and our friends. Robert, who sat on my other side, whispered that she was a very religious woman, a widow and most intelligent, but also eccentric. I did not dare to ask him in her presence what he meant by that. My father would say that, by definition, religiosity and high intelligence cannot go together, but I believe that is too simplistic. I think religion is mainly a matter of fear and hope, and intelligent people get scared, too. Perhaps even more so than most.

When we left the church, Mrs. Thomson tapped me on the shoulder.

"Should you ever need a chat, about Bible stories, about life in Dundee, come and call on me," she said. Her watery blue eyes were cheerful and serious at the same time. "And if you ever need help of any kind, I'm here."

I did not quite know how to respond. Eccentric—she certainly was. So I nodded and then I was carried towards the road with the flow of people.

I SPENT THE time that remained before dinner mending one of my gowns, the hem of which was starting to fray from my walks around the area. After dinner, Johnny asked us to go outside with him. He had found an anthill that afternoon and was very keen to show us. Isabella was tired, Mr. Baxter was busy, so only Robert and I accompanied Johnny. Finding the anthill again proved difficult. Johnny led the way, looking around with a frown on his face. Robert and I followed him. I was smiling to myself at Johnny's seriousness and, judging by the wry grin on Robert's face, he felt the same. Behind us, the sun was beginning to spread across the horizon, the occasional quick black shadow skimming past with a sharp, angular flight—bats, Robert said. It was a fine evening; the sort that carries within it oceans of time and calm surrender to all that might happen. But little did. Perhaps we were not heading in the right direction for the anthill, perhaps Johnny had forgotten exactly where it was, but after half an hour he seemed to become discouraged. I asked him if he wanted to turn back and at that precise moment his eyes widened and he stormed ahead of us.

"Mary! Rob! I've found something. Come quickly!"

Johnny was kneeling on the path, crouched over something.

"Look!"

When I peered over his shoulder, I thought my eyes were deceiving me. It was a fish head, or at least the bones. The eye sockets had a deep emptiness, the mouth was open in vacant shock.

Johnny prodded it with a stick.

"How did that get here?" I said quietly.

Robert looked up. "A bird, I should think."

"I'm keeping it," Johnny said breathlessly.

I looked at Robert. Should we put a stop to this? Can touching a fish head make a person ill? But I saw a smile on Robert's lips. Perhaps he remembered how it felt to adventure through the bushes, with streaks of mud on your trousers, a new world, finding treasure.

On the way home, Johnny walked ahead of us, but now he was no longer aware of his surroundings. He seemed not to hear our voices and walked calmly, his hands in front of his stomach, wrapped protectively around the fish head. Now and then, he seemed to talk to it, but his words were too quiet to hear.

July 10, 1812

We were all at home, even Mr. Baxter, who for some reason did not have to go to work, but I had not yet seen any sign of Isabella. By mid-afternoon, I no longer felt like reading, embroidering, or working on my French. Mr. Baxter and I had already had a game of cards, I had played a little piano and then hide-and-seek with Johnny, and then I decided to knock on the door of Isabella's room. I heard nothing. I stood there in the hallway, outside her closed door, and thought about a few weeks ago, when I had seen Isabella for the first time, her white nightgown hanging over her body as if she were wading through water, her pale feet delicate yet strong on the floor. Then, finally, the door opened.

"I thought it was you." Isabella turned and walked to her desk. She had been writing a letter. Her inkpot was open, her quill lay beside it, and there was a sheet of paper filled with angular, uneven handwriting. She placed a drawing portfolio over it. I pictured the smears it would make: words smudging across the paper like angry bats. She stood there, said nothing. I went and sat down on her bed. I do not know what made me so bold. There was, after all, a chair, and she had not even invited me in. Maybe I thought I was entitled to it. That if—after we had spent days on end together, developing an unutterable but substantial bond—she chose to shut herself away in her room, I had the right at least to know what she was up to. She did not seem at all surprised. She did not ask me what I wanted, she just looked at me. She seemed so different from before, when we visited Margaret and Mr. Booth, and at the fair; she had been so free and amiable and now I felt a peculiar coldness radiating from her.

Rain pounded against the windows behind her. It was as if

someone were standing on the roof and pouring a bucket of water over the glass; it was inconceivable that this waterfall was ordinary rain. Isabella gave a deep sigh and came to sit beside me on her bed.

"Would you like something to eat?" She pointed at a tray with a teapot, half a sandwich, and a scone on it.

"What are you doing?" I simply asked.

Isabella smiled slightly. "Writing letters. Reading. Drinking tea." She looked at me. Her eyes seemed to be telling me more than she was saying, but in a language only she spoke.

"Do you feel like doing something?" I asked. I felt as if I were eight. Couldn't I just come up with a suggestion?

"Wait," she said. She stood up, stood on her toes in front of the bookcase, and snatched a book from the top shelf. It was *The Sacred Deep*. She sat against the headboard and patted the bed beside her as a sign that I should come and sit beside her.

"It's so fascinating," she said, opening the book. There was a wave of warmth in her voice. I felt something glowing behind my eyes.

"Look." She searched for a moment and then turned the pages to a creature called an *each-uisge*, a water horse. "This is one of the most malevolent water spirits," I read. "It disguises itself as an ordinary horse or a handsome man. If it is in the form of a horse and you mount it, you had better not be near water. Its skin will become as sticky as the strongest glue as it seeks out the water and heads for the deepest depths, where a certain death awaits the rider. When you have drowned, the *each-uisge* will devour you."

In the illustration, I saw a horse-man, its chest like that of a human, but scaled, the head a horse's. Its arms were the most hideous part: a man's arms with long claws, sharp, as thin as seaweed.

Isabella looked at me with a delighted grin on her face. I laughed.

"There are many creatures like this," she said. "Here, and farther to the north, and on the west coast too, and in Ireland. But I've mainly been looking up the creatures that live around here, in our waters."

Those last words gave me goose bumps. Did Isabella believe all this? I did not dare to ask—the idea was ridiculous. I had simply assumed that no right-minded person believed in myths and fabulous creatures and therefore neither did she. But what if . . . ? I was fourteen. I came from London. What did I know about life? What did I know about other parts of the world? And wouldn't life be more fun, more interesting in any case, if we did not immediately dismiss as nonsense those things that are inexplicable, seemingly impossible?

"We're going on a little trip tomorrow." She looked at me with a grin.

"What are we going to do?"

"If the weather's better, I'm going to show you something. Have you ever heard of Grissel Jaffray?" Isabella's eyes were big and brilliant.

I shook my head.

"She was one of the last witches in Scotland. Burned at the stake, not far from here. Lots of witches were burned around here, and she was the last of them, over a hundred years ago. I'm going to show you the spot. It's quite extraordinary."

I wondered how many times she had been to that place. And what she did there. But I was also becoming curious. Isabella's enthusiasm was contagious, and yes, I wanted to see things. Eerie, evil things. I wanted to know how it might affect me. How fast would my heart pound when she showed me the place? How anxious would I be when I lay in bed that night? How intensely would

I imagine the burning? The fire licking and biting, with death the only escape.

"People used to say that witches could enchant people by giving them an object." Isabella's eyes sparkled.

"What kind of object?"

"It could be anything. Many objects can carry such a spell. In any case, it was wise not to accept anything offered by someone suspected of witchcraft. If you took it, the witch would have you in her power."

We sat side by side for a while. The rain eased. We heard only the splashes tapping against the windows. It was cozy in the room. The fire in the hearth burned low, but Isabella's body felt warm against mine. Sometimes we said a few words, something meaningless. About the rain. About Johnny's fascination with everything about nature. Sometimes we laughed. We sat there beside each other and talked, but we did not look at each other, almost as if we did not dare. I was about to ask her who she was writing to—it was none of my business, and I was timid, but I wanted to know, had to know—when she laid her head on my shoulder. Warm and heavy. I smelled her soap, and a longing sang through my body. Like a glowing knife ripping me open from my heart to my lower belly in the most loving way.

"I used to think everything I could imagine was true." Isabella chuckled. "Or at least that it *could* be true. It seemed so logical to me." She raised her head.

The warmth disappeared from my body.

"All the strange animals, all the unpleasant people, if they can exist, why should the terrible things that sprang up inside my mind not also exist? What is inside my head—it must come from somewhere, mustn't it?" She looked at me, and I saw that she still believed in such things. She was seeking my agreement. But I was thinking about my father. My father, a man of the world. My father, who knew everything, who debated everything, who could fathom everything with such evident self-assurance. He knew so much because he read and wrote, and wrote and read, more than anyone else. I had always relied on him, he knew what was true, what could exist. He was my point of reference. But suddenly I realized how far away he was. That I was in a new world, with different people, different stories, and different rules. In a way, my father was now a story. The story lived in London, sending its daughter the occasional letter. The story was one of order and reason. It loved its daughter's mind, but not her imagination. And Mama. Mama was a different story. Mama was a nonexistent story about fairy tales at bedtime, the sweetest kiss, the softest arm, never leave, stay forever, the hand that would always be there, because mothers do not die. If mothers could die, then there was something wrong with the world.

"Did your mother use to read to you?" I looked at the fire in the hearth. The flames were slowly gnawing away at the wood, as if it had become tough.

She did not appear to have heard me. No one spoke about Isabella's mother. As if she had never existed. As if one might forget, if only one were quiet enough. Is grief the middle ground between wanting to hold on and wanting to let go? Between wanting to remember and wanting to forget? Was I unable to grieve because I was unable to remember?

"I could read by myself from a young age." She said it very quietly.

"But before that? When she put you to bed?"

It was quiet for a while. My heart was pounding like a thing possessed. The skin of her hand against my arm seemed to transmit some kind of energy: pushing, tingling, penetrating into my blood.

Isabella sat up a little, her hand still against my arm. "Mama did not read. She told stories. She knew a lot of fairy tales, a lot of legends. And Papa said later that what she didn't know, she made up."

"So your mother loved stories."

"Very much so."

I wanted to ask her something, but not one single question reached my lips. I would have liked to ask what had happened. Why no one spoke about her death, spoke about *her*.

"It is such a shame that you never knew your mother," she said. "I've read her work. She was so wise. So brave."

I knew she was. People told me that, and I hated it. She was *my* mother. I should have been able to have my own opinion about her. I should have known her best. But even before my birth, thousands of people knew how she thought, who she was, what she was like. And before I could come to know even a fraction of her, she no longer existed. I was her daughter, but I did not know who she was.

I stood up, lingered around the bedroom door. For a long time, she just sat there, staring outside, where the wind still raced, the rain fell and fell, and the clouds were fleeing from one another or from something else. As I opened the door, she said, "Tomorrow, Grissel Jaffray."

I nodded.

July 11, 1812

"Here it is."

We were on top of a hill, a little way outside the city. The weather had cleared up; the sky was dazzlingly white and the air was cool. To the other side of the hill were meadows and farms. Isabella took my hand and pointed towards the city.

"Look. This hill is where Grissel was burned. Can you imagine that this was her view as she stood on that stack of wood, tied to a pole? And then, when they came to light the wood, the flames slowly growing larger, coming closer, getting hotter? The city where she had lived so many years of her life, which she knew so well, where people had accused her of witchcraft and even her friends turned against her. That city was what she had to look at as she died."

"Why did they think she was a witch?"

I could not imagine why. Were people really that scared back then?

"I don't know. They say her body is buried in the Howff, not far from here. Come on."

Isabella walked ahead of me, the path was narrow. Her hair was so very black against the bright sky that it hurt my eyes.

The church tower struck eleven as Isabella pushed down the latch of the cemetery gate. It opened with a solemn scrape. We walked along the rows of gravestones, Isabella searching, me looking around. A grandmother, a father, a sister, a child. Their graves were nearly all overgrown by plants and moss.

"Look." Isabella had stopped in front of a small gravestone, which had been placed just a little too close to the stones beside it. As if there had been no room left for her.

It was hard to read, but if you looked closely, you could see her name carved into the stone: GRISSEL JAFFRAY. That was all. No dates, no other words or wishes.

"When did it happen?" I asked.

"The end of the seventeenth century. My grandma says we're descended from her."

"From Grissel?"

She chuckled. "My grandma was fond of stories too. They say that if you're in trouble, you should give Grissel some money and she'll help you."

"From beyond the grave? A clever witch."

Isabella laughed. "Goodbye, Grissel," she said.

We walked on and I whispered over my shoulder, "Bye, Grissel."

In the last row, I spotted a double tomb. I stopped to look. The rough stone was plastered with white moss, but the names were still legible. JOHN BOOTH 1752–1794 and ELEANOR BOOTH 1756–1794.

"Were they Mr. Booth's parents?" A vague unease prickled the back of my neck.

"I suppose so." Isabella came and stood beside me. She peered at the stone.

"They died in the same year," I said. "Do you know . . . ?"

"I didn't think he had any family."

"Everyone has family."

"He's never spoken about them."

"You never talk about your mother either."

She looked at me sharply. "Let's go back."

Without waiting for me, she headed to the gate and the whole way she walked a few steps ahead of me. I kept wondering how I might take back my words, even though I had meant them. I do not know where the feeling came from, but it upset me that she barely wanted to speak about her mother. As if she were hiding a part of herself from me, while I wanted to see all of her; her darkest memories, her untamed wishes and naked thoughts. I wanted to be inside her head, and I wanted her to want to be inside mine. And the longer I thought about it, the angrier I became. She treated me so dismissively, and then *she* got angry with me?

But this anger was different from the anger I knew at home. When Papa did not come to the dinner table because he wanted "a moment" to finish something, which then took all evening, when he did not listen to what I was telling him, but only pretended to, when Mary Jane thought she had some authority over me, perhaps imagining she was my new mother, when Claire stole my writing paper, kept me awake with her tuneless singing, when Fanny just stared ahead like some kind of rag doll as Mary Jane made some waspish comment about Papa. It used to make me furious. Sometimes Mary Jane grabbed me so hard by my upper arms that the mark of her fingers was soon marbled blue in my skin.

This anger was different. Less furiously charged, but many times sharper. It cut me, tore something open, raw, and that made me even angrier.

I CLIMBED INTO bed, even though it was far from evening. I pulled the blankets far over my head and thought about home, about London. How simple things had been there. I was happy. I was angry. Sometimes I was sad. Things were clear. Here it felt as if everything were dangling on a rope. Nothing had a fixed place, and everything might simply, with one sigh of wind, start swinging, colliding with other things that were hanging from ropes, and I was standing among them, and had to keep looking around, staying on my guard, so as not to be crushed when one reality touched another, creating a new reality.

It started to rain, and for the first time since I had stepped off the boat, I missed home, London, my own bed, my safe girlish dreams.

July 18, 1812

I had not spoken to Isabella for days and had hardly seen her. When I did happen to encounter her, in the hallway or in the kitchen, she looked straight past me. Yet she did not seem to be angry. The expression on her face suggested more a deep sadness. Sometimes I was about to say something, but she was already gone. I tried to read, but my thoughts wandered. I played with Johnny, sometimes went for walks with Robert. The days were long, pallid, sedate.

I sat with Johnny at the bottom of the garden. It was just warm enough, the sky was gray and the light was cold. Johnny was showing me his card tricks. He made a card disappear and reappear in his fingers, guessed which card I had picked, and turned the five of hearts into the seven of spades. I thought he was very skilled for such a young lad, and I told him so. He laughed, fiddled with something beside him on his chair.

We went on playing for a while. I taught him snip-snap-snorum, which I often used to play with Fanny, and he was so enthusiastic about this new game that he could barely stay in his seat. I had to laugh. Then Elsie called him and he ran back to the house.

I felt no desire to get up, to read, or to continue with my French. So I stayed there and listened to the birds in the nearby orchard. Mr. Tysell, our immediate neighbor, had said he left one tree in his orchard to the birds. They were not allowed to touch the others, but they could feast on that one tree. I asked him how he managed to keep the birds out of his other trees. He said that birds were clever creatures, that they knew by now that they were allowed in that one tree but not in the others, as then they would be chased away. I thought it a curious tale and was not sure if I should believe him. Were the birds I could hear chirping now all sitting in that one tree?

I did not think Johnny was going to return, so I started tidying away the cards. Two of them slipped off the table, and as I bent forward to pick them up, I saw, on the chair where Johnny had been sitting, the fish head. For a moment, I could not move. It was staring at me, with its empty sockets, its mouth open in a bite that would last forever. I was not sure what to do. Should I throw it away? I found it an unspeakably unpleasant idea that the thing was in the house with us, that he actually played with it. But I did not want to upset Johnny. He had found it, and it clearly gave him pleasure. And what harm was he doing? I should not be making such a fuss. I picked up the head—it was lighter than I had thought, and smoother—and I carried it to the house. A song began to play inside my head, but I could not place it. Quietly, I began to hum along.

◆ ◆ ◆

"Postponed by a week, especially for David, but no less wonderful: the great Baxter story night!" Mr. Baxter had red cheeks, gleaming eyes, and in his hand a wineglass that had already been refilled a few times. He stood in front of the hearth, trying to say things that would put us in the right mood, but we were mainly chuckling to ourselves at how he occasionally had to hold on to the mantelpiece.

Margaret had come with Mr. Booth this time. She sat in her invalid chair beside Robert and was the only one who was not laughing. I had not prepared anything. The continued distance between

Isabella and me had me so in its grip that I could not focus on anything. They were days of boredom and brooding. Isabella sat beside me on the sofa. She had come downstairs late, and it was the only place that was free. I often glanced over at her. I wanted to make her notice that I missed her, that I did not understand, but I did not dare to do anything but look at her. She did not look back. I did not exist.

As usual, Johnny was allowed to go first. All of a fidget, he sat ready and waiting on the stool by the fireplace. He held the fish head in his hand, stroking it now and then. His story began with a boy who found a fish head, which he put on his windowsill. After three days, the thing began to talk to him. The boy was obviously startled, but it was a very nice head, and they became friends. Then the story was over, and Johnny looked up at us happily. Robert said he thought it a particularly fine tale, and Mr. Baxter agreed. Isabella did not wish to tell a story. She took small bites of bread and large gulps of wine. Then it was Mr. Booth's turn. He stood up, glass in hand, and began to walk slowly through the room. He told us about a demonstration by the physicist Giovanni Aldini, at which he had been present years ago, when the corpse of a criminal was more or less brought to life. Aldini used electrical stimuli to make certain parts of the body move.

"His jaw tensed, and one eye opened. It was as if that blue eye looked directly at the audience, accusing us. It was impossible, but it seemed as if there was still life in that body. Or as if life had returned to it. The room was deadly silent. Only the hum and the rattle of the machine could be heard. Aldini himself seemed as staggered as we were. He appeared to forget that he was giving us a demonstration and began to examine the body, listening with his ear on the chest to see if he could detect a heartbeat, drawing blood. There was a commotion; some people in the audience wanted to leave, others crowded forward to get a better view. Luckily, I'm tall. I stood at the back and saw everything. It was clear to me: as soon as the electrical stimuli stopped, the body returned to its original state of lifelessness. He could not bring dead matter to life."

"Bravo!" Mr. Baxter stood up and applauded. "An interesting anecdote," he said. "Most intriguing. And yet more proof that the breath of life is the preserve of God alone. Without a soul, the body is no more than an empty vessel."

Mr. Booth sat down, an amused smile playing on his lips.

Grace brought the soup, and I caught a glance from Isabella. A hint of complete helplessness. Maybe she was missing me. Maybe she was thinking about me as much as I was about her.

We talked while we ate our soup, and Johnny occasionally put his spoon to his fish head's gasping mouth. No one said anything about it. After the soup, Robert told a story he had heard from his friend Thomas about a girls' orphanage near Aberdeen, where the children were raised as animals. They were not permitted to talk, had to walk on all fours, ate from troughs on the ground, and were not allowed to wash. Mr. Baxter looked increasingly perturbed.

"That's enough," he said in a voice that was stern yet unsteady.

The room fell silent.

"I'd like to go home," Margaret said quietly.

Mr. Booth sent her home in the carriage. Although our story night was over, he wanted to stay awhile. Mr. Baxter obviously thought that fine—he would never object to anything Mr. Booth said. He himself headed upstairs and he asked Robert to put Johnny to bed.

Mr. Booth, Isabella, and I stayed by the fire. For a while, we sat in silence. Then Isabella said quietly, "I thought Robert's story was good. And scary."

I nodded.

"So did I," said Mr. Booth. "Very good, very frightening. Your family has a talent for this, Isabella. Even little Johnny is learning." He smiled. Then he turned to me. "Did you not want to tell a story, Mary? I so enjoyed your tale of Marie Fish's-Eye last time." His face seemed more open, reassuring. His gray eyes were cheerful.

"Thank you," I said. "But I couldn't think of anything this time."

"That's a pity. Don't you agree, Isabella?"

Isabella looked for a moment as if she were about to shrug, but then she looked at me. "Yes. Quite a pity."

I burst out laughing and I saw she was doing her best not to laugh as well. Lightness overcame me.

"Have you girls ever heard of the Draulameth?"

Isabella sighed with relief and topped up our wine from the bottle by her feet on the floor.

I shook my head.

"It's a very old story, goes back at least four centuries. Very much a regional tale. The Draulameth is a sea monster that can grow very old. In fact, it's the oldest creature on Earth, almost as old as the Earth itself. It's not very large, not some huge monster, but about the same size as you and I. The strange thing about the Draulameth is that it can understand humans. Most monsters are rather stupid, as you know, but the Draulameth understands every word you say. In addition, its hearing is second to none. If you're standing by the water and you say something, it'll hear, even if it's miles out to sea." Mr. Booth lit his pipe. The smell stabbed at my throat. He smiled broadly, leaned back in his chair, and took a swig of wine. Isabella's eyes were fixed on him. "The Draulameth prefers to be in the deepest waters, at the darkest bottom of the sea, listening to all the conversations on beaches, in harbors, on board ships. It wants to get to know humans—and there is a reason for that."

Out in the hallway, I heard Elsie or Grace going into her room and closing the door. It was getting on for twelve. Mr. Booth took a puff of his pipe.

"It's because the Draulameth is truly dangerous only when it knows you. Once it knows your fears, your dreams and desires, then it will call you. It happens at night. It calls you, but so quietly that only you can hear. It doesn't wake you from your sleep but lulls you into a state of slumber in which you get up, start walking, follow its voice to the sea. And that is when you wake up. It doesn't lure you into the sea—you choose to go yourself. Because, as you stand there on the water's edge, it shows you how your life could be: all your fears become reality, your dreams dissolve in the foam of the waves. Every moment of your life will be filled with horror, bitterness, sadness, and loss, or: you go with the Draulameth. The water feels gentle on your feet, warm and clear, a welcome comfort. The deeper you go, the more firmly the sea embraces you. Your head goes under, you go to the Draulameth. Breathing no longer means anything. You think you are happy. Then it appears, its tongue licks your temples, and your heart flips inside your chest. The beats last hours. And with every beat of your heart, a piece of you disappears—until you no longer exist."

We were silent. Mr. Booth looked at us and smiled.

Isabella took a swig of wine and folded her legs beneath herself on the sofa.

"Is that a well-known story?" I asked.

"Not too well known. It's a very old one. It's not told very often

these days, though. Only the oldest residents of Dundee will still remember it. Did you like it, Mary?" He looked at me with a friendly
expression, as if he were young, maybe even younger than I, with a
kind of childish delight.

"Well, I should head for home. Margaret will be glad to see me."
He stood up, Isabella and I walked with him to the hallway. He took
his hat and coat and kissed our outstretched hands. His kiss was warm
and tickled. Outside, he called for a carriage and was driven away.

ISABELLA AND I sat by the glowing embers of the fire, waiting for it to
go out. I kept wanting to ask if all was well between us once more,
but I did not know how. Besides, it still did not feel at all good. I
only hoped that such a question might make things right. Eventually, I said, "I'm sorry."

She looked up. "What for?"

"For saying that about your mother. About you. I didn't mean to
upset you. I thought we were friends, that we told each other things.
Everything."

Isabella did not look at me. She breathed deeply in and out. She
looked glum. "In the past few weeks, since you arrived, have you
seen me talking to anyone else?"

I thought for a moment. Apart from the usual pleasantries, she
did not talk to anyone, except for Mr. Booth sometimes, and to
Margaret when we went to visit.

"I talk only to you, Mary. Don't you see that? You're the only one.
I don't want to talk about my mother, about her death, about all that
darkness. Talking about it only makes it worse. At night I think about
her, and horrors haunt me that you can't even imagine, but during the
day I want nothing to do with that. In the daytime, I want to talk to

you about ghosts and monsters. I want to walk with you and laugh with you. Please, believe me: if I wanted to talk to anyone about my mother, it would be you." She still had not looked at me. The dying fire glowed in her eyes. It was becoming very dark in the room.

"Sorry," I said again.

Still without looking at me, she laid her hand on my arm and smiled.

"We should have asked Mr. Booth what he was doing at the fair," I said.

"Maybe it's just as well that he doesn't know we saw him."

A dark feeling climbed up inside my chest. "Why do you say that?"

There was no reply. She was still looking away from me. Then she said, "Mary, everything is fine between us now, isn't it?"

I nodded. "Yes," I said.

"You're not angry with me?"

"I love you," I said as quietly as I could. I looked at the hand that was resting on my arm. A brief tremor went through that hand.

Finally she looked at me. For a moment, I thought she was going to cry. Then she took me in her arms and, with her lips on my neck, she whispered, "I love you, my dear friend."

That night, we slept close together in my bed. Isabella fell asleep almost at once, I lay awake for a while, listening to her deep breathing. With every inhalation, I loved her more; with every exhalation, I feared I would lose her.

July 23, 1812

The heat held our bodies in the grass. The walk had taken over an hour, and now we were clammy and thirsty and tired. It was too hot for boots. We untied our laces, pulled the boots from our sweaty ankles, stripped off our stockings, and lay in the grass, which tickled our bare legs. What did it matter? We were alone, in the hills. We had not seen anyone for hours. All the life around us came from insects, sheep, birds, and the occasional rabbit. A bluebottle kept landing by us. On Isabella's hair, on the red, flaking skin of my arm, on the rim of my glass, which was balancing on the picnic cloth.

"We should always go bare-legged," said Isabella. She tucked a loose strand of hair behind her ear and yawned.

"We should always go without corsets," I said, trying to look fierce.

"Yes!" Isabella nodded vigorously. She stood up and turned her back to me. "Help me."

"Madame," I said, making a small bow as I loosened the ribbon at the back of her gown.

She pulled her gown down to her waist. "Can you help?" My fingers undid the lace. Isabella removed the corset. I could not help but look. She had minuscule red dots speckling her body from her neck down. A flash of her breasts, white, pointed, pink nipples. A Botticelli, but for real. So soft that I could feel it with my eyes. I looked at her face. She was radiant. Her eyes sparked with mischief and fun. "Just need to fasten this." She pulled the gown back up. I laced it tight.

"How about you?"

I turned around as well. Her fingers touched my back. Her breath my ear. The fly landed on my nose. My gown lowered, my breasts, my nipples naked to the world. A deep sense of freedom ran through me. I was like the grass under my feet or like a young tree. I could sway in the wind. Then she pulled me against her, her hands on my bare stomach. My heart lost its rhythm. She said, close to my ear, "You are so beautiful." Sun, air touched my stomach, my breasts. Isabella pulled my sleeves up over my arms, laced me back into my gown. I turned around. We were free.

"I need to go," I said.

Isabella fell back into the grass. She lay there, stretched out, and took a swig of wine. I walked away from her. In the distance was a small rock formation. I looked at my feet, so free in the grass. The skin between my toes was turning black. We would never wear corsets again. We would never wear stockings again. We would be naked wherever we could. I could breathe again, as deeply as I wanted. I could see my stomach move when I sighed, like an animal with a will of its own. I skirted the rock to where Isabella could no longer see me and looked around. Still no one. Then I heard a sound I did not recognize. It sounded like an animal, and yet also human, like a short, stifled primal cry. I looked up, as it made me think of a bird of prey, and out of the corner of my eye, I saw movement. Something crouching in a crevice. It had the proportions of a human. But it was larger. Wider. The skin was dark, and it had hair on its back and legs. The arms were long, as with an ape, but it was not an ape. The head was big, coarse, it had human features, but not in the right proportions. It had small eyes and a small nose, but the mouth was huge. The thing made wild gestures, appeared to be trying to do something there among the rocks, in that cave, but I could not see what. I changed position and realized that I could not control my own movements. I was trembling, and the tremor came from the very depths of my soul. What if it were to look around? It would see me, and I could not imagine that it would ignore me. I thought about all the monsters we made up together, Isabella and I.

About all the stories we told each other, at night in bed, in the garden in the daytime, at Margaret and Mr. Booth's. I thought about *The Sacred Deep*, how convincingly the sea monsters were described, as if the writer had seen them, as if he knew them. I thought about fairy tales, about the ghost stories Claire and I told each other at home in London, on my bed by the light of a candle. Maybe they were not all fabrications, as we had learned when we were growing up. Every child believes in witches. In ghosts, in the devil. Maybe, when we got older, we started to believe that it was not true because we no longer dared to believe that it was true. But maybe children are right, maybe they see the world as it is, before the pragmatic seriousness of adulthood throws a veil over it. Maybe only they see the entire world, in which all things exist, everything in which one might believe.

I tried to calm my breathing. Then, slowly and carefully, I crept away from the rocks and hurried back to Isabella. She laughed and poured some wine for me.

"I mean it," I said. "You have to see it."

Chuckling to herself, she came with me. I told her to be very quiet, not to laugh and not to say a word. She looked at me, and I believe she realized then that I was serious. That I was convinced that I had seen a monster. But two minutes later, she believed it herself. We stood behind a low rock and watched it.

"Look at those arms," I said. "That head. All that hair everywhere. Do you see how wide he is? Look, I think he's chopping something. Wood perhaps. Do you see those muscles?"

Isabella just stared, breathlessly. I think we stood there for a long time and then I looked at her, her eyes fixed on the monster. I took her hand, tried to pull her away, back to the world we knew, where we could talk about what we had seen, or thought we had seen, but she would not come. It was as if she wanted to know for sure that the monster would not vanish into thin air. After quite some time, she looked at me. I could not gauge what she was thinking. How she was feeling. Was she afraid? Confused? Incredulous?

"This . . ." she said and fell silent for a moment. "Mary, this is amazing." She held my head in her hands and kissed me on the cheek.

That night I had a dream. The dream was vague but terrible. It was more atmosphere than situation, more feeling than event. I remember that something was buzzing, all the time. Throughout my entire dream, I kept wondering what it was, until it came and sat on my cheek. It was the fly, in exactly the spot where Isabella had kissed me. There was an open wound there, and the fly began to eat from it.

May–June 1816
Cologny

What wants to live, what is keeping watch

She is standing on the beach. It is not quite real, she knows that, but
it is real enough to feel the grains of sand between her toes, to hear
a gull cry, to fear a presence. The sun has just dived into the water,
the sky is the hue of earthworms. What is she doing here? Suddenly
she sees a boy sitting on the sand by her feet. He is drawing with a
twig, and she cannot see his face. Yet she knows him.

"Johnny," she says. "Johnny?"

He nods, does not look up.

"Johnny, how are you?"

"Fine." He goes on carving with his twig. There is a tangle of
scratches and lines in the sand at their feet.

"Where are the others?"

Johnny goes on scribbling.

"Will you look at me?" she says.

He shakes his head.

"Why not?" She kneels down and places her hand on his shoulder, but Johnny turns away from her.

"What's wrong?"

"You're not Mary."

And then she feels it too. This is not her face. These are not her hands. These are not her feet that are held here by the signs in the sand. And she hears herself starting to cry, at least, she thinks it is her, and then she sees it. Something falls, she let it go, something important, and then everything is dark. She is entangled in the sheets. She does not know what she saw, but she feels it, in every heartbeat that hits her.

She wipes her wet face. It is a long time before her heart calms down, before she dares to move.

No one is lying beside her. Of course, Willmouse is at Chapuis, with Elise.

"Percy?" she asks the empty room. Mary's voice sounds tired, not yet awake, not yet able to face the day. Certainly not ready for conversations with Claire, for Percy, for John and Albe. She is not ready for anything; not her voice, not her head, not her body. Her stomach hurts from all the drink. As if a rat is chewing away at her abdominal walls. Her head thumps to the rhythm of her heart. Her pale hands tremble.

She imagines everyone lying in bed. Albe half-naked on his back, snoring. John sitting upright on the edge of his bed, unable to move, for fear of vomiting. Claire on her stomach, fast asleep, a thread of spittle on her pillow. Percy. Next to Claire. Separate from her, as he cannot sleep right beside anyone. Or does he feel that way only with Mary? A hand on Claire's hip.

And then she, Mary, awake far too early, because she always is;

even if she were sick, even if she were on her deathbed, she would not sleep if it were after six. The shutters at Diodati are better than the ones at Chapuis. They let in barely any light. And the tall trees around the house take care of the rest. The sheet feels clammy. The rain of recent weeks has seeped into the house.

A knock at the door. Mary shoots upright, the sheets neatly wrapped around her.

"Yes?"

It is Claire. She is wearing the same gown as yesterday—of course, they have not been home yet—but Mary can see that she has slept in it. She climbs into bed beside Mary, rests her head on her shoulder.

"How do you feel?"

"Hm." That is all she can manage to say. Ah, she does not know why Claire annoys her so much, even when she is not being obviously irritating.

"I couldn't keep my eyes open last night. Percy said you're all going to write a ghost story."

When had Percy said that? When he had crawled into bed beside Claire, befuddled, full of ideas, folding his body around her contours, thinking her his sweetest one, at that moment, because she demanded nothing from him, because she was not his?

She nods.

"So, are you going to write a story, too?" asks Claire. She shivers and snuggles up close to Mary.

Something is there. She feels it as she lets the idea of herself writing a ghost story sink in. It is wild and so vulnerable that she does not dare to seize it. She could crush it to death, it is that fragile. And it might bite her, furious as it is.

"Are you going to take part, then?" She looks at Claire. For a moment, she feels that rare affection, which she sometimes turns out to be capable of after all, not only for William and Percy, but also for others, for Claire, and she hopes for it, does not begrudge it, for a story for her. One that will surprise the men, making them see Claire in a different light, making *her* see Claire in a different light.

"Oh, I wouldn't dare," Claire replies. "That's not for me. That really is something for the men." She looks at Mary with a half smile. "And for you, of course."

Mary throws off the sheet, sits up, starts putting on her stockings, her corset.

"Shall I help you?" asks Claire.

She allows herself to be helped. She is alone.

◆ ◆ ◆

The rain the rain the rain. And now she is sitting on her bed at Chapuis, William beside her, Albe's manuscript on her lap. She needs two candles, because it is refusing to become day outside. She reads and she thinks. Occasionally she says something to her sweet Willmouse. He is holding his rattle as if it is his life, sometimes shaking it unintentionally, which startles him so much that it seems he has forgotten that the thing is not a part of him. Still, he does not let go of it and neither does he start crying. So the excitement is perhaps enjoyable.

Every day, she watches this little person and still he is an enigma to her. And yet. And yet she is connected to him in every way. Just as at times one does not understand oneself and yet one knows that it does not matter, because explanations are not sacred, because it is about affection and recognition of one's own. Maybe she does not understand William because he is hers. She often sings for him. "Lavender's Blue" and "Oranges and Lemons," but sometimes she makes up a song herself. Thinks up sweet creatures, kind words. They are theirs, theirs alone.

Albe's poems are terribly good. She can barely formulate a single point of criticism, which is annoying, because she does not want to give the impression that she has not read them carefully enough.

Percy bursts in with a smile on his face and, when he sees what she's doing, a frown. He sits on the edge of the bed, beside William, lets him grab his finger, smiles at him. "Well?"

It is barely a question, of course. She glances up. Percy is still not looking at her. He wants her to detach herself from the work, to pay him the attention he deserves. Percy is not good at asking for attention. Percy *receives* attention.

"I think it's very, very good," she says. She sees his nostrils twitch. Otherwise, no reaction. "Albe knows how to tell a tale with such elegance. Everything is exactly right, as far as I can tell, as far as the rhyme in the verses is concerned, but told in such a way that it is only logical that this rhyme should emerge. Almost as if there were no other way."

No, she cannot see if it truly pains him, this praise, but she suspects it does. Then he puts his hand on her foot. He slides it upwards, his fingertips over her stocking, into increasingly sensitive territory. It is surely intended as a caress, but it feels like a demand. And she does want to. But she thinks she should not want to. Let him beg a little, her head says. Surrender, her belly nags, come, come, take off your stockings. She has never been good at resisting, the desire is too strong. She must love him too much. Because she does.

PERCY GETS DRESSED, kisses her, leaves. Outside, the rain falls as if its source is inexhaustible, invincible. They will always be defeated by the rain. The rain settles in cracks one has never seen, grows mold under the closet, behind the edge of one's bed, in one's boots, in the wine. And it is inside her, the rain. It will have entered her body, through her eyes and ears, through her mouth as she spoke. And now she is full of it, full of that rain. Slowly, she is starting to cool down. She climbs under the blanket, covers William, beside her. She looks at the full, small lips, soundlessly making words, at the veins in his eyelids, delicate strands through which life flows. She recognizes those strands, her daughter's were just as delicate. Everything was complete. Small, but complete. When she was cold, when the strands still contained color but no life, they took her away. She cried out words. She begged, cursed. The first few nights, she kept forgetting about it. No, she did not forget, it was simply not true. Those nights, her child was alive, every night she sucked her nipples raw. It was so painful, but it was a pleasant pain. A mother's pain, indistinguishable from happiness. And in the morning, when the pain had subsided, the realization came. There was no child anymore. The pain had not existed. The days were crippled. Gray, rain, cold. No fire, no tea, no water bottle helped. Percy did his best, those weeks. He sat with her, washed her, kissed her. But she did not want to be washed and she did not want to be kissed. She wanted to go back to when her child was still there. She wished she had stayed awake, forever if necessary, so that she could have heard death approaching.

She would have hidden her little girl in her bed, against her breast under the covers, she would have kept her alive and warm with her own life. Her child had died because the flame of her life went out and no one was there to rekindle it. She was alone.

Mary's bed was, from that moment, a deathbed, and in her mind it was the same bed as the one in which her mother had died. The first night after giving birth, her mother had fixed her eyes on the curls in the gleaming woodwork, in a delirium that her daughter was no longer alive. The next night, she had dreamed she herself would die, leaving her daughter alone, and that it was not her fault, but her daughter's. The third night, there was a monster under her bed. She heard it growling, but her husband did not. The monster wanted her, or her child—and she could choose which. She was a mother, the choice was already made.

Mary was alone.

◆ ◆ ◆

The Italian lesson is not going smoothly today. John is doing his best, but she can see that his thoughts are elsewhere. As are hers. She puts her book aside, sighs.

"Is something bothering you?" she asks.

John leans back in his armchair. They are in the library at Diodati. There are four armchairs around the fire. Behind them are seven bookcases with Italian volumes, in front of them seven with German titles. The cabinets beside the door are filled with objects: figurines, vases, paintings. There are two high, narrow windows looking out onto, yes indeed, trees, and if you look closely between the branches you can see the lake in the distance. Mary and John use the library for her Italian lessons, and she wonders why they do not spend more time in this room. Percy and Albe rarely go there, Claire never.

"I am afraid I have resigned myself to defeat." John's eyes wander along the bookshelves.

"Defeat?"

"How can I write when I know I am competing against Albe, against Percy?"

"They have never written a ghost story. Besides, they are poets, not story writers."

"They have so much more experience." He looks defeated. Already.

"With ghost stories, it is also about originality, about mental vigor. About inspiring a sense of horror, of dread. They are no better than you at that, not necessarily. What monster lives in your dreams, John? Which nightmares do you know? That is what you must write about. That's the point."

John leans forward, smiles. His right eye is slightly narrowed. "What are you going to write about?"

She laughs, to cover up how she is doubting, pondering, ignoring her own advice. "I don't quite know yet."

He stands up. "Do you mind? My migraine is really starting to torment me now. I need to rest for a while."

"Of course."

"We'll continue tomorrow. Conjugations." He does a sort of bow, and it is not clear to her if he is serious or not. Usually he kisses her hand, but she can tell just by looking at him that even that is too much of an effort at the moment.

Mary leans sideways in her chair and closes her eyes. Her story will be about the most frightening thing in existence. Longing, loss, grief. But there is still so much in her way that she cannot push aside. It has been there for a long time, the idea. It has existed for many centuries, ever since the earth awoke, and still it roams the world. It has seen her. It has chosen her. But the time is not ripe or she does not dare to take a look. Because if she looks, she will have to see everything. Not only the beautiful truth, wrapped in a story, trembling with wonder, ancient yet newly born, but also the cruelty, the defiance, that which screams and shrieks at her to open her eyes. And all of it is true.

She is dreaming. It is a dream. She is sitting in the library at Villa Diodati, eyes closed, leaning to one side in the chair. My goodness, she is getting thin. John has gone to bed with a vicious migraine. On his side, legs drawn up, hands crushing the pillow. His cheeks wet with tears. Albe is sitting in his study. He hums, looks in amusement at a poem he has written: it is grotesque and vulgar, it is a joke and so it is good. He takes a puff of his pipe. He wants wine. In the drawing room, Percy is in the red armchair by the window. He has a book by Lucretius on his lap, he is not reading. He looks at Claire, lying on the sofa in front of the fireplace, her hands up over the armrest, breasts rising and falling with her breath. Is she asleep? Claire knows that Percy is looking at her. She feels it on her skin. She often wonders what she wants. She does not know, but she wants only that which she cannot have. As soon as she gets it, she wants something else. She will never be happy. At Maison Chapuis, Elise is putting little Willmouse to her breast. It does not hurt her, her nipples have become tough, callused from all the suckling. Her nipples are mother nipples, she knows what they must do because she is a mother. They are exactly the right size, give exactly the right amount of milk with every gulp. He never splutters with her. He never cries with her. She is good to him, but he is not her child, and she feels that and he feels that. This is not his mother's milk. This is just the milk of a kind lady with lovely big nipples.

Mary sits upright. She can hear something. It is Claire, crying. Or screaming. Or both. She rubs her eyes and walks to Albe's study, where the sound is coming from. It is Albe, scathing but muffled, she cannot make out what he is saying. The door is ajar. Claire says something in her weepy voice, also unintelligible.

Should she go in? Then she hears footsteps. She ducks into the room next door. It is dark, the shutters are closed, and she can barely see anything. She hears Percy's voice, he is asking a question. Claire bursts into tears. Albe says something, short and loud. Then the door slams shut. Two sets of footsteps in the hallway. Claire's sobbing sounds farther and farther away. She hesitates, but she is too curious. She knocks on Albe's door.

"Yes?"

Mary thinks he was expecting Claire. His gaze softens when he sees it is her. He sighs.

"Did you hit her?"

Albe smiles. "I would never hit your sister."

"Stepsister."

They are silent. He is not smoking his pipe. There are no poems on his desk, only an open book.

"I do like her, you know."

She thinks he means it. His eyebrows lend gravity to his face. She does not often see him like this.

"She is like the wind. She pulls at you and pulls at you and rages in your ears and blows in your face and she wants so much." He looks at Mary. "I'm sorry. I do not wish to be hateful about your sister. Your stepsister."

Mary stands there in front of the writer's desk. He looks her in the eyes, and she sees that he respects her. Respect of a different sort than he bestows on most women. What makes her different? Why does he treat her as an equal? Like a man?

"I'll go and see her," she says, leaving before he can say anything more.

MARY HAD EXPECTED to find them together, but Claire is alone, God only knows where Percy is. She is sitting with her feet up on the wooden bench on the veranda, huddled up, sadness hunching her shoulders. Mary sits beside her, rests her hand on one of those shoulders, it feels warm, intense. After a while, Claire starts breathing more calmly. Then she looks up. Her eyes are rimmed with red, with a pale pink tinge to the whites. With a heavy sigh, she nestles up to Mary, who was not expecting that and woodenly puts her arms around her stepsister.

"He's such a terrible man," says Claire in a thin, unsteady voice. "Oh God, Mary, I love him."

Of course, thinks Mary, and she hates herself. It is sometimes so difficult to love Claire. Mary does her best, doesn't she? And sometimes she knows for sure that she does love her, that she is her sister, but often she does not feel that way. Maybe she can love her if she impresses upon herself that Claire is also afraid, not in the hysterical Claire way, but in a human way, because everyone is afraid, including Claire, because everyone is human. Including Claire.

CLAIRE HAS REMAINED at Diodati, and she is now sitting next to Mary with a stony expression, drinking her wine. She does not look at Albe, she is doing her utmost not to. Percy and John do not appear to have noticed the chill emanating from Claire. Percy has been on the laudanum since this afternoon and is exuberant, lively, humming songs, grinning.

"This one." Albe holds up a book that Mary recognizes. "Samuel Coleridge. I was allowed to read it before it went into print. This poem in particular is so fantastically spine-chilling." He looks at Mary. Smiles. This is what they share.

"Inspiration," cries John, coming into the drawing room with two bottles of wine.

"The wine or the poems?" Albe leafs through the collection. "Here," he says. "This is what I mean."

John puts the bottles on the floor, sits next to Mary, too close, looks at her. What does he want? Applause?

Albe reads aloud. Mary knows the poem. It is wonderful, terrible. Christabel, a young woman, a girl in fact, meets a lovely lady in the midnight wood. She takes her home. Watches while she undresses, she is so beautiful. Maybe she wants to kiss her. Maybe she wants to lie in her arms. Her silken gown falls at her feet and then, oh heavens, she is not a woman. She is deformed, a witch!

Percy shrieks. It is a sound Mary has never heard before. He was sitting on the floor just a moment ago, his face upturned, paying attention, the wine between his feet, but now he has buried his head in his arms and is groaning. He is sobbing. Mary goes to sit beside him, puts her arm around him, but he fends her off, pushes her away.

"Jesus." Albe stands up and pulls Percy into one of the chairs by the fire. "Shelley, what's wrong?"

Percy's reply is unintelligible. The high notes in his voice are full of panic. John runs to the kitchen and fetches water. Claire sits down on Percy's other side and puts her hand on his cheek. Mary stands there, in the middle of the room, rejected by her beloved.

In a soft, fragile voice, Percy says, "I once heard a story about a woman who had eyes where her nipples should have been."

Claire shudders.

"She," says Percy. He looks up at Mary, points at her, *points*. "I saw it. She has them, those eyes. In her breasts. Oh God, I can see it." He sobs.

Albe, John, Claire, they look at her. She is still standing there in the middle of the room, as motionless as a statue, and she feels that they can see the eyes on her breasts. And suddenly she is afraid. Maybe Percy saw correctly. Maybe he has seen who she really is. Deformed, a monster, a witch. Maybe those eyes are not really on her breasts, but inside her. But the eyes inside her are just as bad, just as deformed. A heartbeat sounds in her ears like loud footsteps, footsteps coming closer and closer. And all those eyes are still on her.

Claire pulls Percy to his feet. "Come on, I'll put you to bed."

Percy allows himself to be led away, sobbing like a child. He avoids her gaze.

THAT NIGHT, Mary sleeps alone at Chapuis. The others remain at Diodati; Claire with Percy, Albe continuing to write, John drinking, smoking, staring out the window, she has no idea. Of course she is not alone, her greatest treasure is there. William is lying beside her bed in his cradle, sleeping, sleeping, yes, really sleeping. Tomorrow, Percy will no longer remember what he saw. He will no longer be able to recall the image. But a feeling will linger. Something that, every time he looks at her, every time he kisses her breasts, takes her nipple in his mouth, will unleash a turmoil within him. He will not be able to put that feeling into words. Perhaps he will not even be consciously aware of it. But something will have changed. A glimpse of her true nature has been shown to him. He will not know why, but he will become afraid of her. He will become afraid of her, and she is the only one who knows why.

◆ ◆ ◆

Mary turns over again. Elise is standing in the doorway, with William in her arms. There is something in the way Elise is standing there, the way she is holding William, that disturbs her. She can vividly imagine that this is the last time she will see him. She understands how it might be that their boat will capsize, she will be unable to reach the side in time, too much fabric around her body to swim, too much fear of what she is losing to reach the shore. Elise will take care of William until Mary's father and Mary Jane come to fetch him and take him back to London. Her father will remain his grandfather, while Mary Jane will play his mother; a repulsive spectacle. No, she admonishes herself, we are not going to die. The lake is calm, the boat is new. We are not going to die.

Percy cautiously steps on board. Although he enjoys sailing very much, he is afraid of water. He cannot swim. It is a curious combination, and it is typical of him. Fear and longing at the same time. Claire steps into the boat, helped by Percy, and sits down. John helps Mary and they perch on the seat beside Albe, who has already hoisted the sails and is waiting at the helm for Percy to untie the ropes. As they leave the shore, Mary feels laughter bubbling up inside her belly. It remains silent, but even so she feels a freedom she knows only on the water. They glide across the surface, cleaving it in two with the bow: lake to the left, lake to the right, they are the central point, illuminated in rare sunlight.

Claire has opened her parasol and asks Mary to come sit with her. Claire sits close to Percy, Percy talks to her, in her ear, no one else should hear his words. Mary shakes her head, turns her gaze to the prow, and lets her eyes rest on the distance.

"Not yet," she hears John say.

"Just try something. Begin. Don't ever wait." Albe's words can withstand the wind. "What about you, Mary?"

Oh, she has so little desire to talk about her plan. She knows for sure that talking about them will kill the ideas, the feelings she has about what might end up on paper. She cannot say anything about it, because the moment it leaves her mouth, everything she says will no longer be true. She will have to wait. They will have to wait. She will start writing, the story will make her write, and then, when it is finished, she will be able to answer.

"I have nothing," she says, looking at a snow-white bird above them. "I don't know yet." That is the most correct answer by far. But even so, it is not true. She does have something. It is coming.

"I'm finding it somewhat difficult, I will admit." Albe moves the rudder back into position, lights his pipe. "I am distracted by my poems, which are so biddable right now, and prose is such a different genre."

"I want it to be so terrifying that you won't dare go to sleep after reading it." Percy sits up straight, his hand sliding from Claire's lap.

"That's difficult," says Albe. "To convince your reader that these ghosts or this monster are real, that they might be real."

"In actual life, you mean? But why?" John eases the mainsail a little. Water splashes up against the bow and a mist of small drops hits Mary's face.

Albe shrugs, looks at John with raised eyebrows. "If it's not real, it's not frightening."

"But in fact everyone knows that a ghost story is made up." Percy takes out a bottle of wine and begins to open it.

"Some of them aren't," says Claire. She is looking at the bottle.

Percy's hands stop moving. "What?"

"There are stories that may not have been made up. That's a possibility." Claire looks argumentative, chin jutting forward.

Albe bursts out laughing.

"It's true! There are so many inexplicable things. I've seen them myself. You *know* that." She looks at Percy, tight eyes, tight mouth.

Percy holds up his hands, the bottle of wine between his knees. "I don't know if . . ."

"Claire, just stop it!" Albe is furious, suddenly. With a stony gaze, he stares ahead, hand on the helm.

Claire's eyes become large, wet. Percy places his hand on her back. John looks, grimaces at Mary. She nearly laughs, but holds it in.

"Open that wine, will you, Shelley?" Albe's voice has its normal tone again.

In silence, Percy fills the glasses that Adeline packed for them. John adjusts the position of the mainsail. Drinking changes them. After one glass, they are looking at one another again. After two glasses, Claire's tears are gone and forgotten, Albe can laugh once more, Percy starts talking. Before long, he, John, and Albe are engaged in a discussion about the consequences of the French Revolution and the Greek people's desire to gain independence from the Turks.

Claire is leaning against Percy, her thoughts seem to be deep under the water. Sometimes Mary feels an urge to contribute to the discussion, but every time she wants to say something, thinks she knows something relevant, she somehow cannot manage to do it. It is as if the men are enclosed in a transparent room. And maybe she does not feel like speaking. Maybe she does not wish to take part in this conversation at all, but since she is a woman, that does not matter. She must participate because she does not have to. If she were a man, she could remain aloof, look at the water flowing past beneath them, at the mountains around them, the thousand-tipped forests on their flanks. She could drink and dream, allow her thoughts to go where they wanted. She could look at Claire, at how sweet she actually is, how pretty, this child. She could wander through a befogged mind and find things there, drag them to the surface and put them into stories, stories that are not from here, which have their origins in incomprehensible sources. But she must participate, as she is a woman and no one expects it of her. She has too many roles to play. She wants to assert herself, even though she does not, solely for the sake of asserting herself.

Mary is startled when Percy leans towards her, fills her glass, kisses her, deeply. The space has broken open. A shivering sun sparkles in the water, spots dance before her eyes.

◆ ◆ ◆

"I am going to write something about my childhood. I had a governess, Miss Claymayer she was called, and there was something not entirely right about her." Percy leans back on the picnic cloth. Albe sits beside him, with a glass of wine. The wine is going down well today.

"My parents left most of my upbringing to her and were often away, so I had to spend all day and evening with her during the week. She taught me, played with me, ate with me, put me to bed. She came when I was six and from the very beginning I felt that there was something strange about her. When I was doing my lessons, I could feel her looking at me. Not occasionally, not just now and then, but all the time. When we went for walks, she always stayed a little too close to me."

Claire yelps. "It's ice cold!" She is standing nearby, up to her hips in the water. John is already in. His head is bobbing triumphantly around Claire. Behind him, the boat is floating.

"In the evenings, she put me to bed. She sang to me. She had a very deep voice, almost like a man's, and the songs she sang were slow and sad. One day, she showed me the attic, where she slept. She had her own room up there, but there was nothing in it. I wondered how a person might have no belongings. Miss Claymayer sat down on her bed and began to unbutton her gown. I didn't dare to look, I was still so young, barely ten, but I felt that I had to. She bared her breasts. I had an instinctive suspicion of what they were supposed to look like, but what I saw did not remotely resemble what I had expected. Her breasts were very pale, with blue veins, and her nipples were like eyes. I knew these were the eyes that were always looking at me. The eyes that followed me when I played in the garden, and she watched me from the bay window. These were the eyes that looked at my naked body when her hands dried me with a linen cloth that smelled of my mother. These eyes looked at me in my sleep, detected my dreams, my fears, and also my fear of her."

"Good heavens." Albe grins and gazes into the distance.

Mary looks at Percy. She sees his taut smile, his expectation. He is looking at Albe, not at her. She drains her glass. "Nice," she says. "Unnerving."

Claire runs out of the water. She grabs a linen cloth from the basket, wraps it around herself. Her long white legs naked to the heavens.

"Cold?" Percy asks with a wry smile.

"So cold." She trembles exaggeratedly, squeezes in between Percy and Albe.

Mary tries to hold back a sigh. Her hand reaches for the wine.

John joins them as well, shivering in his underwear. Water runs down his body in rivulets. Mary hands him a linen cloth to wrap himself in. He smiles at her.

"I'm just going for a walk," she says—and she is gone before anyone can say they would like to go with her.

SHE WALKS AWAY, bottle in hand. Away from Percy's story, from Albe's infuriating nonchalance, from Claire's flirtatiousness, John's friendliness. She does not know what is annoying her, what is annoying her so much that she can no longer be in their vicinity. She knows it is excessive, whatever it is, that it is her fault, that *she* should be reasonable, stop being so childish, my God, she is acting like Claire, but there is nothing she can do about it. She needs to be alone for a while.

When she has gone around a corner, along a path, is now truly alone, she takes a deep breath, for the first time today. In the branches above her, a blackbird sings. In the shade, it is chilly. Her goose bumps show her despair. What is wrong what is wrong what is wrong, all the things around her ask. She has no answers, only questions. More questions than she thinks she can face. But she will do it; she will begin. She will go inside this story and discover what is awaiting her there. What wants to live. What is keeping watch. What cannot exist without her.

"SHOULDN'T WE WAIT?" Claire's voice is thin.

Albe pulls on the rope, secures it. He tells them to get on board.

Percy helps Mary, helps Claire. The rain pours down on them in a relentless outburst of violence. Finding shelter is no longer an option—the sky has found them. Their clothes stick to their arms and legs, their boots chafe their feet.

"Damn it!" Percy pushes the boat from the shore but loses his balance and steps with one foot into the shallow water. John helps him into the boat.

Mary looks up. The air around them is cleaved by rain. She fears that she can hear rumbling in the distance, but when she listens more closely, she hears only the rain. John bails water out of the boat. Claire has hidden in Mary's arms. Their shaking seems to be making the boat heave. Now and then Albe yells something from his place at the helm, and Percy shouts something back from the gangway. When you are drowning, at what point do you know you are going to die? Or do you go on hoping until nothing remains? When you are pulled down because your body no longer wants to keep going, because you are needed there, because you are no longer needed above the water, because there is something that wants you down there, something drawing you into the cold depths with fingers like hooks, commanding the water to close over your seeking lips, your thoughts diluted to thin dreams, until they too dissolve, deep under water, into the depths, where everything is heavy, from whence nothing returns to the surface.

"PERCE," MARY SAYS that night, her lips against his neck. "That morning, when we found her, our little girl, it made me think of my mother."

Percy turns to look at her. He has just washed, he smells of soap, his breath of sweet tea.

She rolls onto her back, to the darkness above her. "It is so strange, one life beginning as another one ends. Exchanged. When Clara died, it was the same, but the other way around. She was the one who died, not I."

He kisses her. His tongue is like words on her lips, but he says nothing. On the other side of the window, the whole world perishes. She thinks about their boat, on the jetty now, and how just a few hours ago they were in the middle of the lake, their tender bodies inches away from the eternal flow.

Her thoughts come back. "She was the first," she says quietly. "Our first."

Percy runs his fingers over her stomach, leafing across her skin as if he wants to open her up.

"And I still think about her, do you understand? When I look at William. Every time I look at William, I think of her. Will that ever stop?"

"You couldn't help it," he growls now with his unused voice.

"And I knew she was quiet. I knew she was so quiet, and I was happy. I would be able to sleep that night. And I slept. I slept so deeply that I didn't hear her go. And when I awoke, she was gone. Suddenly. Maybe, if I hadn't slept . . . Maybe if I had tucked her in again, given her a kiss."

"She was too small," says Percy. "You know how small she was. She should still have been inside you. She was still far too small for this world. That wasn't your fault." He kisses her, he kisses her. Her tears trickle down her temple.

"And when William came, I was afraid. I was so afraid, Percy, and he was so small."

"Not that small."

"He was so small and so blue. So white. But when he drank from me, I knew he would stay. He will stay." She nods and stares into the darkness.

"Yes, he will stay, my love."

A few minutes later, she hears Percy snoring. The sound sends her into a state of rage and relief. She is alone again. Her little girl would not drink enough. After every gulp, she fell asleep. Mary fed her and fed her, her breasts insisted, were filled only for her, but she did not want it. Her little girl was as pale as her milk, and her cheeks, her stomach, her little arms simply would not take shape. She was an angular baby with eyes the size of walnuts, sea blue, until they became deep gray pools as time passed. Just as the sea changes color according to the time of day and the time of year. What color will the sea be when her own time is up?

THE NEXT MORNING, she remembers nothing of her nocturnal thoughts. She sits down at her desk and begins. At first, it is single words. Then they become sentences. Ideas hook on to memories, weaving a story that could even be true. And suddenly she sees how what she is writing was there all that time, how, stamping its feet with impatience and denial, it cracks out of its cocoon, ugly, colorless, and vague because it thought it was unfit to be seen. How it tries out its voice, flayed and urgent, how it screams. She writes and it shakes back its colors. It is horrible. And here it is.

July–August 1812
Dundee

July 26, 1812

Everything happened at the same time. There was no opportunity to talk to Isabella about it. Her father and Robert were called to the factory, Isabella had to go into town with Johnny because he needed a new suit. I entered the world of idleness. I wandered around the Baxters' house, opening doors I should not have opened in all decency. I visited the bedrooms, I looked out the windows, just to see what their view was. I studied their bookcases to see if any of the volumes attracted my attention, but Robert had already shown me his books and Mr. Baxter owned mainly books about procedures in the textile industry and treatises on religion. For a moment, I sat on his bed, on the side where he slept—I could tell by the candlestick and the book on the bedside table and the slippers on the floor. On the other side, the bedside table was empty. Just a year ago, Mrs. Baxter slept on that side of the bed and now Mr. Baxter lay there alone, next to a memory. I ran my hand over the smooth bedspread, but when I reached her side of the bed, a grim feeling came over me. My hand did not want to go any farther, or I did not want to go any farther, because it did not feel right. I cannot explain it precisely, but I knew at that moment that if I extended my hand any farther, I would be able to feel the contours of her body under the covers. Startled, I pulled back my hand, and only a second later I could not believe that I had felt such certainty. Only the memory of the feeling remained. An absurd memory. As I closed the bedroom door behind me, I felt guilty, and I was glad that I felt guilty. What I had done was improper, and it would most certainly have been inappropriate to feel nothing. Silently and with a heavy heart, I walked downstairs. At that moment, Elsie hurried into the hall with a letter in her hand. Panic sparked in her eyes as she searched for the Baxters but found only me.

"Miss Mary, we need a messenger. Someone must go and fetch Mr. Baxter. Things are not good with Margaret."

A cold blast that seemed to come from the depths of my body spread all the way to my fingertips.

Grace came in with a full shopping basket and was immediately asked to send a messenger to the factory for Mr. Baxter. We had an hour to wait. Elsie mumbled prayers as she made tea. I paced back and forth—from the windows at the front to see if Mr. Baxter was coming, to the dining room windows to see if there was any sign of Isabella and Johnny's carriage yet, to the kitchen to report that still no one was coming, and back again to the front. The tension had reached a level at which all we could do was think, utter short sentences, perform simple actions. The letter Elsie had opened an hour ago, which had been delivered by a messenger from Fife, had been so urgent that the sender, Mr. Booth, had given permission to anyone present in the Baxter household to open it. As I, too, was now part of the Baxter household, I believed I could also read it. It was not a long letter. In rather forceful handwriting, it said that, two days ago, Margaret had suddenly been taken unwell with a severe fever. As the fever rose higher and higher and Margaret lost consciousness several times, Mr. Booth had sent for the doctor this morning. The doctor did not foresee a favorable outcome, and Mr. Booth wished to convey Margaret's wish to see Isabella. That was where the letter ended. Elsie looked at me with hopeful eyes, as if I might have read something different from her. I knew she could read—perhaps nothing too challenging, but this letter should not pose a problem for her.

"Where has Isabella got to?" I asked.

I was not expecting an answer. Outside, I heard a vehicle slowing down. Elsie, Grace, and I ran to the door and saw Isabella and Johnny stepping out of the carriage. They were carrying two boxes, and Johnny beamed as he ran towards me. Dark clouds drifted overhead. A strong wind had picked up, seemed to promise something.

"We bought such a fine suit for me!" he shouted.

"Come on," said Grace, "Elsie has baked biscuits." And she led him to the kitchen.

Isabella clearly knew that something must be wrong. Elsie and I stood straight-backed, waiting in the doorway while she paid the coachman. As she walked towards us with the boxes of clothes in her arms, I saw the curious sadness in her eyes. But not only that. I also saw anger. Anger at so much injustice in one place. Someone else? Again? She stood before me, my dear friend, and all I could do was open my arms to her, hold her tight, and whisper in her ear, "Margaret is not well. In fact, she's very ill."

And all Isabella could do was lean into my embrace, sob, and know that she was going to lose someone else.

◆ ◆ ◆

Mr. Booth and Margaret's house was suffused with forlornness. You could see it in the light that came in through the tall windows, illuminating the fireplace, the four-poster bed, the sheets, and the way it seemed to have lost some of its brightness, as if it had always brought in reality but was now struggling to do so. It was in the walls, in the ceilings. The ornaments were somehow more sharply delineated, as if they might come to life, the angels' heads extricating themselves, revealing their bodies, which had been concealed within the plasterwork, descending into the drawing room, the library, the hallway, and Margaret's bedroom. Though in my memory the wallpaper on the landing was green, with ornate grapevines in purple and gold, I saw now that it was brown, with roses and branches.

I sat and waited on the small sofa opposite Margaret's bedroom. When she read the letter, Isabella had been so upset that she wanted me to accompany her to her sister's. Mr. Baxter was still not at home. After waiting for an hour, Grace sent for a carriage to take Isabella and me to Fife. When we arrived, a Mr. Woltham opened the door. I had never seen him before. Mr. Booth was nowhere to be seen.

It was getting dark, and the wall lamps had not yet been lit. One elongated window provided a diffuse light. It was so very quiet. I heard only the occasional gust of wind around the house, like an animal circling its prey.

"Mary."

I gasped and then felt like a fool. Beside me stood Mr. Booth with a candle in his hand. He seemed taller than on the previous occasions I had seen him. His sideburns thicker, his eyes larger. He sat down beside me.

"I'm so sorry about Margaret," I said. "You must be very concerned."

Mr. Booth nodded. He did not look at me. His gaze was fixed on the door. For a time, we sat there. Occasionally I glanced at him from the side. The candlelight cast sharp shadows over his face. His expression was a mix of gravity and resignation. When he began to speak, his voice was softer than I remembered. "I wish I could say otherwise, but Margaret is not strong. She does not have a strong will like her sister. Like you."

I looked at him. His expression was unchanged, his eyes still focused on his wife's bedroom door.

"I've been having such strange dreams lately." Mr. Booth placed the candle between us, folded his hands in his lap. He seemed like a different person as he sat there. Powerless, almost diffident. "Margaret is not my first love, but I would have liked her to be my last."

"But she's not . . ." I was unable to continue. What could I have said?

"I believe it is inevitable." He shook his head, slowly, as if gradually recognizing that the world had never promised him anything.

"Can I do anything for you?"

Mr. Booth smiled briefly. "No, that's kind of you, but no. I have staff for the necessities. I can arrange everything myself."

"When do you think . . ."

"That she will die?" Mr. Booth looked at me. His eyes seemed almost black. "She does not have much longer."

"Is that what the doctor said?"

"No. Doctors won't be able to save her now. Two more nights, three at most, and then it will be over."

At that moment, the bedroom door opened with a soft click and Isabella came out. Her face was wet with tears, and she tried and failed to smile at us. Mr. Booth stood up and opened his arms wide to her. Trembling, she fell onto his chest, and he stroked the hair that tumbled down her back. I stood and watched her sighing, resting her wet cheek on his shoulder. She had closed her eyes. She was barely aware of me standing there, looking at her. He held her tight.

TWO DAYS WENT BY. The mood in the Baxter household was tense and somber. Robert made no more jokes, Johnny was less boisterous and noisy when he played. Isabella spent a lot of time in her room. I often came across Mr. Baxter somewhere in the house, lost in thought. He would be sitting at the window, staring outside, or halfway up the stairs with his hand on the rail, gazing ahead for seconds at a time. Only Elsie and Grace continued their daily activities, although they, too, were in low spirits, moving around the house as unobtrusively as possible, as if they would prefer to disappear, not to be a part of this tragedy.

Mr. Baxter went to visit Margaret every day, along with Isabella, Robert, and Johnny. I stayed at home. Isabella did not ask me to accompany her again, and I did not wish to impose on her. I read Milton's *Paradise Lost*, ate the madeleines that Elsie baked, and drank tea all day long. In the evenings, everyone gathered by the fireplace and we drank cognac, except for Johnny, who was given warm milk with honey. We did not talk about Margaret, especially not about Margaret, but we all knew why we were sitting together like that. We talked quietly and said very kind things to one another and told beautiful, loving stories. Isabella sat beside me, sometimes taking my hand, giving it a quick squeeze. Those were the happiest moments.

Isabella knocked on the door of my room. That was early this morning. I opened the door for her, and she threw herself into my arms. She did not make a sound. Her body trembled and shook, her breath came in irregular gasps. I held her tight, smelled her sleepy scent; deep and warm, a little spicy. My hand stroked her back, my other hand clutched her tightly to me. After a couple of minutes, she detached herself and looked at me. Her eyes were red and small from crying, her cheeks as pale as a ghostly apparition. Her dark hair was loose and tousled. I thought her very beautiful and very unreal.

"You need to come downstairs," she said in a voice that had lost almost everything. "We're all there."

DOWNSTAIRS, MR. BAXTER and Robert were sitting side by side at the kitchen table, conferring. Grace had Johnny on her lap; he was crying quietly and constantly. Elsie was bustling around the kitchen, lighting candles, boiling water, letting tears roll down her cheeks without wiping them away. When Isabella hugged her father from behind and put her head on his shoulder, he began to shake and made a terrifying hollow sound that seemed to come from the depths of his soul. Robert looked at them, laid his hand upon his father's. It was all so wretched, so terribly sad, and I stood there and saw it all and had no part to play and so decided to go and help Elsie. She looked at me with confusion for a moment, but then let me go ahead. I sliced bread, laid the table, brewed tea.

Breakfast had a solemnity to it, as the light from outside barely penetrated into the house, because of the early hour, and we let in the day with the candles between us, knowing that this was what we had to do. It was the day when all manner of things would have to be arranged. The day full of practical matters, the day suddenly filled with untamable grief. We talked softly to one another. Johnny did not eat much, but the others seemed to know that consolation and courage are impossible without food, and in some way I felt as if I had helped them to face this day, if only by slicing bread.

After breakfast, Mr. Baxter and Robert went to Mr. Booth's house to help make arrangements for the funeral. Isabella, Johnny, and I remained behind in the house, where day slowly dawned. Johnny forgot his grief now and then, so at times we forgot it too. Then the three of us went into the garden, played catch or sang a song together. But most of the time we sat in silence or quietly sobbing and staring into the distance.

"What did she die of?" I asked as midday approached. I was sitting on the bench in the back garden with Isabella. The sun had broken through the clouds and was warming our arms and faces.

"Mr. Booth says it was an infection. A week ago, there was nothing wrong." She rubbed her arms, she had goose bumps.

I could barely imagine it. How could a person go from healthy to desperately ill within a week and then die? But I knew it was possible. It often happened. My mother had died of an infection. A force so strong that the doctors can do little about it. An invisible force, but no less real for that.

"It's so terrible for Mr. Booth," said Isabella. "He loved Margaret so much."

"It is terrible," I agreed. "For Mr. Booth *and* for all of you." I laid a hand on her arm, stroked her gooseflesh.

Isabella did not say anything else. Johnny's reedy voice came from inside the house. He was calling her. Isabella jumped to her feet and hurried to him.

July 29, 1812

The Glasite Chapel was full. The Baxters sat at the front, together with Mr. Booth. There were prayers and singing. Johnny did not join in. He looked around with a still face, kept fiddling with something in his pocket. It was not his first funeral, of course. Perhaps he was wondering who would be next. Mr. Booth wore an expression of a pained tranquility; it was hard to look at him. Isabella did not appear to have noticed me. She sat next to her father, holding his hand, stroking Johnny's head. Mr. Baxter cried and cried, in a soundless stream of sorrow. Robert was pale, his eyes swollen. He was the only one who looked at me from time to time; then he would give me a small smile.

The walk to the Howff, where Margaret was to be buried, did not take long. As we passed through the gate, I realized that Isabella's mother must be buried here too. When we were there a few weeks ago, she had not mentioned it. We had not even walked by her grave. This time, we did. Margaret was given a grave beside her mother's. It started drizzling as the minister said his final words and some of the men lowered the coffin into the earth. Isabella fell into her father's embrace, Robert hugged Johnny close. Johnny was still fiddling with something in his pocket. What had he brought with him? Mr. Booth stood as straight as a pillar beside the hole. He seemed deep in thought, as if he were doing some complicated calculation. When the minister had finished speaking, he nodded, turned around, and walked away.

The mourners headed to the exit. I turned off down a path just before the gate, walked to the end of the row, and stood still for a moment. Her small stone with the worn letters was still the same, of course. And yet something was different. I studied the soil around it, the graves next to hers, the earth beneath my feet. I could not detect anything. Grissel Jaffray's grave looked exactly as it had a couple of weeks before. And yet I was convinced that something was different. It was abundantly clear. There was a certain presence; animate, weighty. Invisible. But it was there.

August 2, 1812

"What are you doing? What is that?" Robert pulled Johnny's hand from his trouser pocket.

We were at the table, eating soup. There was meat, bread. Johnny sat beside me, kept fiddling in his pocket. In his hand he held the fish head we had found weeks ago while out walking. Not only had he kept it—he was carrying it around with him.

"Have you cleaned that?" asked Robert.

"What is it?" asked Elsie at the stove.

Johnny looked around the table. He seemed terrified that we would take his toy from him.

"You shouldn't be playing with that, should you?" said Elsie.

"It's clean!" Johnny held the thing up. It was indeed dazzlingly white, almost gleaming. He had clearly done his very best to clean the bone.

Mr. Baxter was also at the table, but he had not said anything for days. He did not seem to notice that those around him were saying things, doing things. He just stared into the distance, ate, drank, slept. When anyone said something to him, he replied, but it was brief, flat. Everything was overshadowed by the loss of his eldest child.

Robert and Elsie said how dirty it was, that there could be nasty little creatures in it, that it was not normal to keep a skeleton, that it was a sin, and then Mr. Baxter said suddenly in a loud voice, "Leave the boy alone."

Everyone around the table fell silent. Robert stared at his father. Johnny put the fish head back in his pocket, with a little smile on his face. Isabella looked at me, somewhat surprised, trying not to laugh.

August 12, 1812

Mr. Woltham opened the door for us. He nodded and took our coats. The house was, at first sight, unchanged since Margaret's death, and yet it felt different. As if this had never really been Margaret's home, as if everything had forgotten her at the exact moment she breathed her last breath. Mr. Booth was in the drawing room. He was smoking a pipe, sitting with his legs crossed in an armchair by the fireplace. He looked up as we entered, and a big smile appeared on his face. He came to greet us.

"Isabella, Mary, how nice that you've come." He kissed our outstretched hands and gave a short bow, invited us to sit.

We took a seat on the sofa, close together, opposite Mr. Booth. On the table was a plate of biscuits and a large carafe of red wine. He poured some for us, without asking what we wanted to drink.

"I feel honored that you accepted my invitation." Mr. Booth coughed. His gray eyes seemed to eddy like the sea.

It was not just the house that felt different. Mr. Booth did not seem quite the same either. As if something that had previously shunned the light had now emerged.

"The two of you always came to see Margaret. This time you have come to visit me."

The pendulum clock in the hall struck eight.

"Wonderful!" Mr. Booth leaped to his feet. "Let's drink a toast!"

Isabella and I stood up and took our glasses. The wine was as dark as the damask curtains at the windows.

"To life," said Mr. Booth.

"To life," we repeated after him. The first sip tasted bitter.

MR. WOLTHAM LED us into the dining room. The fire was roaring brightly. The candles in the chandelier were all lit. There were dishes and tureens on the table with green beans, pie, salmon, and Madeira cake. Isabella and I sat opposite each other, with Mr. Booth between us at the head of the table. Mr. Woltham served the food and then left the room at Mr. Booth's request.

We began to eat. Mr. Booth talked about his brewery, asked Isabella about her father's textile factory, asked after my father, whom he turned out to know well. He had written to him after reading one of his books and they had corresponded regularly since then.

"In fact, it was Mr. Booth who ensured that Papa invited you to stay with us," said Isabella. She put a bite of food into her mouth and grinned at me. "My father didn't really know your father at all."

My father had not told me that. Everything he had told me had been about Mr. Baxter. Mr. Booth filled my wineglass again. How many times had he topped it up already? Suddenly I pictured my father. A glass of wine in his hand, or cognac, a book in the other, telling Claire and me to be quiet. In his eyes, only his work, his work, work. He did not have to tell Fanny to be quiet. She was naturally silent, she was not there, the child who belonged to no one. And when he thought he had reasoned with us for long enough, he kissed me on the forehead and left for his study again. And I truly wanted to do my best to be quiet, I enjoyed reading in silence, but then Claire came out with another ridiculous story she had heard, or she started annoying me with her out-of-tune violoncello playing, or she dressed up as her mother, imitating her voice, surprisingly convincingly, and said something suggestive and then I could not read any longer and started laughing so much that I feared I would never be able to stop. And there he was again, my father, his glass more empty, his eyes more full, and unable to suppress a little smile himself. She was more my sister than Fanny was, I thought, although Fanny and I shared a mother, and Claire and I shared nothing.

I looked at Isabella. She was eating and drinking and laughing. She was talking with Mr. Booth. She had no sister now. I could be her sister, I realized, but immediately rejected that thought. I did not want to be her sister. My sister but I kissed her. A line of poetry, not my own thinking, I thought. Not my thinking. I looked up. Mr. Booth laughed, loud and exuberantly, his head tipped back. I could see down his throat, a black hole into which he could swallow everything. Isabella's eyes seemed to be glued to him. Or he had enchanted her. With his wine, with his eyes, with his hands that could do as they pleased, which promised safety but brought wild adventures. My plate had been empty, I was sure of that—but now it was full again. More beans, more fish. I looked at Mr. Booth. His shirt was open. A dark marsh grew upon his chest. Gleaming black aquatic plants, among which it was impossible to breathe. Isabella should not stroke it with her fingers—you never knew what might happen. She could run her fingers across my back, over my belly. They were so soft, her fingers, far softer than mine, they must be. Those fingers, those Isabella fingers sparked and tickled, as if driven by an electric charge, as if twinkling lights shot out of them, into my lap, dancing between my legs, sparking through my marsh, slithering like a serpent through my sensitive spot, which glowed, which sparkled, which radiated at their touch. Again, he filled my glass, Isabella laughed loud, her teeth large and white. Mr. Booth's eyes had become dark oceans.

"I can't eat any more," cried Isabella, pushing her plate so far across the table that a few beans rolled off it.

Mr. Booth got up, went and stood behind her. He laid his hands, which were monstrously large—why had I never noticed that before?—on her shoulders, his nails were claws, his skin breathed, had gills. Isabella tilted her head to one side, against his arm, and she was the most beautiful princess I had ever seen. She was the only woman, she was beauty. Her eyelashes fluttered in front of her eyes, which held all that sorrow, she looked at me, she wanted to leave. I nodded, but I could not stand. It felt as if my body were no longer mine, but belonged to the room, as if I were part of the furnishings, the food in the dishes, which looked untouched—how could that be? I looked at Isabella to see if she could not stand either, but Mr. Booth's paws had become ordinary hands again, he had let go of her, was standing with his back towards us, looking outside. Dark clouds raced across the sky. I heard tapping on the window; the rain was embarking upon a long night.

There was a shift in the evening. A shift without a sound, but after that our setting changed. We were in the drawing room. The three of us sat on the sofa, Mr. Booth in the middle, but sometimes he was suddenly back at the window. The embers in the hearth glowed as if wanting to prove their existence one last time before they perished.

"There's a storm coming," said Mr. Booth, and it sounded as if he were glad.

My hand made a strange movement and my glass fell to the floor and broke. Wine ran like blood into the wooden boards.

Isabella looked at it. Her breath seemed to have stopped. She whispered, "Mary, we have to go back." The sharp seriousness in her voice tightened itself around my throat. Isabella stared at the floor, her eyes large, lost.

I felt heavy, as if something were holding me back, fastening me to this room, this house.

"We have to go home," I said. At least I think I said that.

"We need to leave." Isabella stood up.

It had grown cooler in the room, Isabella and I were once again the people we were, not parts of a whole, only of ourselves. I was able to stand. Mr. Booth led us to the hall, where Mr. Woltham was waiting with our coats to escort us to the carriage. I felt that I should not look back through the window as we drove away, that I should not want to see what there was to be seen, but I could not resist, precisely because I was too afraid of *not* seeing it, of leaving it behind, as if it did not exist.

So I looked.

On the steps stood a man, probably just Mr. Booth. He was standing perfectly straight, with his arms behind his back, and I went on looking until our carriage almost rounded the bend, because I knew something was going to happen. And I was right. Just before he disappeared from sight, I saw something that made me whimper inside. Mr. Booth was moving on the spot where he stood, with his legs, his arms, and his head, like a snake. He was moving smoothly and purposefully, as if in a lithe and graceful dance, as if he had to rearrange his skin, to slowly cast it off.

I SUSPECT THAT I fell asleep after that. This morning, I was lying in my bed, half-dressed, with a pain that had sunk into all the crevices of my head and a sick feeling in my stomach that intensified when I moved. I remembered nothing after the moment the carriage had rounded the bend. I had no recollection of how we got back home, how Isabella and I went to our rooms, how I—apparently—partially undressed myself. It felt as if there were gaps in my memory. The curtains hung heavy around my bed, the flowers on the wallpaper trembled skittishly before my eyes, the room twisted and wrapped around me. I closed my eyes but could not keep them closed. Something forced them open, wanted me to see, wanted me with bed and all to spin around and around as if on a merry-go-round, to see everything, becoming sick from seeing, from the pain, from the stories forming within me that could find no escape. For a moment, I thought I was going to die. And then I fell asleep.

THROUGHOUT THE MORNING, I awoke from time to time and the waking became less and less cruel. Around midday, I decided to see how Isabella was faring. I put on my dressing gown and crept along the hallway to her room, where I knocked on the door. I heard only a slight, tired groan. I waited a while but then opened the door. It was dim in her room. The yellow curtains at the windows filtered the light, lending the room a cheerful sunny glow. Isabella lay with her back towards me, her face to the window. I suspected she was awake.

"Isabella?" I went a little closer. The floor creaked. Isabella mumbled something. I slid under the covers beside her.

She gave me a nudge. "Lie still." She had cracks in her voice.

The warmth of her body attached itself to mine. I felt her breathing against my stomach. In and out. A sigh.

"I feel so wretched."

I put my arm around her, lay closer to her. Her curls tickled my neck and smelled of the night. Of this night in which sleeping and waking embraced so intimately that they were indistinguishable, becoming a long, sacred moment of uncontrollable thoughts and elusive meanings.

"I think I'm going to be ill."

How much wine had Mr. Booth given us? What had I seen and what had I dreamed? There were images of intoxication in my head, and I did not know what they were based on.

"What do you remember about yesterday?" I asked.

"What do you mean?" It seemed as if she moved away from me a little.

"What it was like? At Mr. Booth's?"

"What do you mean, what it was like? Of course I remember." She sounded impatient, almost resentful.

I decided to change the subject. "That monster, by the rocks, I want to go and take another look. We need to find out what it is."

Isabella shrugged. She mumbled something.

"Will you come with me? This afternoon?"

"This afternoon?" She laughed, snorted. "I'm not going anywhere at all today."

I fell silent. It annoyed me when she was like this. So distant. As if something had happened that I did not know about. But even more than annoying me, it made me sad.

"But aren't you curious to find out what it was?" I asked in a last attempt to get through to her, to touch her.

"What *what* was?"

"That monster, that thing."

She did not respond for a while. Then she said, "There are more important things, Mary. My sister is dead. I can't keep making up entertaining stories with you."

I was so furious that it was an effort not to give her a shove. As if she spent time with me only as some kind of favor. My breathing became deeper, all my muscles trembled. With a sharp movement, I threw back the cover and I left her on her own. Back in my room, the anger became softer but clearer, the trembling turned into shaking, and with the shaking came the tears. Something was not right. Something was not right at all.

I GOT DRESSED, pinned up my hair, put on my boots and coat, and asked Elsie if she had a bottle of water for me, because I wanted to go for a walk. She gave me water, a cake, and a pear and suddenly I was very hungry and was sure that everything would be better after I had eaten.

AFTER A FEW miles along the path, I did indeed feel better. The food had done me some good, and the air was cool and clear. I saw birds, rabbits, and a fox, but to my delight not a single human being. Almost my entire life, I had lived in London, beautiful, filthy, jangling London, but this was where I belonged. It was as if I could breathe more deeply, as if new thoughts could simply come blowing into my mind. Nothing was impossible here. Everything you could imagine could be true somehow, and that struck me with a joy I had never experienced before.

I recognized our picnic spot. I recognized the rocks. They looked different than they had a few weeks ago; innocent and unknowing beneath a light gray sky. I walked closer, almost fearlessly because I was so eager to see that creature again. I hid again in precisely the same place behind the rocks. My heart pounding so violently that it seemed to want to escape from my chest, I looked around the stone.

Nothing. The crevice in the rock where he had stood before, where he had uttered that stifled cry in his animal voice, was abandoned. I stood up and walked cautiously towards the rocks, but the closer I came, the more certain I was that there was no monster here. No monster and no trace of him, not even any remains of the fire with which he kept himself warm at night. There was nothing and, as far as this spot was concerned, there never had been anything. A chill ran over me, sending a shower of goose bumps across my skin. I pulled aside bushes, walked around the other rocks, listened, looked. Nothing.

On the way back, I no longer felt happy and free. I felt like a fool, a foolish child. How could I have believed in a monster? I was fourteen years old. I knew better than that. It was still a long way back to the Baxters' house and I tried to enjoy the birdsong, the cool air on my cheeks, the wide-open landscape, but the whole time I was thinking: How did that happen? How could I believe that? Accepting as true something that did not exist, something that obviously did not exist, purely and simply because I saw it? But, said another part of my brain, that isn't so peculiar, is it? Is seeing not proof? There you see a flock of swallows in the sky, and you believe that they are real, too. You feel the grass under your feet, the brambles on your skin, the tears on your cheeks. Of course you believe in them.

I had already come quite some way on the journey home when I caught sight of a large figure. He was standing with a horse at the side of the road, near a tall tree. For a moment, I was not sure what to do. Going out walking alone had its risks, I knew, but how many people were not to be trusted? I wanted to go home. I did not know what the figure was doing, but I was not inclined to wait until he rode on. Besides, maybe he was coming my way and I would be unable to avoid him. So I walked on, and I suddenly saw that it was not a stranger; it was Mr. Booth. It was almost as if he was waiting for me, so at ease as he stood there beside his horse, looking in my direction.

"Good afternoon, Mary," he said, doffing his hat when I reached him.

"Good afternoon, Mr. Booth," I said. "I was just out for a walk."

"Good for body and soul, a walk. I chose to go out for a walk with Duchess here today, but I could do with a little exercise myself. May I accompany you to the Baxters'? At least, I assume you're on your way back there?"

I nodded.

Mr. Booth took his horse's reins, and she walked along beside us.

"Do you often go riding?" I asked.

"Not as much as I used to. When Margaret was still alive, when she still had use of her legs, we often used to ride together."

"You must miss her terribly. It's so dreadful."

"Of course I miss her." It sounded somewhat brusque, but I blamed myself for being too familiar.

We were silent. In the distance, I saw a buzzard alight on a branch. It seemed to have something in its beak, but it was too far away to see properly. The gray sky became a warmer shade of gray in the west; the sun slowly rolled away from us. I was craving some hot food; a pie fresh from the oven or the potato gratin Elsie was so good at making. I longed for a chair, a hearth fire to warm my tired face, to sit by and forget what I was no longer so certain of. I suddenly realized how far I had walked today, how little I had eaten, and how much I had missed Isabella.

"It is perhaps better if you don't mention this to her," said Mr. Booth, and I could tell by his voice that he had held those words in his mouth for a long time, "but I am concerned about Isabella."

My thoughts shot to the previous evening. His hands on her shoulder, Isabella shrieking with laughter as she pushed her plate across the table, her gaze suddenly frozen on the floor, as if she saw something moving there.

"Why?" I asked.

"You may have noticed that her character is not as well balanced as yours or mine, or as Margaret's was, or their father's. One moment, she is cheerful, pleasant company, affectionate, and it seems as though she takes great pleasure in life, and the next moment that all changes. She becomes sullen, somber, averse to well-meaning attention, and withdraws into herself, where no one is able to reach her. Isabella has always been like that, to a certain extent. But since her mother's death, this erratic behavior has become one of her main characteristics. And I might add that Margaret's death has not helped. This is clearly very difficult for those who love her, but also, I think mainly for herself, most unpleasant."

It was true. I recognized everything Mr. Booth said. And somehow it was a relief that her erratic behavior had nothing to do with me, but that it was her character. Maybe I would be better able to bear her unpredictable rejections now that I knew this.

"I am telling you this with the utmost discretion. I do not like to talk about others in their absence, but in this case I must make an exception. I do not assume Mr. Baxter and Robert have told you anything about this. However, I think it important that you are aware, since you and Isabella have become so close." Mr. Booth had a bitter twist to his mouth. The conversation seemed to be difficult for him.

"I am not solely concerned about her changeable nature, Mary. I am also afraid that you have come to consider her too much as a friend."

It felt as if a warm blanket, which had lain over my shoulders since my first meeting with Isabella, were being pulled away. Mr. Booth looked at me. There was a flatness to his gaze, as if he were very tired. He sighed.

"Isabella is an intelligent, engaging young lady. But she is incapable of friendship. I believe that Isabella does not understand—or even realize—this herself."

I stared ahead. What Isabella and I shared—how could I describe it as anything other than friendship? A very tempestuous friendship, and perhaps that was what made it so intimate.

Mr. Booth continued. "You might be wondering what happened between her and Margaret. I imagine she has told you something about the reason for the chilly relationship between them, but perhaps not everything."

She had told me nothing. But now that Mr. Booth mentioned that chill, I saw it clearly in my memory. The lukewarm greetings, the brief, polite conversations, the little we saw of Margaret. I had thought this was because of Margaret, because of her accident, or because something made her inherently unhappy, but now I realized it must be to do with their relationship.

"Margaret was a troubled girl when I first met her," began Mr.

Booth. "Whenever I visited the Baxters, she would take refuge in a corner of the room. I tried to talk to her from time to time and came to see that she was a very gentle person. She was interested in the world, in me, but felt no need to talk about herself. Whenever I asked her a question, her expression darkened and she gave short and evasive answers. One day, I chanced upon her alone at home, and that time she was more open. We drank tea in the garden, and I discovered that she not only had a good heart but was also caring and intelligent. She told me that—although she was the eldest child—she never felt like a part of the family. Isabella, who was twelve or so at the time, was spontaneous, a tearaway, full of ideas and imagination, independent and clever; Robert was the joker, a pleasant brother who would undoubtedly take over their father's textile factory. Johnny was coddled by their mother, adored by their father—they were so delighted that another child had come along so many years after Robert. All the children in the family had a function, a quality that made them loved. But what did Margaret have? It seemed almost as if the big sister's classic jealousy of her younger sister had never left her. She thought herself mousy, quiet and inconspicuous. I believe she enjoyed talking to me. I think I was the only one who talked to her at such length about her feelings. After a number of weeks, I decided to ask for her hand. She said yes. We were happy. During the preparations for the wedding— which we wanted to keep very simple—I noticed that Isabella was drawing more attention to herself than usual. She normally had no reason to complain about the attention she received; people enjoyed her company. But now that her sister was getting married, *that* was the big news. Mr. and Mrs. Baxter, the neighbors, the people from the village—they all came to talk to Margaret at the fair. At the grocer's, they asked Margaret how things were going, how she wanted to decorate our home, how many children we wanted if we were granted the good fortune. Margaret had entered the realm of adulthood and she realized that she had every right to be there, that she mattered too. That she was perfectly cut out for this new life as a married woman. She was radiant as she led people around my house, where we would live together. You know the house. Many people find it quite imposing: large windows, the extensive library, the high, wide staircase in the hall. The visitors were impressed."

I pictured the staircase. I could never walk past it without thinking about what had happened to Margaret, and every time I saw it, I could feel her fall in my stomach, a painful fluttering.

"Margaret paid particular attention when she led Isabella around. She hoped her sister would be pleased for her, but Isabella just shrugged at everything, said she was bored, wanted to leave. That really hurt Margaret. During the wedding, Isabella entertained herself by letting her mouth run away with her. She and Robert made jests. At one point, Margaret took Isabella outside. She begged her to stop. Told her she was ruining her big day with her attention-seeking. That now, for the first time in her life, this was *her* day, and that Isabella clearly could not stand it. Begrudged her for it. I went out to see where Margaret had gone and at that moment I heard Isabella say to her sister in a cutting voice, 'Well, I hope you fall down your beautiful high staircase and break both legs, Mrs. Booth.'"

I could both imagine it and not. Isabella was headstrong, she could be both blunt and sharp, but to say such a thing? On the other hand, she had been only twelve. When young, one can do terrible things, things one would never even contemplate doing when older.

Mr. Booth gazed into the distance, and his horse snorted. "From that moment, Margaret and Isabella did not speak to each other for a long time. When Margaret and I visited the Baxters, they ignored each other. I thought it was terrible, encouraged them to reconcile for a while, but although Margaret was inclined to do so, Isabella did not care. She was hurt, jealous, I think. Not accustomed to her sister receiving the attention she deserved. And then too proud to patch it up."

"And then Margaret had her fall," I said.

"Indeed. She fell. Less than a year after the wedding—Margaret and Isabella still had not spoken a word to each other—Margaret tripped over the hem of her skirt when she was at the top of the staircase. She fell down all twenty-four steps to the bottom. Broke her collarbone, sprained her thumb and forefinger. And the damage to her spine left her legs paralyzed. Several doctors examined her, but they all said the same thing. The damage could not be undone. Margaret would remain an invalid for the rest of her life. According to the doctors, she had been very lucky. Such a fall, from such a height, could easily have proven fatal." Mr. Booth's bottom lip trembled, and I felt as if I were witnessing something very rare. I wanted to console him, to stroke his arm, but I did not dare.

"Terrible," I said.

The sky took on a swollen dark purple hue. I heard a barn owl screech and saw a bat swooping through the tops of the trees. The buzzard had disappeared, along with its prey.

"I am a man who does not believe in the supernatural, in witchcraft. But I have always found it puzzling that Isabella predicted Margaret's fall."

Had she done so? Or had she uttered a dreadful curse that happened to come true? If all our stories are true, was it not possible that Isabella had known what would happen? Or had she set something in motion? I felt sick. I thought about home, with the Baxters.

"I do not want to worry you . . ."—and with those words he drove a deep anxiety into me. "I do not believe that Isabella is a bad girl. I am merely saying: take care. That is all."

I nodded. I had no desire to question Isabella's intentions. Yet something within me urged me to take Mr. Booth's story seriously. If only for safety's sake.

A DETERMINED WIND picked up. It was almost completely dark now, and it was only just possible to distinguish the path from the surrounding greenery. Suddenly there was a tug on my arm, and I tumbled back into the bushes, together with Mr. Booth. Something sharp scratched my cheek and I felt my ankle twist strangely. I heard Mr. Booth's ragged breathing close to my ear.

"Mary, did I hurt you?"

I felt his hand in mine and he pulled me to my feet. "No," I said, "what happened?"

"I am so sorry, Mary. I saw a snake."

"A snake?" Something hot flashed up my back.

"An adder, I suspect. I couldn't see it clearly."

CLICK. **A MEMORY** surfaced like a bubble in water.

Mr. Booth is looking at Isabella with fascination. "You saw her already, eh, in the dining room?" he asks.

By the light of the candles in the chandelier, her eyes seem to be crying slightly; flecks of light on her cheeks, her throat, her breasts.

"She has followed us." Mr. Booth stands up and walks past, be hind the sofa. At the door, he stoops and then, suddenly, he has a snake in his hands. The snake is black and has yellow bands around its body.

"What is that?" whispers Isabella. She is pale, I see her hands trembling.

"Have I introduced the two of you to Emilia, my pet?" Mr. Booth is holding the snake in his arms as he might carry a baby: close to him, the body over his arms, over his shoulder. The snake's head is raised, alert, looking at us.

Isabella stands up from the sofa, swaying.

"No, no, no," Mr. Booth says soothingly. "No need to worry. Emilia is very sweet. She always listens to me."

Isabella stands there, one hand on the back of the sofa, her eyes on the door.

"Sit down," says Mr. Booth curtly, and Isabella sits again, looks away from the door and at the snake.

Mr. Booth walks towards us, the snake in his hands like a precious gift. The place between us is intended for Mr. Booth and his snake. Maybe we are under a spell, I think as he sits down and takes my hand, placing it on the hideously cool skin of the snake, its scales so smooth and unearthly. Then he takes Isabella's hand and lays it on the snake too. And she is too afraid, I think, to do anything. Or she is no longer afraid. She has surrendered to whatever it is that is happening now. I look away from the snake, at her. She is looking back at me. We run our hands over the cool scales in synchrony. I can feel the wicked shiver beneath my hand, as if it is having to hold itself back. But Isabella and I look into each other's eyes, we see a depth we have never known before. I am not scared.

"Face what you fear," says a deep voice between us.

Isabella smiles, but only at me.

THERE WAS A draft when I lay in bed that night. The curtains around the bed moved with an insatiable desire, driving me into a state of slumber. There was no monster, but the presence of a monster was undeniable. His breath could be felt in every dark corner, heard in every crevice in the floor. Wherever I went, he was there. He was not a monster in a fairy tale, he was not a story. He was the loneliness I felt without Isabella. He was my mother's kisses, which I had made up for myself, my accumulated grief, my collected childhood dreams. He was the one who saw into the future. He consisted of intense desire and the deepest sorrow. And he was more real than a monster by a rock.

We stroked the snake. This wonderfully cool, hypnotically calm, possessed snake. Isabella had stretched a cobweb of flesh across our laps. Mr. Booth, whom we called David, had unbuttoned his shirt, and the snake disappeared between layers of clothing. Somewhere in the house, we heard Margaret laughing. Isabella and I went on stroking, we looked into each other's eyes and, for a second, I thought we were kissing. When I looked down, I saw David's hairy, dark pink member, twitching like a caught fish, and we stroked away, we could not stop. This living, idiotic, quivering thing has our monster's name, Isabella said to me under the web of flesh, so that David would not hear. It stinks, I said, and I thought I might vomit. That's because of the sea, said Isabella. What did you expect?

June 1816
Cologny

❦

Monster, come

There are, in essence, two reasons to be unhappy. The first, of course, is death. The knowledge that everything is ultimately meaningless, as it is finite. That everything that has once been will one day be no longer makes it, by definition, futile. Even so, it *feels* significant when a loved one dies. The discrepancy—that is where the pain is. She knows all about that. And everyone who has ever lived knows it. And that is in fact the second reason: life. Life is all there is, all we have, and that makes it of the utmost importance. Of such importance, and we suffer. If it is not the suffering of the body, then it is the suffering of the spirit. People are born with a will. It is the driving force behind their lives. But do people ever get what they want? In rare cases. And then? Then they want more of it. Or of something else. Satisfied people do not exist.

Mary gently slides her little finger into the corner of William's mouth, breaks the vacuum, turns him, and puts him to her other breast. Carefully. A small piece of tooth is starting to emerge in his upper jaw, and it sometimes presses fiercely into her nipple. She strokes his thin, reddish hair, barely a layer of down. Thoughts run away with you when your mind has nothing to do. Sometimes she sinks into a dream while feeding; not a daydream, a dream. She sees what her brain concocts. Parties, Fanny laughing behind her handkerchief, her father with a glass of gin, Mary Jane with drunkenness in her moist eyes, her own mother with a baby in her arms, at her breast, on the sofa. She looks languidly ahead, as if she, too, is dreaming. That baby is Mary, of course. Things she can remember merge with what never happened, what never existed. She sometimes thinks she can invent things into the world. A myth that feels so true, that is so inherently present in every human being that it opens up a recognition, an awareness: I have seen this. I remember this. A knock at the door.

"Mary?" Claire comes in, on stocking feet, pale face, hair loose. Her brown curls tumble over her shoulders. She lingers at the dressing table. Moves Mary's bottles around.

With difficulty, Mary pulls herself back into this reality. "Is something the matter?"

Claire turns around. So many tears on her cheeks. Then she throws herself onto the bed beside Mary, shaking silently. Albe or Percy, Mary wonders. Claire goes on shaking, says nothing.

William lets the nipple slip from his mouth, hiccups, a drop of milk slides down her bosom. Mary grabs him under his arms, lays him on her shoulder. She tries not to sigh.

"What's wrong?" she asks.

Claire makes a sound. It is a high, deep sob, which must have been plaguing her for minutes. Mary rests a hand on her back. William burps, milky spittle drips down her neck. There is the sour smell that she associates with love.

"Albe is so mean," sobs Claire. "I don't understand it. Sometimes we laugh together, sometimes he kisses me, makes love to me, but then the next day he tells me I get in the way, that I rob him of his inspiration, that I'm foolish. What am I to do?" She turns her face to look at Mary with small, red eyes.

Mary sighs after all. "You know what I'm going to say, don't you? Maybe that's why you've come to me. Maybe you want someone to say it, one more time. He doesn't want you, Claire. He doesn't love you. He doesn't even like you very much. And you should not want him."

Motionless, Claire looks at her. Then her lip begins to tremble. She hides her face in the sheets. "I knew you would say that. How can I not want him? I believe you are capable of that: of no longer feeling love for someone who is beastly to you. You can do that. But how do you do it, Mary? How can you remain so unmoved? How can you deny your own heart? I love Albe. I love him and I don't even know exactly why. Tell me how to do it, how to turn my love into indifference."

She does not think that Claire intends to hurt her. Is she right? Is she unmoved? Is that what people see?

"You don't know why you love him?"

Claire scrambles up, sits beside Mary against the headboard. She strokes William's nose, and he makes a happily startled noise.

"Strange, isn't it? He is not kind to me. Not usually. But when we are enjoying ourselves . . . I always want to be with him. Sometimes people say they love someone because that person makes them feel good about themselves. I think I love Albe because he does not do that." Claire shakes her head. "I am insane."

Mary grins. With her free hand, she pulls Claire close. "Disturbed," she says.

◆ ◆ ◆

"I've started." John's cheeks are bright red, as if he has a fever.

They are sitting on the veranda at Diodati. Beyond the mountains, the sky is pink, purple, and red, almost the color of John's cheeks. It has been an exceptionally beautiful day; barely any rain, not too cold, and at the edges of the sky a little light blue actually shimmered through the gray of the summer. They all went for a walk together along the shore of the lake, played card games in the garden, and ate on the veranda. Now only she and John remain. Albe wanted to work. He had to catch up on the work he had missed today. Claire did not feel well, ate only a little, did not drink, and wished to return to Chapuis early. Percy offered to walk back with her, down the short path. Chivalrous, probably. Tiresome, thought Mary, hating herself for it.

"I have an idea. A good one, I suspect. And I've found the right tone. When I've made a little more progress, I would like you to read it, Mary."

"Good," she says. "I'm pleased for you."

John turns the flame of the lamp a little higher. "How's it going with your story?"

What is she to say? She is working on it. All the time, or so it seems. On paper, but mainly inside her head. It is a story that is already there, that she is discovering, separating from the other stories. That does not mean it is easy. Or that she thinks she will succeed. There is so much in the way. Fear, she thinks. Fear of what happened, but also fear of what never existed. Fear of her own memories. And that process is something she cannot put into words. More precisely: something she does not wish to put into words. Not to John. Not to Percy or Albe. She feels that she can free this story only if she lets it surface within herself. And that she can free herself from this story only if she does not reduce it to a narrative, to an idea, a form, and a series of events. It will have to mature within her, until it has acquired its own existence, until it has become so true that it flows from her quill as the truth, until no one can deny it, not even Mary herself.

She smiles. "I don't know," she says. "It's happening. I'm writing. I've mainly been thinking a lot."

"I spend too long thinking. Just start writing. That's what helped me. I was in the library a few evenings ago. The curtains were closed, there were two or three candles, the fire. It was pleasant. Albe was lying on the sofa in front of the fireplace. He had opened Coleridge, but he was not reading. He was staring into the fire with those pale eyes of his. There was something strange about him, something unfathomable. It was as if he were not entirely here, as if things were happening inside his head that extended far beyond our mundane reality. And suddenly I had it. I returned to my room, sat down at my desk, and, there and then, that night, I wrote the first two chapters."

This is the first time she has seen John happy. She takes his hand.

"How nice, John. How wonderful."

John raises his glass. "He inspires me, Albe. I don't know why that is."

"He is a great writer." Mary clinks her glass against John's.

"No, that's not it. Or yes, it's that, too. But it's more than that. It's the way he is, the way he lives. He is so . . . so pure."

"It's not as if he's some kind of god."

The sky is almost black. No stars.

John laughs. "Of course not."

They stare at the lake, which is starting to lose more and more color, like the mountains behind, like the trees around Diodati.

"Are things going well between you and Percy?"

"Of course." She was not prepared for the question.

In the distance, a wolf howls. Or a dog.

"You both believe in free love, don't you?"

She doubts whether they believe in free love. Increasingly she thinks that believing in free love is like believing in God. It is an ideal, the ideal. But ultimately, it does not work. Cannot work. You lose something, every time you give yourself and once again stand alone. Without illusions. Percy would laugh at her. He is the most fervent atheist she knows. And yet the analogy is right as far as she is concerned. Maybe free love does not work for her because Percy is the only one she wants to love.

"Yes," she says. "Absolutely."

"I think it's beautiful," says John. "You and Percy and Claire. The ease with which you get along."

She feels something rocking inside her stomach. Is it the burned flan that Adeline reluctantly carried in from the kitchen this morning? The wine, which may have been poured less generously this evening, but has somehow hit her differently, more urgently? Is it the slowness of the evening, the haughty look on Albe's face (because his poem is going well, he is pleased with himself), Percy's grin (because of wine, because of Claire), Claire's giggling (because of wine, because of Percy)? She can feel the wind rising. She wants it to be night, for it to remain night for days. Hours and hours to think, to drink and to dream. Hours when she can escape, can retreat, each of them remaining on their own island. Hours in which she can stare at William, sleeping in his cradle with animal warmth. She will stroke him; his softness hurts her fingertips, his newness pains her eyes. This is their human. They made it themselves, out of nothing. No, not out of nothing. Out of love.

"I know that, as a doctor, I can do good deeds, but as a writer I can achieve so much more, don't you think?"

Did she just drift off? She shivers at the blackness outside the veranda, pulls her coat more closely around herself. "You're a very good doctor," she says. "Not many people can do what you do."

"I want to be able to do what you can do." John's head is close. His wispy mustache looks like a shadow. "Mary, you are my angel."

She wants to laugh, but she controls herself. Then she feels hands on her waist, wet lips on hers. A strange tongue, thick, rough, longing, so longing, demanding. She can think of so many reasons not to do this. She thinks of Percy. She thinks of William. Of Claire. She thinks of Albe. But there is another reason. As that big tongue collides with her own, and too much strange saliva enters her mouth, too much strange breath, she suddenly knows that there is only one question. Does she want this? And as she asks that question, she extricates herself from John's kiss. Shocked, disheveled, defeated, John looks at her.

"I'm sorry," she says. Then she stands up. The table, the bars of the veranda, the black shadows, they begin to spin. From left to right, from left to right, again from left to right. She tells herself nothing is wrong. She follows her feet as she walks away, down the veranda stairs, cautiously. The walk back to Chapuis is a dark one. She has no lamp, no candle. The sky is black. The bushes are black, the trees, the path is black. She tries to feel where she needs to go. She thinks there is a light at home, she sees it dancing in the distance. She hears her own breathing, as if someone is walking beside her. She tastes the strange taste of John, as if he is still inside her, his tongue still against hers like a snake, strange and bitter as it penetrates the mouth.

She begins to run. Strands of her hair come loose, she is panting. Please let everyone be sleeping when I get home, she prays.

The house is filled with a deep silence, one that tires her through and through. A few more steps and she will reach her bedroom, and then she can slip between her sheets, away from this day. In the darkness, she undresses, finds her nightgown by touch. With a light hand, she feels inside the cradle; child, warm breath. She slides into the sheets, the bed is empty. She does not know what she was expecting. She is good at crying quietly. Thank goodness she is.

◆ ◆ ◆

Her father says she came into life quietly. Hair as dark as the blackness she came from. Eyes as light as the day beginning for the first time. She is a girl, and although they were anticipating a boy, they are delighted. Everything went well. It is twenty to twelve at night. The wind has the strength of a giant's breath and hailstones as big as coals are falling from the skies. Her mother's womb is the gate through which reality can be found, the painful white surfaces of life, the cold that makes her gasp for air. Tonight she has been brought to life.

Mrs. Blenkinsop, the midwife, arrived in time, her father is waiting downstairs, in the drawing room. He makes a cup of coffee, he knows how to, since her mother does not always have the time to do it, let alone the inclination, and he waits until he is allowed to come and see his daughter. Although Mrs. Blenkinsop has informed him that the child has been born, is healthy, she does not let him come upstairs. He waits. And waits. Around two in the morning, the midwife comes down with an alarming message: they need to send for a doctor. So her father hurriedly takes a carriage to Westminster Hospital, and an hour later he returns with a French doctor, who tries with all his might to pull the placenta from her mother, if needs be in pieces.

That pain, so bitter and hostile, is unknown to her mother until this moment. The hands of the doctor deep inside her, as if clawing away at an open wound. The birth has not until now driven her to such despair, awakening thoughts within her of grotesque internal devastation.

She is her father's first child. He knows nothing about this, now that her mother lies bleeding on the bed, moaning softly but bleeding profusely, the sheets wet with sweat and blood, her mother's face pulsing with misery, with delirium, with every vicious contraction forced by the doctor's hands. Is it going to be all right? Does her mother know? And if she knows nothing, if she is only breath, snarl, muscle power, animal, then who would know? Her body?

All the books he has read in his life, all those conversations with writer and philosopher friends could not prepare him for what is happening now. This is of a different order. This is another domain. The domain of women, although her mother, if her spirit had been there, would undoubtedly have given him a mocking look. The domain of women? Because the child was carried to term within her and born from her loins? That hardly seemed sufficient reason to grant her this domain exclusively. Had it not been the man, he, who together with her, both to an equal degree, had formed a child, who in brief ecstasy had fired a shot, within her, so that their particles might find one another and make a new human being: this child? The fact that the child had grown within her could not make him an outsider, could it? This life they had made, and everything about it, she would say, was the human domain.

And her father, always ready for meaningful discussion, would want to bring up some kind of counterargument. Something about nature, about motherhood, about instincts, but he loves her too much. He would look at her, another contraction, the candlelight splashing off her damp face, a brooding ghost, sunk deep in pain, and he would say she was right.

But her mother does not give him a mocking look. She does not put him in his place. Her mother is no longer in the room. Her body is working for her, but her mind is free. Her eyes see but no longer comprehend. And her father looks at her, discovering depths to his panic whose existence he never suspected.

The doctor leaves a few minutes after half past five in the morning. It is still raining and the gusts of hail push angrily against the windows. The child is wrapped up tightly, lying in her father's arms. He does not dare to look at her mother, at least not with the eyes of a husband, not with the eyes of the father of their child. He looks at her with the dispassionate gaze of a doctor. He sees a pale body, goose bumps, on her face and throat the glimmer of drying sweat, dark patches around her closed eyes, and, if he looks very closely, a chest that gently rises and falls. And farther down, a tangle of sheets, wet, deep dark red. There he sits, her father, with his child in his arms. All that can be done now is to wait and see, the doctor said. Mrs. Blenkinsop fetches water, linen cloths, clean sheets. The child has still not cried, not made a sound, but she is breathing and her eyes are open, and he knows it is fine.

Nothing is fine. Ten days pass and, after her mother's condition initially seems to improve, she slowly but inevitably slips away into the depths of her own thoughts, if they are still thoughts. The hope and slumbers of the night flow into the chilly reality of the morning; dazzling white, cold through to her fiercely exhausted bones, a no-man's-land.

Five days later, they take her mother to the churchyard of St. Pancras. The child has learned to cry in the meantime.

THAT IS HOW she pictures it. If we do not fill in the details, there are no stories. Mary cuts a slice of bread, spreads it with butter. She has moved the cradle into the kitchen. William is lying on his stomach, has pushed himself up, and is watching with wide eyes as Mary takes a bite. She tickles him under the chin. The stamping by the door indicates that Percy has returned from wherever he was. Stamping mud off their boots has become second nature. Cold. The door slamming. The creaking of floorboards in the hallway. Percy puts his head around the kitchen door. It must look cozy: three candles, tea, bread, the woodstove lit, fogged-up windows, a mother and baby at the kitchen table.

"Hello, my love," he says. "Is Claire not here?"

"Claire's at Diodati." Percy takes a cup from the dresser and pours tea for himself. He kisses her. Kisses William.

"Come and sit for a moment."

Percy pulls up a chair. Smiles at her with that mouth.

It was the first thing she fell in love with. That mouth said everything. Those full lips spoke silently of a world she did not yet know; the gazes that evening, those wonderful eyes she wanted to know forever, his feigned diffidence in her father's office, his knee against hers, his fingers on her back, the words that were meant for her alone, the kissing, his breath on her throat as he gently pushed her up against her mother's gravestone, the loving, the drinking in bed while he read poetry to her, his cold feet on hers, the laughter, the traveling. It was those lips that carried her forward in time, the lips she *knew*, even then, because they described a life that was to come. And since then, those lips, that face have been her anchor point. From there, she could move forward and back in time, because this was the face of her entire life. She would never be able to lose this face, even if that was all she could think about. Because she would lose it, and, with it, everything.

"Do you want to take a walk this afternoon?" Percy takes a sip of tea. "I think it's going to stay dry and Elise will be here soon, won't she?" He looks at her and, at the same time, he looks past her.

She nods. They have been for relatively few walks since they arrived here. Oh, she has. With John, with Claire, alone. But hardly at all with Percy. They do very little together anyway, here. Or is that how it has been since William came along? Even before, says someone inside her head. Don't you remember what it was like during your pregnancies? The child growing inside her united them, she knew that, she felt that, but for Percy that bond was something different. He tried not to see how she was changing, outwardly of course, but that was not the main thing. The changes in her body and in her mind made her stay at home, read, sing songs quietly. She wanted less wine, it disagreed with her. Percy tried not to see how she was awakening as a mother. He went into town with Claire, to the theater. Sometimes they did not return until she was getting up.

She wanted to know what Percy and Claire were doing together, and yet she did not want to know. So she did not ask, but she was angry anyway. Imperceptibly angry, silently angry, angry with herself. And then, one day, she knew. The link that the child had forged between them was not for Percy a bond, but a bind.

As they move through the wet blades of grass that afternoon, their boots heavy with greedy mud, sending birds flying up from the undergrowth towards the cloudy sky that, like a gray blanket, closes the world off from the clear, the eternal, the calmly indifferent, she worries about what to say. She wants one sentence, a sentence that will reduce everything to normal proportions, that will right all that is wrong, that will show her love, ask for his, transport them back in time and deeds, transforming their monstrous incomprehension of each other to something that could never arise, because they knew each other, loved each other, loved only each other in the world.

"John kissed me."

It is not the right sentence.

Percy smiles. He continues to look ahead, as if there is something to see there. Mary feels something cramping up inside. It is hard to keep calm, to keep breathing, to keep walking, beside him, to wait. What exactly did you expect, she asks herself mockingly. This is what he wants, isn't it? You knew that. Had she hoped for shock, even if only slight? Some small sign that, even though this was how they wanted to live, even though he believed in it, fought for it, it still hurt him?

"How was it?" he asks.

She tries to answer him without remembering it, but that is impossible, because it is inside her; that broad, languid tongue making a wound in her that would never fully heal. She is unsure what she will say.

"What do you think?" she asks, her tone as neutral as her body will allow.

Somewhere far off, worlds away from here, she hears a child laughing. In the bushes along the path, something is startled. It darts away before Mary can see what it is.

Percy stops, takes her hand, looks at her. "You will not admit it to me, but I know you find it hard when I'm with Claire. But that will pass, truly. I wanted to make it easier for you." Perfectly calm. He means it.

"John?" As if she has something revolting in her mouth.

There is a beast inside her, a monster. It wants to scream, it wants to tear things apart. It wants to stamp through the world independently of her and suffer no consequences because it has no conscience.

She is not shocked. She recognizes it. As if she has spent her life observing it in a cracked mirror, thinking she saw herself. It curses. She pants. Looks at Percy. With the palm of her hand, she slaps his pale pink cheek. Percy takes a step back. And another step. He frowns. His cheek is the color of the setting sun. He turns around, leaves her.

Inside her, it howls. It is awake.

HOURS LATER, she is home. She did not want to come home, so she walked. She walked farther than she had ever done before. She got lost and did not much care. Only when it began to rain, when her toes went numb, her fingertips began to throb angrily with the cold, did she ask for directions. A surly farmer with a cart drove her to

Chapuis. She gave him five centimes and he drove away without saying goodbye. At Chapuis, there was only Elise with William, who was asleep. Elise left and Mary sat at the kitchen table. For a few minutes, she just sat there. She looked at the mantelpiece, the little white porcelain bird gleaming sharply in the lamplight. Curiously animate, yet motionless, as if sleeping. She cut two slices of bread, poured wine into a glass, picked up her notebook, ink, and her quill, and began, finally, to write.

SHE WRITES HAPHAZARDLY, almost without thoughts, without cause and effect, without conscience and consequence. It is an urge. She knows nothing of what she writes down, as if it is dictated to her, and yet it is her story, hers alone. Her body drinks the wine, her body eats the bread, her hands write words, try to keep up with what is happening inside, forming the story that rages within her. Sometimes she stops. It has become midnight. Still it is only her: little Willmouse and her, and that is how it should be. She would not be able to tolerate Percy now. The looks, the apologies, the substance of what she has done, what she would never have done, what can never be made undone, and yet she does not regret. And she does not regret that either. William is sleeping. Every half an hour she goes to check on him: he is still there, he is still there. Then she continues with the story, her ghost story, which—although she cannot explain how—is her own. It is her monster, this monster. She has always carried it with her. She carries it under her bosom, keeping it warm, keeping it wild. But now the time has come to set it free. Into this shadowy kitchen, into the light of this oil lamp, into the color of her ink. It overcomes her, exciting and frightening her in equal measure. It is like the night that, after a long day of heat, hope, and bright colors, finally falls. The night in which everything is possible because it belongs to the spirits, the monsters, to all that dark inner reality.

William begins to cry. It is a soft but intensely sorrowful sobbing, as if, deep in his dream, he has understood what his life will be. Mary takes him from the cradle, wraps a blanket around him, places him on her breast. He does not manage to take the nipple, but a drop of milk that she drips onto his bottom lip calms him and he takes it. At the kitchen table, in that same light, William in her arms, pages full on the table, pages she could never have written before, because she had forgotten what existed, what was abhorrent and angry but nevertheless real.

"Come on," she whispers, "come on."

William tenses his jaw, she feels a bit of tooth and an angry spark flies from her nipple up through her breast.

"Show me what you can do." She closes her eyes.

August–September 1812
Dundee

August 24, 1812

These past few days, I have been unable to find any rest. Isabella was reading in her room. She came out only to eat, because Mr. Baxter would not allow meals to be taken to her any longer. He asked me yesterday if I could get through to her. We were sitting on the porch in front of the house. Elsie had made tea, and brought shortbread for Mr. Baxter, Johnny, and me. She asked if she should take some up to Isabella, but Mr. Baxter shook his head.

"She's not talking to me, either," I said.

Mr. Baxter took a sip of tea and closed his eyes. "I tell myself she's been doing this since her mother's death, but that's not true. Isabella has always had a tendency to shut herself away. It is as if it takes her a great deal of effort to connect with other people. If she does that for a while, then she needs to rest. To come back to herself."

"Are we going to see Margaret?" Johnny danced around Mr. Baxter's chair.

"Margaret? Oh Johnny . . ." I didn't know how to respond, but Mr. Baxter beat me to it.

"We'll go in a minute." He looked at me, puzzled. "We're taking a walk to her grave. And to her mother's. Would you like to join us?"

I shook my head. "I'd like to read for a while. Go without me."

As the light of the day began to dwindle, turning the garden a deeper hue, and a moving curtain of swallows flew over, like a sheet on the washing line in the wind, I heard something in the house. I headed inside and paused on the threshold of the vestibule. At the top of the stairs, one hand on the rail, the other on her heart, stood Isabella. She was wearing a long, dark green gown that seemed too matronly, with a high neck, long sleeves, trimmed with lace that fell almost over her fingers. She had a peculiar expression on her face. As if surprised to see the house still standing, that I was still there, that everything had continued in her days of absence, and I felt anger. Did she not understand that people cared about her? She walked slowly downstairs, her eyes on me. I wanted to go on looking at her, but I was unable to. She took my hand and led me into the drawing room. We sat down in the window seat, the sun shining in at a low angle. She looked at me.

"I am sorry I have not seen you for so long," she said.

"Why?" I asked.

"I couldn't talk about it. Mr. Booth was so . . . so different from normal. And, well, you know what happened then, and I believe I was ashamed."

"It was a very strange evening," I said.

"And at the same time, it was very pleasant. I don't know if I'm making it worse by saying that. Oh Mary, please don't hate me. I believe it was only your closeness, your strangeness, and yet your attention, maybe your scent, that made me feel so at ease, that I thought I felt things that might explain my behavior." Isabella looked at me. I felt the radiant pond green of her eyes making me softer, because I knew that color. I knew this face. It was the sweetest face I knew, the sweetest of all.

"Would you please forgive me? Can we forget what I did and never speak of it again?"

"What exactly do you mean?" I asked. "The wine made us unsteady, both in our actions and in our minds. But I cannot think of anything for which you should ask for my forgiveness." I saw that Isabella did not know if she should believe me. She pulled a loose thread from the sleeve of her gown. Then she said very softly: "That we kissed, Mary."

A hot diamond shone inside my belly. My lower body was seized by a sweet ache, and I felt betrayed, knowing that its sparkle was piercing my skin, for all to see.

I raced through my memories, which were disjointed, dark, and viscous. I could not remember any kiss.

"Was that before or after Mr. Booth let the snake into the room?"

Isabella looked at me, her eyes full of astonishment and doubt. "What do you mean?"

"That snake. We were in the drawing room, on the sofa. It was black and yellow. Mr. Booth held it in his arms, like this." I brought my arms to my chest, as if cradling a baby.

Isabella shook her head. "I know nothing about that," she said.

I believed her at once. Just as I believed she had kissed me that evening, if not in reality, then in her imagination or a dream.

"How is this possible?" She stood up, resolute, restless, walked to the bookcase, walked back, lost in thought.

"We both remember different things," I said. "But what about the rest? Do you remember the storm?"

"Oh yes," she said. "And the meal in the dining room was so strange. I can't explain it. I do not believe that I know for sure what I think I saw."

My memories of the dinner were the same, I thought. I could not clearly describe them, just as sometimes one cannot capture one's dream in words. There is only feeling. There are only vague, ludicrous images. Something ineffable that has entered your soul and remains there, stored in the pool of subconscious impressions, experiences. "If we both have a memory of that evening that we do not share, why is that? How can that be?"

Isabella came to sit beside me. She took my hand. Hers felt so warm, almost like a brass bed warmer. "We had drunk wine," she said. "My father says it can sometimes make one imagine things. Things that didn't really happen. If I can't remember a snake, and you can't remember a kiss, that seems to make the most sense, doesn't it?"

I nodded. "That must be it." I thought about the kiss. The kiss I could not remember, but so wished I did.

◆ ◆ ◆

"There!" Mr. Baxter pointed at the horizon. The sharp sunlight flashed on the water; glints that were almost too bright for my eyes. In the distance, I saw a dark dot.

"I see it, I see it," cried Johnny. He jumped up and down, as if that might help him to see the boat more clearly.

"It will be a while before it moors," said Robert. "Come on, let's take another walk around the harbor."

"No," said Johnny loudly. He pulled his hand free and stared at the end of the world, at the dot that, excruciatingly slowly, was becoming larger.

Isabella stood beside me. A restless wind blew tears into our eyes.

"I think it's carrying a load," said Mr. Baxter.

We peered. In the distance, the dot appeared to split in two. With a little imagination, one might see the second dot as a whale.

"Come, come," we heard behind us.

A graying man with a furrowed face was smiling at us and nodding in the direction of a tavern opposite the harbor, which was called the Siren.

"Come and wait inside, Mr. Baxter. I have a good port that you'll like." There was something servile about him, I thought, but he had a cheerful manner.

"Ah, Les," said Mr. Baxter. "That would be nice, thank you. Come on, ladies and gentlemen, we might as well have a quick drink."

It was quiet in the tavern. At a small table in the corner sat a broad-shouldered young man with a tankard of beer in his hand and a plate of ham and eggs in front of him, and there were two older men playing cards by the window. On the walls and above the bar were pictures of fishing boats, whales spurting water, and mermaids with round breasts and fiery red nipples. An anchor hung on the wall at the back.

"Sit down, sit down." Les led us to a big table by the window. The harbor was visible through the uneven window, but the sea barely.

"Port for the ladies, too?" Les asked Mr. Baxter.

"The ladies will have tea," he said. "And so will young Johnny."

He soon returned with a full tray. A black bottle of port, glasses, a teapot, cups, sugar, milk, and cake.

"Rosa's ill," he said, as he arranged everything on the table. It sounded apologetic.

"Nothing serious, I hope?" Mr. Baxter took a small, appreciative sip.

"Let's hope not. I can't run this place on my own. When the boat comes in, and in the evening . . ."

I hoped Rosa was the barmaid and not his wife. He did not sound too concerned about her.

"They'll be coming in soon, with their tall stories." Les pulled up a chair. Did Mr. Baxter know him well? Or did he not care about etiquette? Isabella chuckled and poured tea for us.

"Have I ever told you my brother's story?"

"More nonsense, I'm sure." Mr. Baxter smiled.

Johnny made four spoonfuls of sugar disappear into his tea.

"What is nonsense? And who cares? A story is never nonsense," said Les.

"What was it about?" Robert had already downed half of his glass.

"My brother Ian is a whaler, sometimes away from home for months. His wife complains, but without his work there'd be no bread on the table. Anyway, years ago, when he was home, he came to see me one night here at the Siren. He and his wife had had a disagreement and he needed to get out of the house for a while. He sat there at the bar, on that stool. I was pouring beer for the guests; packed, the place was, because all the sailors were back home. I barely had any time to listen to his story, but for some reason no one was bothering me. Rosa was helping, which obviously made a difference. Well, when Ian told me what he'd seen at sea, I got the goose bumps. All the way up to here." Les pointed at his neck.

Johnny listened breathlessly.

"He told me that one morning, so early his shipmates were still in their bunks, he went up on deck. It was already light enough to see without a lamp. He could make out the surface of the water, as smooth as a mirror, a purple-red glow at the end of that expanse joining the sky to the sea. He stood there for a while, his hands on the rail, watching the gulls flying overhead. And he felt something strange. He could not have known, because he was standing with his back to what had appeared in the sea, but he felt a presence with an energy that was not human. He turned and saw, swimming along the side of the ship, a man. At least that was how it seemed at first. But it wasn't a man. It was almost twice a man's length, and thinner. It had gills like a fish, but the thick, greenish scales of a snake. And it had legs like a wolf's, but longer. Long, thin fingers with claws that were almost as long as the fingers, strong and yellow-looking." Les gave me a crooked grin. "You don't come from around here, do you? Then you won't recognize the signs of what my brother saw. But those who live in Dundee and along the Tay know that they exactly match the description of the sea witch."

Under the table, I felt Isabella's hand gently slip into mine, and there was a painful tingling in my stomach.

"The sea witch lives in the Tay and the waters around Arbroath. Legend has it that he—because it's a man—is fish, snake, and human being. He can change his form when he wants to. Once upon a time, so they say, the sea witch was created when a flash of lightning struck the sea, a few hundred yards off the coast of Dundee. The energy in the water was supposedly multiplied by the heat of the lightning strike—and a living creature emerged."

I brought my hand to my teacup, but I felt that it was unpleasantly cold.

"My brother was shocked, of course. No, he doesn't believe in seamen's tales and legends, but when you see something, when you see it with your own eyes, well, that changes everything. This sea witch, so the story goes, doesn't do anything to you, but at the same time he does everything. Physically, he'll do you no harm. He won't drown you, he won't drag you to the bottom of the sea, he won't rip you open with his yellow claws. And yet he's one of the most dangerous creatures out there. He gets inside you. He hides inside your dreams, hooks on to your thoughts, disguises himself as your own senses. And that means he can make you do anything. If he manages to get inside you, if you let him in—and oh, it happens so easily, before you even realize—then you belong to him."

There was silence. All we could hear was the sound of the cutlery on the young man's plate.

"That's a fine story, Les." Mr. Baxter poured himself and Robert another glass of port each. "I was aware of the legend, but you tell it with such glorious detail."

"What happened to him?" I asked. "To your brother?"

"Ian? Nothing out of the ordinary, actually. He couldn't remember much about the return journey. He slept, he said, and he had strange, terrifying dreams. Back in Dundee, he began to feel better. Ah, suggestion can do a lot to a person. Or maybe he really did see the sea witch. Who knows?" Les shrugged.

Isabella was gripping my hand so tightly that I wanted to pull it away.

"Look!" Johnny pointed out the window. A colossus was trailing behind the boat. It had to be a whale, but from here it looked like a monster.

Mr. Baxter jumped to his feet. He placed a shilling on the table and urged us to come with him. Les stood up and collected our cups. He began to sing softly, a sad melody.

> *The whale sails into the harbor but where is his bride?*
> *Lonely in the waves, she calls across the ocean wide.*
> *Soon to be a widow, her husband turned to oil,*
> *she will always remember him, far away on foreign soil.*

Outside, the wind had picked up. I buttoned up my coat. Some of the locals had come to the harbor to see the arrival of the boat. Mr. Baxter had told me that whale oil is of the utmost importance for the industry of Dundee, which certainly includes his textile factory. So the return of a whaler was cause for celebration. Children ran around, were scolded by their mothers if they came too close to the water's edge, young women held the boat tightly with their gaze, afraid of losing their husbands again, even before they had returned, their eyes shining with fear and longing. The smell of salt and fish and ocean wind mixed with a scent I did not know. The closer the ship came, the stronger the smell became. It had a hint of cesspit, of something that had started to rot, but also something else, something cloying, something that reminded me of a dream whose outlines I did not remember, only the weight, only the scent, only the resonance. And there it was. It was hard to believe that this creature was here, in our harbor, seized by the harpoons of this ship. The animal was colossal, its skin shone as only creatures of the sea can shine, with an infinite sense of pride, as if it could not be captured. And when that did happen, as it had now, the defeat was not in its heavy, black, bright eyes, but in those of the hunters on the ship, to all appearances triumphant and exhausted. You had to look closely, but then you saw it: in their half smiles, in their slightly too fixed gazes. They knew that catching this sweet monster had a different significance than they had imagined. They knew this could not be undone. They knew they had done something that was unthinkable.

August 30, 1812

When I came downstairs this morning, everyone was ready for breakfast, including Isabella. The table was lavishly laid with various sorts of jam, sheep's cheese, sweet and savory bread, tea and coffee, fruit, and two bouquets of wildflowers. The Baxters got up from the table and kissed me.

Robert said that, this afternoon after the church service, we would be going for a picnic at Lindores Abbey.

"Mr. Booth is coming with us. He would like to congratulate you personally on your fifteenth birthday," said Mr. Baxter.

Something crawled through my stomach. I tried to look at Isabella, but she was concentrating on slicing an apple, her shoulders rigid and unyielding.

"I'M GOING TO show him my fish head." Johnny's face was filled with joy. He was sitting beside me in the carriage, his happy eyes looking up at me. There was a small bag around his neck; he had put his hands over it protectively.

"A little more patience." Mr. Baxter looked outside, as if searching for something. It was a beautiful day for a birthday. Above us, the sky was bright blue with rippling white clouds around the edges. Isabella was on my other side. Her gown, like mine, had short sleeves and our arms touched with every gentle bend in the road. I thought about her neck, about the curve of her breasts, as I had seen that afternoon when we saw the monster, but both images now seemed so implausible to me.

"He's never afraid," whispered Johnny.

I looked up. "Who?"

"Fingal." Johnny smiled as if he were dreaming.

"Who is Fingal?"

"Fingal Fish's-Eye." He gently patted his bag.

I looked at the others, but no one seemed to have heard what he said.

"Why is he never afraid?" I asked.

"What is it that you're afraid of?" asked Johnny.

It was a moment before I could answer. "There isn't something that I'm afraid of," I said.

Johnny looked right at me. "Yes, there is," he said. The carriage was slowing down.

"Look! There's Mr. Booth!" Johnny shouted, as if a heavy thought had suddenly lifted from him.

Mr. Booth helped Johnny, me, and then Isabella out of the carriage. Then he turned to me, leaned forward, and kissed my hand.

"I wish you many more years, Mary," he said. "Many more years of happiness."

For a moment, I fell into his eyes. The deepest, coldest, most sensuous sea. When I returned, Isabella was halfway through a sentence—something about the abbey we were standing in front of—Mr. Booth was talking to Johnny, and I saw Mr. Baxter and Robert walking ahead of us with the picnic basket.

"Don't you think?" Isabella seemed to have shaken off the lethargy that had overcome her in the carriage.

"I'm sorry. What did you say?" I tried to smile, but when that did not work, I hooked my arm into hers, so that she would look ahead, and not at me.

"I said they had to work very hard, those monks. There were so few of them."

I nodded. I had no idea what she was talking about.

"There were fewer than thirty monks. Can you imagine that? Such a big abbey?"

It was no more than a ruin. Some of the walls were still standing, but everything was overgrown with moss in all shades, and there were dry blades of grass poking between the tiles. There was no sign of any roof. Despite the sadness of this dilapidated place, the old abbey had an atmosphere of tranquility. Crows flew to and fro. Now and then I saw a robin.

We found a spot in the shade of what must once have been the chapel. Robert spread a picnic cloth over the knee-high grass. Isabella started unpacking the basket, putting down plates, bowls of salad, sliced meat, bread, cake, and butter. Mr. Booth took charge of the drink, pouring wine for us and lemonade for Johnny. Sunlight floated on my wine.

"A toast!" Mr. Baxter had stood up. "To our Mary, our dear Mary, whom we have welcomed into our midst. We are glad you are here, Mary, and we wish you a wonderful fifteenth birthday and many happy years to come."

We drank. The wine tasted heavy and sweet. It burned in my throat.

"What's that you have there, my young friend?" asked Mr. Booth, pointing at Johnny's bag.

Johnny's eyes flashed brightly.

The sun seemed to be gaining strength in every minute. Not only was I warmed so deeply that I felt it into my core, but a ferocity also spread across the sky above us, forcing our gazes downwards. The grass under our feet, the rough stone walls, the cake on our plates, the wine in our glasses—it was all we could see. Anything could have happened above our heads, and no one would have noticed.

"A fish head?" Mr. Booth bent over Johnny and his prize. "Beautiful," he said.

"It came from the sky," said Johnny.

Mr. Booth raised his eyebrows.

"I found it on the path, all the way past Ninewells. So it must have fallen out of the sky."

Mr. Booth nodded. "I suppose it must. Have you cleaned it properly? It could make you ill."

Johnny shook his head. "It's not dirty. Look." He held it up, right in front of Mr. Booth's face.

It was strange—Mr. Booth seemed to be startled. For the briefest moment. Then he chuckled.

I closed my eyes. In the minutes that followed, I lost my thoughts in the warmth of the day. Ideas, memories, and wishes drifted into one another like circles on a pond. Somewhere in the middle of that haze, I heard Johnny whisper: "He's called Fingal."

"I see," said Mr. Booth's voice. Very slowly, he repeated the name. "Fingal."

It was silent again.

Seconds later, maybe minutes, Mr. Booth said, "Do you know what Fingal means, Johnny?"

Johnny shook his head, I think. Or maybe he was concentrating on stroking his fish head and could not take his attention from it for more than a few seconds.

"White stranger," said Mr. Booth. "An excellent choice."

I felt a movement beside me. My senses bristled.

"Mary, might I ask you to walk with me?" asked Mr. Booth.

I opened my eyes and looked up, into the middle of the bright white sky, and saw nothing but a patch of black. My eyes sought Isabella, but she was lying on her back, her head on a rolled-up coat, her eyes closed. It seemed as if no one else were here, except for Mr. Booth and me. The others, even Johnny, were like a mirage. As if they were in another world, a world I could not enter now that Mr. Booth's hand was reaching out to me.

WE HAD WALKED some way from the abbey, Mr. Booth going a little ahead of me to make a path through the long grass. I had to lift my skirts to avoid getting stuck, and I concentrated on my feet on the tussocky ground. After five minutes or so in silence we reached a path, which allowed us to walk side by side again.

"An adventurous birthday," said Mr. Booth.

"It's beautiful here," I said—and it was. Around us were low hills and, here and there, a rowan tree. The scent of heather penetrated my nose.

"I would like to give you something. It's old, but I think you'll like it." Mr. Booth took out a small wooden box and handed it to me. When I lifted the lid, it seemed for a moment as if he had wrapped up the sun for me. It was a bracelet; dark blue, sparkling stones framed with gold filigree. I took it from the box and laid it over my wrist. A deep, tingling spark traveled along my wrist through my arm to my heart, and it was as if a passageway were being closed off within my mind. The day became lighter, brighter. I took it off and put it back in the box.

"It's magnificent," I said. "Such a big gift. Too big."

"Nonsense. It's for you. You are a special young lady, and a special lady deserves a special piece of jewelry." Mr. Booth stood with his hands behind his back.

"I can't accept it. I would feel terrible about it."

"Please, Mary." He looked at me.

I shook my head. "I'm sorry. I can't." I held out the box to him, so that it almost touched his chest. Then he accepted it.

"A shame," he said.

We walked on. Neither of us said a word, and I wondered if he was offended. Had I been impolite? But he must know that it was an excessively expensive gift, inappropriate even.

"I would like to warn you," said Mr. Booth.

For a moment, I wondered if I had heard him correctly.

"What about?"

Mr. Booth said nothing for a time, which made me start to doubt. Then he said, "I see how you and Isabella are becoming closer and closer. Some time ago, I told you to be careful. That I suspect that—perhaps without realizing it—she has a certain effect on people."

I nodded. It was a conversation I did not wish to remember. Somehow it was as if it had not really happened. When I saw Isabella, talked to her, laughed with her, it seemed inconceivable that my association with her could do any harm. More than that, everything was good whenever I was with her. When I was around her, I was myself. When I was around her, my heart started beating faster, my senses awoke. When I was around her, my imagination became my finest quality.

"But now . . . it seems to be getting more serious, Mary. Sometimes she makes things up. And it is as if she then starts to believe them herself."

I did not know how to respond. Could it be that Mr. Booth knew Isabella better than I? He had known her far longer, that much was certain, but did he also know her more profoundly? Was it possible that there were things, important things, that I did not see? That she did not let me see, perhaps did not even see herself? I thought of those periods when she stayed for days in her room, not wanting to see anyone, completely shutting herself off.

"I understand that you like each other. I like the two of you as well." He smiled at me. "But I want to keep you from forming too close a bond with her."

"I'm sorry, but you've already said that." It slipped out before I knew what I was saying. It sounded snappy.

Mr. Booth sighed. He stopped walking, took off his thin coat, dropped onto the grass beside the path, and laid his coat beside him.

"Come here."

I did as he asked of me. The long grass surrounded us as if in a dream. A small white butterfly landed on one of the coat sleeves.

"It is not appropriate to admit it," began Mr. Booth. He did not look at me. For the first time, I saw doubt in his being, which changed his face, his expression, and his attitude to such an extent that he seemed like a different person: younger, more friendly, more familiar. "But I sometimes fear that what happened to Margaret happened because Isabella wanted it to." There was a deep sadness on his face. But at that moment Mr. Booth was more human than I had ever seen him.

"Witchcraft does not exist," I said, and it sounded certain, but in that certainty I heard my own fear.

Mr. Booth smiled weakly. "No," he said. "No, of course not. But . . ."

Slightly stooped, he sat beside me, his fingers plucking at a cornflower. Had Margaret's death affected him more than I had imagined?

"Then I don't know what it is, Mary. All I know is that you need to be careful."

"But she has never done anything to harm me," I said. "I don't have the impression that . . ."

"She sometimes comes to visit me."

This announcement came so suddenly that, for a moment, it was as if it had not happened.

"She comes to visit you?"

Mr. Booth nodded. "Three times in the past week. She wants to talk about Margaret. I understand that she needs to do that, but it is the way she does it."

I did not understand what he meant. Besides, what did it have to do with me?

"She asks me what I still feel for Margaret. How much grief her death causes me. She wants to know if we were happy, if I made Margaret happy."

"Maybe she feels guilty," I said. "Because of what happened between them before."

"I considered that too," said Mr. Booth. "But it's more than that. She wants to know what I think of you. What I feel for you. And when she leaves, I feel ill. I have a headache, as if she has attempted to put her thoughts inside my mind."

A veil was lowered before my eyes, shutting out the day. The colors around me, the pale green grass, the airy blue sky grew dark and gray, as if the color were running out of them.

"It sounds foolish, I know. I don't know exactly how," he said, "but Isabella is capable of things we do not believe possible. Do you understand what I mean, Mary?"

The darkness persisted. In the distance, I heard someone calling and although I recognized the sounds, I could not place the words.

"I mean you're in danger. Isabella is not who you think she is."

THE REST OF the afternoon was bathed in a calmness I had never experienced before with the Baxter family. Mr. Booth, Mr. Baxter, and Robert talked together, the three of them, quietly and a little apart from the others. Johnny played with his fish head. Sometimes he seemed to talk to it. I could not understand most of what he said, but when he walked past us, his index and middle fingers in the fish's eye sockets, carrying it like a bag, I caught a couple of snatches—"Like with Mama" and "a grave full of eyes, a fairy tale." Isabella lay drowsing in the long grass most of the time. Maybe she had not slept well the night before. I tried to see signs on her face that might indicate the disturbing things Mr. Booth had told me, but I saw only what I always saw when I looked at her: an angel. A sweet, stubborn, sorrowful angel. She opened her eyes, those pond eyes immediately filling with daylight.

"I dreamed I had a small creature." She stretched. An ant walked across her neck. "A little bird or something, but with sharper features, a little frightening. I had found it and I was trying to take good care of it, but it was always so angry. It grew bigger and sometimes it bit me, pecked me, with its beak. I remember having all these holes in my skin, lots of them, in a line." She held up her arm, pale and flawless. "I wanted to protect it, not because I loved it, but because I knew it was my task, that it mattered in some way." She sat up, brushed a loose lock from her forehead. She looked at me. "One morning I awoke and found it dead. It was lying beside me on my pillow. And it was no longer the bird creature with the sharp beak. It had fur, not feathers, and it was soft and gray and round, a little ball with sweet little narrowed eyes. And I thought: I should have taken care of it. With love." She smiled. "Maybe it was because of this." Isabella took a parcel from the picnic basket. As I unwrapped it, I had to look away for a moment, because the sun skimmed across the porcelain like a knife. It was a bird. A white bird, lying in my hand, shaped as if it might be perching on a branch, or perhaps as if it might be dead.

"It can stand upright," said Isabella. She took the bird and placed it on the picnic cloth. It promptly fell over. She smiled. "Well, maybe not here."

"It's beautiful," I said. It was indeed. There was something unearthly about it. It was not immediately clear to me why that was, but when I placed it on my hand and balanced it upright, I noticed that its eyes were shut. Perfectly upright, head up, its crown to the heavens, shining in the sunlight that hit it, the bird was present and yet it was not. Behind its closed porcelain eyelids, there must be wakeful little eyes, eyes that had seen things I knew nothing about. Things I might not believe.

"Thank you," I said. I kissed her. Her cheek felt soft, a little sad.

"THERE'S A STORM coming." Mr. Baxter began putting the things into the basket.

We looked into the sky. Within just a few minutes, the summer-blue sky had been hidden behind a gray veil. In the distance, a dark blanket was pressing forward. You could see the almost black layer of clouds moving our way, and a wind rose around us, rustling the blades of grass.

We walked as fast as we could to the carriage, chased by splashes of rain that could not wait. The horses impatiently scraped the ground with their hooves.

The journey was a silent one. We listened to the wind, the rain on the windows, and the snorting of the horses. I kept thinking: it's just a storm. But then I looked at the faces of the others: Mr. Baxter with his eyes closed, his head against Johnny's, his arm around him, Johnny with gleaming eyes, staring outside, his hand clasped around his fish head, Robert looking seriously, almost sternly at the cloudy sky. Isabella sat beside me, holding my hand, and in that grip I could feel her holding her breath with every gust of wind. The only one who did not seem disturbed by the weather was Mr. Booth. He looked with calm eyes at the drops of rain that left long strands down the windows of the carriage.

September 2, 1812

The night of my birthday, as I slipped into my sheets, there was a knock at my door. It was Isabella. We stood facing each other in the doorway, both in our nightgowns. Her hair lay in a long plait over her shoulder. The candle in her hand trembled. Without saying anything, I let her into my bedroom. I threw back my sheets and she slid into bed beside me.

"I'm frightened," she said, so quietly I could barely hear.

I moved closer to her, took her hand, which was as cold as the rain beating against the window.

"You do love me, don't you, Mary?"

"Yes, of course I love you," I said. "You're my best friend."

She shook her head. "No, don't say that." Her wet eyelashes were sticking together.

"What is it?" I asked. "Dear Isabella, I really do love you."

She shook her head even more wildly. "You must not say it like that. Sorry, but I'm confused. I'm so afraid. I thought tonight about what you told me about the evening we spent with Mr. Booth. About the snake. And about what I remember, the kiss. And how we feared we had imagined things. That we did not truly experience what we thought we had experienced. And then I thought: maybe it's not that we remember things that didn't happen. Maybe there are even more things that actually happened, things that we cannot remember." She looked at me with big eyes.

"That would mean that what we can remember is all true," I said.

"And that there may be other things that neither of us is aware of." Isabella was shaking. She laid her arm over my stomach. "I think about Margaret very often. I can't believe she's gone. And Mr. Booth seems so unaffected by it. Almost as if . . . I don't know."

I said nothing. First that conversation with Mr. Booth, and now this. It seemed almost as if, with my arrival in Scotland, the world had opened up, had gained more possibilities. The world of knowledge, of truth and logic, had given way to a world in which anything might exist. A world from which stories sprang, a world in which everything could be true.

"Witches don't exist, do they?" a little girl's voice said against my throat.

And it sounds ridiculous, but I did not dare to answer her, for fear of being wrong. So I soothed her. I rubbed her arm, I stroked her hair and said over and over and over again: "Everything is fine. Truly, everything is all right," and I heard the wind outside howling with laughter.

THE NEXT DAY was a day for sitting inside. We played cards, read, and drank tea. Two letters had been delivered for my birthday. One was from my father. He wished me a pleasant day, told me how he regretted that he could not spend it with me. He wrote about the shop, about the latest books, and about Mary Jane, saying that she was doing well and sent me her best wishes. I pictured them at the table. My father writing the letter to me, Mary Jane looking out the window, bored, asking if my father wanted another piece of cake. He would shake his head; my father did not care for cake, ate more out of necessity than pleasure, and Mary Jane would give a little shrug, slide the last double piece onto her plate, sending a bit more filling into her already overfull belly, subduing something restless, the fear of loss. She would look at my father, at her husband, as he wrote, chewing on the cake, which was too moist, as she had bought it from the wrong baker, and wonder if she was doing everything wrong, with her child, with her husband, and if he would continue to love her, if he loved her now, if she should ask him, or if that would actually make him love her less.

It was a friendly letter, a nice letter, but without a word of love. And although I had known him for fifteen years, I was still not sure if he was unable to express that love because it was stuck within him, shackled to all those rational thoughts somewhere deep inside, or because he simply did not possess it.

The other letter was from Claire. Congratulations and kisses and then a lot of questions and musings, mostly about the people she spent time with in London; people I knew, but also others, those she had met since my departure. Some gossip about a pregnancy, an adulterous relationship, and the dramatic suicide of someone neither of us really knew. She also thanked me for my reassurance after reading *The Castle of Otranto*. She said she was aware that it was all fabrications, as I had written to her in my last letter, but that she liked the thought that she was not the only person she knew of who was familiar with the story. As if, by reading it, I had stripped it of its malice. At the very end, she had left some room for Fanny, who preferred not to write letters. There were congratulations from her as well.

I gave the letter to Isabella to read and she could not help laughing at the events in London, which were so very different from what happened in Dundee. We were on the wide window seat in the drawing room. The fire in the hearth provided more or less the only light in the house; it was only three o'clock, but it seemed like evening.

Isabella closed her book. "I shall play something for you." She walked to the piano, sat down on the stool, and ran her hands lightly over the keys. She was no longer looking at me, just gazing ahead, across the grand piano, at the window, as though she saw something there, something other than the rain swirling across the windowpane.

From the moment she struck the first deep note, I could no longer think clearly. I saw her sitting there, from behind; hair pinned up, the loose, thin tendrils on her neck, her skin underneath, giving off a certain innocence, a kind of sweet ignorance. Images of us during that walk, the feel of her soft skin under the corset, her breath on my neck as she slept beside me, her fingers as we took each other's hands, her mouth, pensive, anxious, full, wet, sweet. How her tongue caressed mine, licking my lips like cream. How I felt that movement in my belly, and deeper, like a warm downpour filling my gut, my fear softening, I saw that rain; a pool of water, a small lake of desire, in which everything that did not matter dissolved: decent behavior, morality, my father, Mr. Booth . . . It simply could not exist. We were here together, swimming in this lake, knew we were beyond reach because we had created this lake. The water was tightly stretched, patches of light among the foliage. And there, among the branches, he stood: our monster. He was there, as real as the time we saw him, and I knew that it was so, that it was real, if we only wished it to be. We floated, Isabella and I, suckered on to each other like magnificent octopuses, my legs clamped around her, my arms, so that I could kiss her, her breasts against my breasts, her belly against the central point from which my desire was driven, hastily, so that nothing might be lost, I pressed myself more firmly against her body, rubbed myself with deeper and deeper strokes, which shot into me, like sparks, endearments coming from my throat, but also curses; her dark hair, her small ear by my mouth as I cried that it came, it came, it came, only because of her.

ISABELLA CAME OUT from behind the piano, smiling. "Did you like it?"

And I could not say anything. I did not dare to say what I

thought, what I found, what I believed, and I wondered what she thought, what she believed, what she had just experienced, in the farthest reaches of her imagination—was it imagination? An almost physical memory vibrated under my skin, seeking ways out, to ask if she, too, if she knew, if she meant. But I could not.

We crawled in front of the fireplace, the drawing room began to cool down, and we stoked the fire.

"Isabel, I want to go back to the monster. I want to go back to the cave. I want to see what it was." I had to go there, once more. With her, this time.

She looked at me. "There is no monster. I think it was not right, what we saw."

"Not right?"

"We imagined it." A little smile.

I shook my head. "I don't believe we did."

"Monsters don't exist." It sounded like a question.

"And yet we saw one."

"Let us forget what we saw." As she looked at me, she seemed younger than I was. "There are some things one should not seek to know."

"But he was standing so close to us! We both saw him. That was not imagination."

"Precisely. Have you ever heard of Alister the Storyteller? He was a young shepherd, around my age. During his long hours on the heath and in the hills, he found plenty of time to daydream. He dreamed up the strangest creatures, the most marvelous stories, and wherever he went, he told them in the form of a song, as he played on his harp, and people hung on his every word. But one day he met a beautiful fairy riding a white horse with bells on its tail and mane.

She took Alister with her to her realm but made him promise never to speak to anyone about it. To seal the promise, he had to kiss her. Which, of course, he did. He was allowed to stay for seven days and seven nights. It was a wonderful place and Alister feared he would forget how much time had passed, so he took a string from his harp every day. On the seventh day, he could no longer make music and he knew that he must leave. The beautiful fairy took him back on her horse. Alister asked if everything he had seen and experienced had been real, if the fairy realm truly existed. The fairy asked if it was important for him to know that. Oh yes, said Alister. It was such a wondrous place that I need to know. The fairy gave him a kiss and told him to go, that he would find the answer to his question when he returned home. When he got there, he found that seven years had gone by, not seven days. At the feast to celebrate his return, Alister wanted to delight his friends and neighbors with beautiful music and song, but he found that he could no longer do so. He could still play, but he could not sing about the creatures of his imagination. In fact, he could no longer even remember those creatures. The stories dissolved inside his head. He still remembered the fairy and his seven magical days in her land—but he was not allowed to tell anyone about that. Suddenly he remembered the spell the fairy had cast over him at their farewell: 'I give you a kiss, I say goodbye, and from now on you may never lie.' Time passed, seventy years. He missed making music and his own imagination. The days seemed gray and dead. He longed to return to the fairy realm because he still believed that it truly existed. One day, when he was walking the hills with his sheep, he saw a white doe with silver antlers. Alister went closer and, as he did, he turned into a white stag. The stag and the doe stood close together. They looked back once and then they disappeared together into the fairy land. Snow fell and the soft tinkling of bells could be heard."

I thought about it. "He had kept his promise. So why was he punished?"

"Because he wanted to know if the land of the fairies truly existed. She asked him if he really wanted to know. And from then on, he could no longer lie."

"So he lost his imagination because he cared about the truth."

"I think so. Perhaps one should not wish to make a clear distinction between imagination and reality."

"It's just a story," I said.

"Is it?" Isabella's gaze moved away from the flames and settled on me. I was not sure if I could see a small smile on her face.

"I still want to go," I said. "I want to know. And you have to come with me. I don't want to go on my own."

Her hand sought mine, stroked my thumb. She sighed. "Fine," she said, "I'll go with you. If it's dry."

I smiled, kissed her cheek, and suddenly, without understanding why, I knew Mr. Booth was wrong: Isabella had never hurt anyone, and something sharp slid through my chest at the thought that I had doubted that.

September 5, 1812

"Well, look here. It's Robert and Isabella! And Mary Godwin!"

I turned around. It was Mrs. Thomson. In the church she was always dressed formally, but now she was wearing a curious coat with tassels and pieces of chiffon attached in three different colors. She waved.

Robert winked and Isabella did her best to smile. We were visiting Rumpton's. The shop was not large, but it was well stocked. It was a little like my father's bookshop, but without the pretension. This was simply a bookshop in a small town, run by a skinny couple who always called each other "darling." Whenever they did, Isabella would look at me with a crooked grin and I tried not to laugh.

Robert stood with Thomas Paine's *Rights of Man* in his hand, but I already knew it. Paine was a friend of my father's, and his books were permanent ornaments on the mantelpiece at home in London.

"Hello, Mrs. Thomson," I said.

"Miss Godwin, how nice. I'm sure you enjoy reading."

"Yes," I replied. "I certainly do. I'd like to buy a new novel."

"I should like to recommend something, but my interest is in the religious titles. I can imagine that the tastes of young people are different nowadays." She smiled as she said it, but she also seemed somewhat upset, and I had the feeling she was lonely.

I gave an apologetic shrug.

Mrs. Thomson nodded. "I should ask Alice for her advice if I were you. She has sound taste." She nodded at the owner of the shop. "And, Miss Godwin, I wish to impress upon you once again that you are always welcome to drop by. Simply to chat, or for any other reason."

"That would be nice," I said. "And please call me Mary."

"I'll see you, then, Mary." She looked at me, seriously. Then she turned and stepped out of the shop and into the rain.

"She's so strange," Isabella said behind me.

"She means well," said Robert. "Come on, let's take a look at the poetry. There might be something new."

I walked with them to the shelves of poetry collections, with the vague impression that Mrs. Thomson had wanted to say something else to me.

September 6, 1812

I kept thinking about the story of Alister the Storyteller. The idea that acknowledging the truth, recognizing it, might impair one's ability to fantasize was something I found intriguing, alarming, and foolish. If imagination is the opposite of truth, would seeing the truth not actually sharpen the imagination? Or did the truth have qualities that might curb the imagination? That could shut it off from the world, label it as untruth and, therefore, irrelevant. That would deprive the imagination of worldly oxygen, until it became thin and transparent, slowly disappearing because no one wanted to see it any longer and so no one was ever actually capable of seeing it.

And the rain just kept on coming. For days, we were housebound. Mr. Baxter and Robert did go out to the factory, where cold and damp prevailed, and they came home in the evening tired, soaked, and grumpy. Johnny spent a lot of time playing in his room. Sometimes I saw him on the landing and heard him giggling, with the fish head in his hand, and every time I saw him, the head seemed less dull, less lifeless.

It went on for a long time. The rain seemed to have found an inexhaustible source. And the longer it persisted, the more I thought about the monster, our monster in the cave. Had he, too, been sheltering for days, shivering with cold and hunger? Or was he venturing out into the landscape, across the boggy grass, with his calloused feet in the mud, his pelt heavy with moisture?

"Come on," said Isabella when she found me this morning in this kitchen. We were alone. I scraped my bowl empty. "Let's go," she said. "It's never going to be dry again."

THE PATH WE had to follow to Kirkton of Strathmartine was a mud bath, so we walked beside it, holding up our skirts. Isabella had given me an old coat of her mother's, which was already soaked through.

The sky was gray, only gray. We did not say much. It seemed important that we hurry, but sometimes she looked back at me, Isabella, and I saw her wild eyes shining among her wet locks of hair, as if she had a secret, larger and more real than the monster, and she wanted to show it to me.

When we reached Kirkton of Strathmartine, there was no path to follow, so we continued straight across the heath, uphill and downhill. Inside, I was glowing, feeling blood and passion flowing through my veins, but outside the cold was biting viciously at my fingers and toes. And there was the rock, as logical as it was sudden. I realized that somewhere inside me I had believed that even the rock would no longer be there, that everything connected to the monster would have been erased or had simply never existed. But here it was. And then I became afraid. Afraid that he would be there. Afraid that he would not be there. Afraid that what we had seen, weeks ago, was real. Afraid that it had been our imagination after all. When I had come the last time, on my own, there had been nothing here, and that had made sense. But now, now that I was walking beside Isabella, Isabella who knew things I did not, who made all my senses alive in a way I had never experienced before, suddenly the possibility was there again. And more than that: he would be there.

We looked at each other. I took her hand. Her glove was just as wet and heavy as my own, but under the cold wool I could feel her warmth. In silence, we walked to the rock, to the exact spot where we had stood before. And even before we could do our utmost to see something, we saw it. We saw him. He was bigger than I remembered. Coarser. His head wider, his torso longer. He sat in the crevice of the rock, by a small fire. He seemed to be cooking something, maybe a rabbit.

I heard Isabella's breathing, deep and full, as if that was the only way she could take in the unreal image before us. She whispered something, but I could not make out the words. Raindrops hit my cheeks and then, out of nowhere, it began. A sonorous sound that must come from a depth that was inconceivable for us. A sound raw and animal-like, but disconsolate, pitiful.

Hot fear flowed down my spine. I felt Isabella's eyes on me. "Let's go," she said quietly.

Our protective clothing had now become ice-cold ballast. We said nothing, we were too tired, too lost in thoughts, too busy explaining the world. The existence of that monster, that almost-human, the rediscovery of this world, the world from which I was supposed to distance myself now that I was getting older, frightened me, but also delighted me. It was growing darker.

THE OIL LAMP in the hall cast our shadows high on the walls. Grace came out of the kitchen. She took a deep breath as she looked at our dripping clothes, shaking her head.

"Get undressed," she said, "or you'll catch your death. Put everything in the laundry. I'll go and heat some water for a bath."

Naked and shivering, we stood waiting in the bathroom for the

tub to be filled. Isabella had lit the oil lamp on the stool, which gave
our skin a warm yellow glow. Grace walked back and forth with ket-
tles full of hot water and buckets full of cold. I looked at the wooden
floor by the bath, which was crooked and decaying from years of
spilled water. I looked at the iron tub and imagined my body becoming warm and calm again. I looked at Isabella. Her skin, her
hair that, loose now, hung over her shoulders, far down her back, her
breasts which seemed soft, so soft, and for a moment, just briefly, I
felt her nipple in my mouth, cold from the rain on the surface, but
soon warm from her own blood, from my mouth, my tongue playing over her nipple, scanning the ridges that arose, exploring the
grooves, the bud of the nipple that stuck into my mouth, bold and
defiant, and which I sucked in, as far as I could, so that I felt it, deep
down in my belly.

Grace brought in the last kettle, checked the temperature, and
left us alone to bathe. In silence, we climbed into the tub. All we
heard was the water sloshing gently against the sides.

"Oh, my toes," Isabella groaned, smiling.

I smiled too. The warm water embraced us and everything I had
to say, about monsters and imagination, about stories and truth, was
covered with an enchanting calm. We gazed at each other for a long
time. At first we looked at each other's faces, but our eyes could not
be stopped. They dived underwater and saw all the warmth of each
other's bodies. They dived and were instructed never to tell what
they found there. Below the surface of the water was a fathomless
depth; a depth of pure beauty, of tangible joy. There were our feet,
our legs side by side; there were our bellies, gently convex fields of
tension; there were our breasts, pale and full and pointed, thrusting
forward as an act of protest, as an act of substantiality. And in the

very deepest depths, there between our legs, was our velvety center, untouchable and unnameable in all its delicious mystery. We were naked underwater creatures falling lamentably in love. At least, I was. Maybe it is more correct to say that I finally knew, that I finally realized what it was that came over me when I saw her. And Isabella? She looked at me with turbid eyes, piercing and unfathomable.

Suddenly, as if we had been given a shove, the moment was broken. What we had seen by the rock, what we now knew with certainty, had to be given words, had to enter the evening. I looked at her, her eyes had lost all their urgency, were shining, bright and serious.

"So it's true," whispered Isabella, and then, more softly still, "Maybe it's all true." Her leg briefly brushed against mine. The water rippled.

"All of it?"

"It can't be."

"We saw it, didn't we?" I said. "We saw it, twice."

"That's not what I mean." A veil of trepidation slid across her face.

I waited. I knew I should not insist, that she would tell me if I just stayed quiet.

"You will not believe me," she said. Her index finger made whirlpools in the surface of the water.

"I think I will," I said. I would believe anything she told me.

"He's a brewer, isn't he?"

"Mr. Booth?"

"There are rumors."

"What about?"

"That he uses his laboratory not only for brewing beer, but also for experiments."

An idea leaped from the depths directly into my mind. It was not so much an image as individual elements of scent and sound; a crackling, a note trembling upwards, the smell of something organic, the stench of burned meat.

"What kind of experiments?" I asked.

"I don't know. That he experiments with life. I don't know anything more than that. It's just rumors." She did not look as if she thought they were only rumors. She looked anxious.

"Why didn't you tell me this before?"

"Because I didn't think it mattered. Because it wasn't true. Isn't true."

"Do you think that the monster . . . that Mr. Booth has something to do with it?"

"No. I . . . no." She took a long, deep breath. The water surged towards me. "I don't know."

We looked at each other, and I knew there was no truth ready and waiting for us.

"Should we be afraid?" I asked, and as I asked the question, I became afraid.

A loud knock on the door made us gasp as one.

"Time to get out, please, ladies. It's late. There's soup for you in the kitchen," said something on the other side of the door, with Grace's voice. Nothing was certain anymore.

As we dried ourselves, put on our nightgowns, we were silent. Even the bathroom had changed. It was difficult to breathe because of the viscous humidity of the air. The light of the oil lamp shone at me, fiercely, viciously. Something had just happened to us, although

I did not know exactly what. Everything was going to be different. And although I longed for it, I feared it. I felt closer to Isabella, but it was a dark and gloomy Isabella. The Isabella I never saw, as she locked herself away in her room. She had let me in now, I had her trust, and I found happiness in that, but somehow I realized that she would continue to shut herself away from the world, creating her own dark exile. And this time she would take me with her.

June–July 1816
Cologny

❧

The whale in the night

All night long, she was awake. All night long, she wrote. Percy stayed away. Claire stayed away. William has been sleeping for hours. As if she is drunk, she stands at the kitchen table, almost too exhausted to remain upright. She has filled forty-four pages, and if you were to ask her now what she has written, she would be unable to provide an answer. Only fragments emerge, as if from a dream that has been covered once more by sleep. There was a thunderstorm. Was there a storm last night? And a smell she cannot describe. Not anymore at least. Something burning, water babbling.

Mary spreads butter on the last piece of toast, eats it like a predator; big bites, fast, almost growling. Then a key is inserted in the lock. Percy or Claire?

"Mary?" It is John's voice.

What?

The angry suspicion that they have sent him bubbles up inside Mary. They spoke about it, last night. They talked about her.

Percy will have discussed it first with Claire, then with John. Albe will have kept out of it, but eventually listened too, given well-considered advice, which Percy will naturally have accepted because it came from Albe. John will have been told to apologize, to clear the way for Percy, as if he might be able to do the dirty work, as if it all happened because of John, as if Percy had in fact had little to do with it.

He comes into the kitchen. His hair, his shoulders, and the front of his coat are wet. Now she hears the rain: a continuous murmur behind the shutters, behind the glass. He is standing on the other side of the table, opposite her, does not move. Mary feels no need to smile, to greet him. She looks at him: his black curls, dripping and flattened by the rain, his eyebrows thick, black, and shiny like leeches, his big nose, the wispy mustache above that eager mouth.

"I should like to offer you my apologies, Mary."

She had expected him to stammer, but he sounds confident.

"What for?" She starts clearing papers from the table, a glass, a cup. She does not look at him. The room remains silent for a long time.

"For our kiss."

"There is no 'our kiss,'" she says.

Mary washes the dishes. She feels his gaze fixed on her. There is nothing she can do about it.

"Yesterday evening," says John, as if she is an idiot.

A cup falls onto the surface. The handle breaks off.

"There was no kiss." She turns around. "There was just your tongue in my mouth."

With the most furious of movements, she walks past him, out

of the kitchen, to her bedroom. He will not follow her. He is not strong enough for that.

◆ ◆ ◆

She has lain in bed for hours, holding William close. When he was awake, she was too, playing with him, giving him his rattle when he dropped it, kissing his nose, his cheek, which was so, oh so soft, softer than anything, so new. She sang to him, made up words to go with the tune. She looked into his eyes, as dark as her own, and stroked his sweet hair. When he slept, she drowsed too, falling into dreams that she could not place, falling deeply into herself as if she would never wake again.

But now she is awake, and rested, and it is evening. William seems to be asleep. Quietly, she slips out of bed, takes the candle, feels her way out of the room, lights the lamp in the hallway. They will be sitting together again. Are they going to leave her here until she goes to them of her own accord? Until she backs down, gives up, until it goes on for so long that it is she who will have to apologize? She walks to the kitchen—and there is Percy. So unexpected that she almost cries in shock.

"Come here," he says.

His arms, his lap so familiar.

"No," she says. She stands in the doorway, pouting. She sees how he sees her. A child. A little girl. Waiting for reconciliation, for attention.

Percy stands up, comes to her, takes her unceremoniously in his arms, and she, Mary, is defenseless, simply defenseless, be-cause of those arms, because of that scent, because of that stubble against her neck, because of the delight of making amends, in spite of the anger, in spite of the rage that coats the inside of her chest like tar.

"Albe wants to speak to you," he says. "About his poems."

They let go of each other. She holds on to his hand.

"Go to him. I'll stay with Willmouse. I need to sleep anyway." Percy gives an exaggerated yawn, kisses her.

Mary plaits her hair, washes her face, puts on a coat. When she looks around the corner of the door, it is dark. Percy is already asleep.

"HAVE YOU EVER read something that was so terribly good that you enjoyed it and yet at the same time it made you feel wretched because you knew you'd never be able to write like that?" Mary takes a sip of the wine John has poured for her. She had accepted the glass, but she did not thank him.

Albe is sitting beside her at the large table in the dining room. On the table, a board with cheese and bread on it, four lit candles in the middle. Claire is in the armchair by the window, with a book on her lap, pretending to read.

"No." Albe gives her his big, heartfelt smile. "No, but thank you."

"I've made a few comments, though," says Mary. She hands him a sheet of paper, torn from her notebook. "They're not suggestions, more like notes. To give you an impression of how it affected me."

"My sincere thanks, Mary. Your appreciation means a lot to me. By the way, I'm stuck with my fantastical story, so you have no need to envy me too much." Albe cuts himself a piece of cheese.

John empties his glass. "Anyone need some L.?"

Claire springs up, longing in her eyes. Albe grins. "Maybe a little. We can celebrate Mary's approval of my poetry."

Mary smiles, but perhaps only because it is expected.

John returns with another carafe, fills their glasses.

"Easy does it," he says when Mary has two big gulps.

She takes a third.

Claire wrinkles her nose with every sip, for a brief moment becoming the old Claire, eight-year-old Claire, sitting beside Mary at the table and struggling with her spinach. Her father chuckles behind his newspaper, preferring to leave education of this kind to his wife. So Mary Jane cannot just laugh about it. A slap rarely helps. A well-aimed taunt works better. With an empty plate and cheeks wet with tears, Claire is allowed to leave the table.

"Polidori, tell me, how are things going with your ghost story?" Albe's expression is a combination of mockery and genuine interest.

John's shoulders visibly tense. He scratches his cheek. "Not too well, to be honest. I do have an idea, but my main character is getting in the way. He is ambiguous. Too ambiguous."

"Will you read something to us?" Albe throws a bit of cheese into the air, catches it in his mouth.

"Out of the question. I will not read it out until the contest is over and the stories are finished. I am not going to give you a glimpse into my newly created universe."

Claire wanders slowly, indirectly towards Albe, as if she does not want to risk chasing him away. Even in this dim light, Mary can see the laudanum swaying in her eyes, but it makes her more beautiful, more sincere. Albe does not appear to notice her until she is standing right beside him.

One look of doubt in his eyes, one look of fear in Claire's. Then she slides her hand down his neck, and Albe closes his eyes.

John sits down, looking sad, probably does not know how to deal with Mary's silence. Mary knows it would be better to forget what has happened. She knows that the men, and even Claire, think she is making a fuss. And she thinks the same in a way. But there is something inside her that is too strong, that does not want to give in. It is not pride. Not an inflated will. It is not a precarious emotion, but an irrefutable sense of justice. The pure, unbending notion that this concerns *her*, that her body belongs to her, and to her alone. And more than that. Her mind. Her thinking, her opinions, her ideas. It all belongs to her.

The others: Claire, on Albe's lap, legs and arms around his body to stop him escaping, Albe, the victim who has everything under control, although he appears to have come off worst. With one hand movement, one small gesture, it will be over, he can banish Claire to her corner. Claire does not see that, is lost in the idea that he is hers, for as long as she can restrain him. She does not see that he is under restraint only because he wants to be, for now. John looks at her, Mary, even though he must be trying to command his eyes to look elsewhere for God's sake, it is as if they cannot, do not know where else to go, again and again returning to that point of calibration, the focus of fascination, the woman who rejected him, the friend he misses. And of course he is not a bad man. None of them are bad. But alongside her understanding of their humanity, another path runs: a path of insubordination. And that path is necessary. It is so very necessary. There must be resistance and anger. And she has anger. It is not new anger. It is ancient anger, as old as the rocks. As old as fire and the sea. It is the anger of witches, of all mothers standing with babies in their arms while cooking for a man who is drinking in the pub, of women who lift their skirts if a man pays enough, of women who owe their place in the home to their bodies. It is the anger that acts against the self-evident, against expectations, against yielding, yielding, yielding.

She notices that it has become dark. Three candles have gone out. Claire and Albe have left. John is still motionless at the table, his elbows on its surface, his head resting in his hands. But he is not looking at her. He is staring at nothing.

"I am not a monster," he says quietly. "I don't know what you think I am." Now he looks at her. He looks at her with the gaze of before everything happened.

Mary's breasts are tight, her milk is seeking a way out, and tears are sliding down her cheeks.

"I'm sorry," says John. "I truly am very sorry."

"Good," she says.

On his lips, a small smile. No, she has not forgotten anything. And yes, she is still angry. However, that cannot be a reason to remain cold. Because she will always be angry. She has no choice.

BACK AT CHAPUIS, Percy chides her for having stayed away too long, says William has been crying for her breasts for an hour. She counts back, to the last feed, she realizes it is true: he must be hungry. Hastily, she swaps her gown for her nightgown and sits beside Percy in bed. She puts William to her breast, and he eagerly latches on, spluttering a few times before skillfully and rhythmically drawing out her milk. Percy sits half-upright, looking a little resentful. After a silence in which only William makes any sound, small swallowing noises, a soft groan, Percy says, "How could you stay away for so long?"

William stops drinking for a moment. Mary's nipple lies motionless in his open mouth.

"What?" she says. William continues to drink.

"You are not here." He shifts position. His elbow nudges her arm, startling William.

They do not look at each other.

"I am *always* here." She feels it again, the anger, hot and sticky in her chest.

"Your thoughts. You aren't with us." The cold reproach buzzes around them.

Mary feels muscles she does not recognize, muscles tensing, bulging in the space between guilt and envy. And she certainly wants to say why that is. She wants to say that she is writing, that she is finally, finally writing, but she cannot. It is the thing that is inside her, that is slowly taking on life, that is preventing her from speaking. It is still too early, it is premature. Like her little—far too little—girl, who already had to live even though she had not yet been able to drink in enough life. She was not yet full and she died, and that is what will happen to this story if she brings it into the world before it is ready, before it has been able to grow, to become life-size, before it has decided to be beautiful or ugly, loving or hideous, before it has been able to grow into exactly what it is in essence: a screaming vessel full of life, so deep that even she does not know its bottom.

Percy is looking at her. She feels it, though she is trying to concentrate on William's regular drinking; the up and down of the little muscle at his temple with every gulp, the peacefulness of that movement purifies the rhythm of her breathing, always. At these moments, she is blissful.

"You simply did what you wanted to do yourself. You forgot Willmouse."

She wants to say that she had not forgotten him. That she could not forget him, because she always carries him with her, wherever she goes, with or without him. That he is always the first thing she thinks about, that nothing in the world is more important, but she realizes now that Percy is right. She had forgotten about Willmouse. For a time, an hour or so, he was present only in the background, something else attracted her attention, something that seemed to need her more, or maybe it was something she needed more. Like last night, when she wrote and wrote and wrote and William played his modest role as an extra in her night; he was there, and yet he was not. She was there, and yet she was not there either. So Percy is right. Something has entered her life and she has seized hold of it. She *wants* this. And even if she did not: it will not depart. Not until it has finished with her.

Later, when everything is quiet, Percy sleeps—he did not say another word, just turned over—Mary is lying on her side, looking at her child. A strip of moonlight lies across his face, from his sweet narrow forehead full of baby dreams, over his closed eyes, his nose as perfect as a rosebud, and his little moist baby lips. He was complete when he gained life. He was entirely ready to be her son.

"Sorry," she whispers so softly she can barely hear it herself. "I'm sorry, little Mouse."

A NIGHT FALLS. William cries and cries. The trees around the house clash their branches together: they will let no one through. In or out, they say. The air cracks, far above Chapuis. As if knives are flashing across the black sky; a fight in shrill sounds, fierce swipes, ruthless. William screams. Percy sighs. He turns and turns. He disappears. To the sofa? To Claire? Mary sits up and hugs Willmouse close: he is soaked from the rain, the sea. She has to hold him tightly, the ship shakes and shudders, as if trying to throw them off, back to the sea, back into the waves. Something shrieks in her ear, but whether it is a seagull, the wind, or William, she does not know. A hard strike. They will surely perish—that is what everything around them wants. The world is conspiring to engulf her, her child, all that is sweet and serene, the peaceful, the good. No one is at the helm; it spins like a runaway wheel. Oh, my sweet Willmouse, your little feet are getting cold. Mary straightens the cloths he is wrapped in, she pulls up the blanket, their own tent, made of sailcloth. Her nightgown clings to her back. She kisses William's hot cheeks. She sings a song, but it is blown away by the wind. She is so tired. William cries and cries. She feels that the ship will be devoured by the waves and then it happens: seawater rushes across the deck, tugging at her feet. The heavens crack. William claws with his little nails, sobbing uncontrollably. "Give him to me," Percy says close to her ear. She does so, and sleep stretches a sheet of surrender around her. Then she slips overboard, straight into the waves, which close over her head. There is no light, no breath, her lungs fill with night.

There is a whale. She sees it from the beach, where she is standing with dry, bare feet. The sand between her toes feels so real, cold and firm. The whale is too big to be right, its teeth too heavy, too coarse, the sonorous noise it makes too unreal. But its eyes. They are heavy with dreams, black and clear, and in them she sees everything that has ever existed. In the sea and on the land, seen by the eyes of childhood, watered down when they forgot how to look. This immense monster, which has seen all that is true, is no fabrication. And it is looking at her.

September 1812
Dundee

September 13, 1812

We walked through the gatehouse, and it was amazing to think what the cathedral must have looked like, centuries ago, before the building was destroyed during the Reformation. It was so peaceful, as if it had fallen asleep after all the turmoil, just wanted to be left in peace for a few hundred centuries.

Mr. Baxter had told us at home about the suffering that St. Andrew's Cathedral had had to endure. Storms, fire, more storms, and, finally, the ransacking, which had caused the greatest devastation. In spite of the destruction, you could see how long the cathedral had once been. According to Robert, it was more than one hundred and fifty yards, probably the longest in the whole country.

We were not the only ones walking around, it was a beautiful Sunday: a clear blue sky and no wind. It was pleasantly warm, although flocks of geese predicted colder weather. Johnny ran ahead, trying to coax Robert to play tag with him. Mr. Baxter walked a few yards in front of Isabella and me, talking to Mr. Booth. Isabella had asked her father to invite him on this outing. That would give us the chance to observe him and maybe to find something out, she thought. Since we had seen the monster for the second time, since Isabella had told me things about Mr. Booth that seemed as probable as they were improbable, I had tried to avoid every thought of him. I noticed that it became more difficult to breathe when I thought of him, as if my lungs were gradually filling with a thick substance. Although he did nothing strange, I could not look at him. I believe Isabella felt the same. We tried to find a subject we might have a pleasant conversation about, but we were too aware of Mr. Booth's presence. Isabella was afraid, maybe even more afraid than I. Every night she crawled into bed beside me, and I felt her trembling until her breath became even and she fell asleep.

Johnny came running to us. "Hide-and-seek! Robert is it!"

Before we could answer, he ran away, and I saw Robert leaning against a nearby wall, eyes closed and counting. Isabella looked at me, smiled. We ran away. I'm a child, I'm a child, I thought as I ran through the tall grass and over the slippery stone paths, in search of a good hiding place. The running made me free, as long as I did not think too much, kept that door inside my head closed, was not curious. Behind the west façade of the cathedral, I found a narrow alcove, overgrown with bushes and plants. I squeezed myself in, arranged the tall bush in front of me so that I was no longer visible. The long wait began. It was late afternoon, and the sun had warmed the stones behind my back. Sunlight pierced between the leaves of the bush, hitting my face. I closed my eyes.

"No, I realize that," I heard a voice saying in the distance. It sounded like Mr. Baxter.

"And of course she has to want it herself. That's the most important thing." That was Mr. Booth.

"Of course, of course."

"I hope you understand that I have thought this through carefully. I am a man of reason."

"I don't doubt that for a moment. You are a valued member of the family, David. And that did not end with Margaret's death, as you know. Yet it would give me great pleasure to see you connected to our family once again in God's eyes."

My heart was beating slowly. The heat pressed against it, the significance of the conversation forced itself upon me. My blood seemed too thick for my veins, my breath too heavy for my lungs. Mr. Booth had said so much about Isabella to me. And it was only then, at that moment, that I began to wonder what he had been saying about me to her.

"PANCAKES!" JOHNNY GRINNED at me, his teeth gleaming black with treacle.

"Johnny, don't talk with your mouth full." Mr. Baxter cut a slice of bread, gave it to Robert.

Mr. Booth sat beside Johnny, mainly eating plenty of the chicken that Elsie had cooked in the oven for three hours that afternoon. Every time the fork scraped past his teeth, the meat remaining behind in his mouth, being ground to a pulp, I had to stop eating for a moment.

Now and then I tried to catch a glimpse of Isabella. She sat beside me, silent, her expression unfathomable. After the visit to the cathedral, I had drawn her to a corner of the porch. She had looked at me, confused and then scornful. She shook her head. I repeated every word that her father and Mr. Booth had exchanged.

"No. They must have been talking about something else. That must be it." She put her hands on her hips.

My anxiety gave way to irritation. "Listen to what I'm telling you," I said. "That is literally what they said."

"Mary, how much longer are you staying in Dundee?" Mr. Booth's voice made my heart do an extra beat.

They all looked at me. Johnny chewing, a trail of treacle running down his chin.

"I don't know exactly," I said. I thought about my arms, how much better my skin was now. "My father has not told me yet." I jabbed a bean on my plate. I could feel Isabella looking at me.

"They must be missing you terribly at home by now."

I hardly dared to move or to look at Mr. Booth. Stop talking, I hissed silently. Stop talking. I could not go back to London. I did not want to go back to London.

"No. She can't go," I heard Isabella saying in her beautiful voice, full and soft yet firm. "Mary must stay a while longer, as I cannot do without her."

A warm prickling on my neck, as if she were kissing me there.

Mr. Baxter smiled. "I think we should like to keep Mary for a time." He gave me a wink.

A stream of relief flowed through my breast.

The conversation soon returned to the latest batch of whale oil for the textiles factory, and Robert asked how Mr. Booth liked the new boiler at the brewery. I tried not to notice, but Mr. Booth often looked at us. At Isabella, then at me. Usually with a smile, but sometimes he forgot, staring at us with his gray eyes like cold daggers in his pale and waxen face.

FAR INTO THE garden, we could see the moon. It was high in the sky and so full that I imagined it might give birth to another moon at any moment. Although he looked tired, Mr. Booth had also joined us. Robert poured wine. Isabella drank too quickly.

"That must be a complicated procedure, making beer," said Isabella. "I'm sure you are very skilled at scientific processes."

"Ah, there's an art to it. I could teach you how to do it." A brief smile.

"I don't believe you could." Isabella took a swig of wine, barely holding in a hiccup. "I think one would need a certain gift for science." She placed emphasis on the word "gift." I was starting to feel uncomfortable. I tried to catch her eye, but her gaze was already too hazy.

"A gift." The corner of Mr. Booth's mouth curled slightly. "I like the sound of that."

"You know a great deal." Isabella leaned forward, letting him look into her big eyes. I saw the shadow between her breasts become deeper. I saw that he saw it.

"I try to research a lot," said Mr. Booth.

"Such as?" There was nothing covert about Isabella's curiosity now. Her eyes were greedily scanning his face. What was this man hiding? Could reality bear up to our suspicions?

"Natural processes. The effect of all manner of substances upon one another. The effect and application of electricity."

"I am going to leave you." Robert stood up, barely stifling a yawn. "Will you take the glasses back inside when you go?"

I nodded. Isabella did not appear to have heard him. She stared continuously at Mr. Booth. I tried to attract her attention by coughing and tapping her boot with my foot, but she had decided to ignore me.

"Might I come and see one day?" she asked. "I think it would be fascinating to see your laboratory."

"The laboratory is private."

"Oh?" She was a good actress. I knew Isabella was not surprised, just as I was not surprised, that Mr. Booth had secrets, that there were things he could never tell us. Only he was not supposed to give us the impression that he had secrets, just as we were not supposed to give the impression that we were aware of that. And although Isabella could have the expression of a sphinx when she wanted, I feared that Mr. Booth would know that gaze and see through it, simply because he had enigmatic powers, even ones—of this I had no doubt—with which we had not yet become acquainted.

"I am sorry, Isabella. It would be too dangerous for two young ladies. I would not dare to risk allowing the two of you to walk around in there. The electricity, the hazardous substances. That would be irresponsible of me."

Isabella nodded, and oh, I knew her so well. Outwardly she was the girl who showed docile acceptance of his obvious paternalism, while inwardly she was burning herself on her own fury. She was holding back. Only her hand briefly clawed at the muslin of her gown. "A pity," she said quietly.

Mr. Booth looked at me. It was perfectly clear to me that he wanted me to leave. "Mary, would you go inside and fetch a glass of water for me? I'm dying of thirst."

"I'll go." Isabella leaped to her feet.

Mr. Booth seemed confused. He coughed and sat more up-right. Isabella tapped me gently on the back as she went by, as if she wanted to pass something on to me, and I realized that it was in fact the case: she wanted me to take over. I stood up and went to sit on the chair she had vacated. A cloud slid in front of the moon, and Mr. Booth took on a bluish glow. It made his eyes fathomless and unknowable, like the eyes of sea creatures that have never seen the light. I could feel his nearness in my entire body; anxiety and excitement were two substances racing through my blood, entan-gled like tendrils.

"Are you keeping an eye on her?" asked Mr. Booth. "She's so wild and therefore vulnerable, because she will never see her own downfall approaching."

For a brief moment, I feared he knew Isabella better than I did. I feared he was right, that, in her reckless, magnificent intensity, she would not for a second turn her attention downwards, at that which crawled in menacing silence at her feet, its gaze raised up to her, able to capture her in an instant.

The question that had been lying in the folds of my mind for weeks took shape, came loose, slipped through my throat and over my tongue. "Have you ever seen an exotic snake?"

Something was happening. Maybe I, too, had drunk too much wine, maybe the wind was picking up. Maybe all the creatures in the forests, on the heaths, in the seas had heard what I had said and were pricking up their ears. Maybe there was a monster inside me that was stretching, shaking its hair, running its tongue over its teeth. Events were increasing in speed, increasing in severity, mak-ing my heart thump to a violent rhythm.

His gaze fastened hooks in me, but looking away would have

been worse. Then he said, "Tell me, Mary, have *you* ever seen an exotic snake?"

HE KNOWS I do not trust him. I should have kept my mouth shut. I have let the evil know that I recognize it, and now the signs are everywhere. In every crevice, in every unfamiliar sound. In the clouds moving through the sky with bestial speed, in the wind that makes the shutters clatter to warn me: it is coming. It is coming. It could even be heard in Isabella's voice, warm and tickling in my ear when she wished me good night; a dark creak that I could not place at first but recognize now: this is where it begins. It begins with one dark scratch.

September 17, 1812

I remember we went swimming. Isabella said the water in Lindores Loch was as clear as glass, so that you could see little fish all around you. The weather was warm, unseasonably so, Isabella said. We looked out through the windows, their glass swallowing up the heat from outside and spitting it back out into the carriage. The heat of the sun was so tightly stretched over the world that movement happened slowly, life preferred to sit still, motionless and silent. We heard no crickets, no birds. We did not talk but looked at each other.

At the edge of the forest, the coachman stopped. He let us climb out, unharnessed the horse and led her into the shade. Isabella and I sought out the coolness of the trees, walking with the basket full of linen cloths, a picnic rug, sandwiches, and a bottle of lemonade between us. In the forest, all I could make out was a buzzing sound.

It was very quiet, but unmistakably present, like a fly on the other side of the room.

"There," said Isabella.

Farther on, through the trees, a mass of water shone. Its coolness, its clarity called out to us. We placed our basket on the grass of its shore. Suddenly in a hurry, we undressed and I saw her body again, although I wanted to keep my eyes on the loch. I saw her, familiar and unfamiliar, like the memory of a dream in the middle of the day. We took our shirts out of the basket and stood facing each other, like twins. We laughed. This was the best moment. Still not cooled down, still full of anticipation, still before everything would begin. Hand in hand, we walked to the water's edge.

With heat on our shoulders pushing us farther into the lake and the icy water around our ankles slowing us down yet pulling at us, as if calling us, deeper, deeper, deeper, we walked into the loch. The water came higher and higher and when it flowed between my legs it seemed like Isabella's touch. I looked at her and wanted to say something. It would have been something foolish, something that would not have sounded as it should have sounded, something superfluous. Something she already knew, as did I. So I remained silent. We heard only the water slipping around us, walked on until our breasts, too, were submerged. I felt a taut line running down from my breasts through my belly to the soft place where I wanted to feel her, her hand there. Suddenly, I feared I was the only one. That this was my strangeness, my inhumanity. But then she came and stood in front of me, against me, and I felt how, in her breasts too, a taut thread began that ran through her body, and she took my hand, placed it between her legs, and I sank, I floated, I felt that she felt just as I did, I saw when I looked up at her face that she had closed her eyes, my touch almost, almost making her burst apart. Then she raised her head, pressed her lips to mine, caught my tongue with hers, gently bit me, and I wanted to kiss back, to chase after her tongue, which would never allow itself to be caught, to bite at her lips, to hold her even closer, because I wanted to feel all of her, but I was paralyzed by the cold of the water, by the heat of shock and desire. She let go of me and gave me a soothing smile, as if I were not fifteen but five. As if I did not know what was happening, as if I did not want what was happening, as if this were not the truest, the most intense thing, as if I did not know that this was also, that this was just as much, that this was perhaps even more than I had ever imagined.

I turned around, the water no longer heavy and nurturing but only annoyingly stubborn. I wanted to wade back, back to the shore, I wanted to wrap myself in a cloth and dry myself, to extinguish in cool linen the flush I felt flaming under my skin. But she held me tight. Her hands were around my belly, her belly and breasts soft against my back, her cheek against my neck, her sweet voice in my ear: "I've never done this before."

She went on whispering in my ear; what she said was sweet and it was exactly what I wanted, but I have forgotten what it was. She enchanted me, my thoughts lengthened, meandered in insane freedom, became delicious and inimitable.

Some time later, we were lying on the shore, wrapped in cloths, on the rug, and looking out over the water. She made me drink lemonade, said I needed it. I remember thinking that the sun was shining with supernatural brightness, as if in a dream, and maybe I said that to her, because she said, "You've had too much sun." I imagined that I had swallowed the sun, not a modest sip, but the whole sun, in one gulp, and I suspected that it was too much of a good thing.

I WOKE UP in a room that smelled strange. My head was pounding as if there were thoughts inside it that did not fit. I could not place the scent. It had something sweet, soapy about it, and it was mixed with something old, something that was sleeping and should not be woken. In what little light penetrated the cracks in the shutters, I could make out a washstand with a bowl and a jug, wallpaper with swallows on, paintings, and a dressing table with a large rectangular mirror, directly opposite the bed. I saw my own form, half-upright against some pillows, as still as a doll. For a brief moment, I was certain that, if I were to move, the figure in the mirror would remain motionless, that the person in that big, heavy bed opposite me had nothing to do with me, but was from here, from this room, was born here and would die here. But when I finally moved my hand, I saw that my reflection did the same. The room around me was strangely quiet, seemed absorbed in its own shadow. This took my thoughts to stories about places that were alive, rooms into which the soul of a dead person had seeped, like wine spilled on a tablecloth.

There was a knock on the door and when I saw the tall figure of Mr. Booth entering, I knew that I had already been aware that I was here, with him. He was carrying a tray with a teapot and toast. His smile was cold.

"Mary," he said. He placed the tray beside me on the bed, sat down on the edge so that the mattress gave way a little and I slid towards him.

"How do you feel?"

"What happened?" My voice did not sound like my own. For a

second, I had the anxious feeling that I was not myself, was not here, but elsewhere, at home, in London. That I was lying next to Claire in our bed, she in half sleep laying her arm over me.

"You fainted." Mr. Booth looked at me intently.

"I was swimming, with Isabella."

He nodded. "Isabella fetched the coachman when you didn't come round. She shook you, but you were completely limp. Then they brought you here because it was closest."

"Where is she?"

Mr. Booth looked at me blankly.

"Isabella."

"She is at home. I said I would take care of you. And that I would send for a doctor. But now that you are awake, that no longer seems necessary." He slid the tray towards me, poured some tea. "Drink this. You're dehydrated from the sun."

He remained where he was. I held the hot porcelain in my hand, not daring to take a sip, not daring to put it down. Mr. Booth looked away from me and at the window. "Swimming weather," he said. "But certainly hot. You girls should be more careful in the sun from now on. Heat affects the brain, Mary."

I nodded.

"Good." He stood up. "Drink your tea. Eat your toast. You're staying here with me tonight. I shall send a messenger to Dundee to say that Isabella can fetch you tomorrow morning." He walked to the door, seemed to hesitate for a brief moment with his hand on the doorknob. Then he left without saying another word.

The tea smelled of flowers, roses I thought. I buttered a piece of toast and started eating. Again, my eyes were drawn to the dressing table. Now I could see a girl in bed, drinking tea, eating toast. As if she belonged there. In front of the mirror were some glass bottles and jars. I saw a few bracelets and necklaces on a shelf. And there, among the other bracelets, was the one with the sparkling blue stones. The bracelet Mr. Booth had wanted to give to me. As if a rope were tightening around my chest, more and more tightly: I slid out of bed, without a sound, my breathing shallow. The wooden floorboards remained silent, felt like candle wax under my feet. Then I was standing in front of the tall mirror on the dressing table and saw the long white nightgown I was wearing. Lace on the sleeves, high-necked. The face above it was my own, yes, but in my eyes I saw something I had never noticed before—something anomalous. It was not about the color, and the minuscule dark flecks in the brown were the same. But a strangeness appeared to have taken up residence in the blackness of my pupil. An entity. So inconspicuous that no one would mistake it for anything other than my own soul. But I knew. I saw it. This was not the blackness of my fears, not the blackness of my lostness. It was not the blackness that had inhabited my own soul ever since the day I was born, since the day I pulled my mother's soul with me from her womb. This blackness was unknown. Pain was building behind my eyes. I had had too much sun. My eyes wandered from the mirror to the hairbrush. I saw my hand, my pale, thin hand, reach out and touch the cold silver handle. When I picked up the brush, I saw, precisely in the ray of light that came between the shutters, a long hair gleaming in the bristles. It was a thick, dark hair and it felt unnatural, wrong, to have this part of Margaret so close to me. That I might touch it, snap it with my hands, break it into smaller, shorter pieces of hair and that no one could do anything to stop me. It would not matter but at the same time it felt like the most terrible thing I could do. I pulled the hair from the brush and wound it tightly around my finger. I picked up the brush. There were initials engraved on the gleaming silver of the back of the brush, but they were not Margaret's. They said E.L. Suddenly I heard a sound, as if someone in the room next to mine had slammed a wardrobe door. I shot back into bed, my heart pounding under the covers. When calmness returned, I finished my tea. Meanwhile I looked in the mirror, at the girl in the big bed, and although it made me uneasy, I could not help it. I had to keep an eye on her, this child. I did not know who she was.

FROM THIS POINT, my memories are hazy, thready, as if someone had pulled them apart. I was very tired. I slept a lot. I saw the strips of daylight fade, the room filling with puzzles. The girl in bed was cheerful. She eagerly drank the tea that Mr. Booth brought for her, she talked to him and said she was feeling much better. She smiled at me in the mirror. The swallows on the wallpaper grew scales. They leaped forward in perfect arcs, like salmon in the river, on their way to the highlands. Ssshh, said Isabella behind the rock. Be quiet. She held him close, our monster. He lay weeping, his broad, angry head sideways on her lap, his hairy arms, the size of a lion's legs, helpless on the ground. She began to sing. The words sounded familiar, but I did not know their meaning. It sounded so mournful, she must be singing about how all things must end. Our monster began to shrink. He groaned and shrank, and Isabella sang and stroked until there was nothing left to stroke. More tea. Go back to sleep, poppet. Yes, that sun. Far too much sun. My fingertip throbbed as if there were something in it that wanted to come out. Then I saw what it was: the hair, Margaret's hair, it was a thread that connected my finger to the room. Thin and almost imperceptibly gleaming, it was stretched throughout the entire room: from the dressing table to the window, from the window to the wardrobe, from the wardrobe to the wall, from the wall to my headboard, and from my headboard to my finger. Like a web that I had spun myself, from which I was unable to extricate myself. This room would not let me go, it whispered that I belonged here.

In my next dream, I saw my mother. She was lying in bed and was in the process of dying. I was her baby, I lay in the cradle and saw how she could not see me because of the leaden shutters that her eyelids had become. Exhausted by hope, resigned to defeat. My body longed for hers but would never get what it wanted. This is your dream, Miss Godwin. I had become blind. There was nothing else, nothing, except for that voice. It is your dream, so you decide. I knew that voice. I knew that I would know who it was if only I were awake. Oh yes? I said silently, then I don't want this dream anymore. I want a different one. More tea. Piping hot this time. Carefully, blow on it first. Are you that thirsty, poppet? What's in my finger, I asked. Nothing for you to worry about, sweetheart. The midwife covers me up to my chin. Don't worry now, the baby will be here soon. She will die, but you don't know that yet. Just go to sleep. And yes, she holds her in her arms. She does not give her a name yet, because she is so small, but she thinks she is called Clara. You must do your utmost if you want her to live, Miss Godwin. But she does not know how. She has never been a mother. Is she supposed to be this small? she asks. The midwife shakes her head. But this is all you've given her, she says. She's not very robust. Look. The midwife grabs her baby by one arm and pulls it off with a short tearing sound. You see? There is no blood, just a detached arm. It's already starting to discolor, the midwife says. She reaches for a leg, but she slides away from her. Miss Godwin, the dying parts do have to be removed. She starts pulling at the little legs. One by one, they come off. Her child does not cry, just becomes quieter. Another arm comes off too. Not the head, she says. Please, not her head. The midwife smiles, she is friendly. She strokes her baby's head, her sweet wisps of hair. Then she places her hand, like a grotesque spider, over her skull and, with a loud crack, she pulls off the head. Parts of her child are scattered over the bed. A sweet little head, eyes half-closed, last gasps of breath from her mouth, six little legs, six little arms. My little girl, she whispers, she's dying. There's no doubt about that, miss, says the midwife. Girls like that cannot exist.

I WOKE UP. It was still dark, halfway through the night, I thought. The moonlight let me see that the room had freed itself from my delusions. I really needed to go. I got out of bed—in the mirror, I saw myself, a little shaky and pale, but nothing strange—and looked underneath, thinking I might find a chamber pot there, but there was only empty space. Quietly, I walked to the door. I feared, suspected, that it was locked, but when I tried the knob and it turned easily, I thought that a ridiculous notion. Of course the door was not locked. The carpet on the landing caressed my bare feet. Blue night light came through the elongated windows around the stairs, which extended over two floors. The sort of light in which things lose their form, but I was determined to keep my clear view. There was nothing strange going on. I had been affected by the sun, suffered a fever, and I had allowed myself to be drawn into the stories harbored by my mind. Now I could once again see things as they were: the floral pattern on the carpet beneath my feet, the delicate rods of the balustrade, the gleam of the wooden banister. I stood at the top of the stairs, indecisive. Where was I going to find a chamber pot? Something behind me moved. I knew there was nothing there, nothing at all, but I felt it: a nudge in my back, the sensation that I was lifting off the ground, the feeling that there was nothing that could stop my fall. I would fall forward, tumbling down the stairs, my arm would swing against the wall and become dislocated, my head would make a strange angle against the balustrade. I would fall with a thud, flat on my back, on the marble tiles of the hallway below; a deep pain shooting through me, as if warm liquid were spreading inside my back, until I could no longer move, my breath could no longer leave my chest, where it fed my panic in short bursts.

My hand clutching the banister was clammy with sweat. The stairs beneath me were strangely real. My knees trembled. I felt the release streaming down my legs, warm and wet and, in a curious way, comforting.

WHEN I SAW Isabella entering the room, I could not hide my smile. Her eyes were sparkling, and her cheeks were deep pink. Maybe she had had too much sun as well, maybe she had been longing to see me.

"I've come to take you home," she said, and it sounded as if I were hers. My heart seemed to be beating in my entire body and something flowed through my innermost being that I cannot express in words. I washed myself and dressed and when I walked past the dressing table, I saw that the golden bracelet with the dark blue stones was no longer with the other bracelets.

Downstairs in the dining room, breakfast was waiting for me. Mr. Booth was nowhere to be seen. Isabella watched me as I ate. She did not want anything, not even tea. She watched and watched and it was as if she were absorbing my every movement. Sometimes

I looked up and my gaze met hers and at those moments there was a spark deep inside my chest. I barely said a word. Isabella told me that Johnny had built a house for ladybirds and that Mr. Baxter had spent all night at the factory because there was something wrong with the machines. I was not really listening to her words. I heard only her voice and imagined that she was saying other things to me.

The peace was broken by the coachman who came hurrying into the dining room. There was no question of leaving anytime soon, he said. The mare appeared to have colic and he had had to unharness her. He had taken her to an empty stable and now it was a case of waiting to see if she would recover. Isabella clasped her hand over her mouth. Her eyes widened.

"Poor Cherry," she said.

"It's best to leave her in peace. I wasn't able to find Mr. Booth, but I assume it's all right that I put her in the stable."

Isabella nodded.

The coachman left.

We went outside, strolled to the stables, tried to calm Cherry, who was lying on her side in the straw, softly whinnying. We were not helping, so we decided to leave her alone.

"Come on," said Isabella, and she pulled me with her behind the stables, into the tall weeds that grew there. A nettle dived under my skirt and grasped my leg, but I was distracted by Isabella scratching something on the wooden corner beam of the stable with a sharp stone.

"What are you doing?" I whispered.

She chuckled. Under the tip of the stone, I saw angular letters slowly emerging. MARY+ISABEL they said. She beamed at me.

The wind was getting up, blowing goose bumps over my arms.

"Where is Mr. Booth?" I asked, although I knew Isabella had no answer for me.

"Maybe he's in the brewery. Let's go and see."

THE SKY WAS full of clouds, and the air was thick as wool. The heat pressed down on our shoulders; I felt as if it were becoming difficult to move forward, as if there were a constant gentle tugging on me. We walked across the gravel that surrounded the house. From the stables came a quiet wailing, which had to be from the mare, although it barely sounded like an animal.

At the large double doors of the brewery, we stopped. They were ajar. We looked at the sky, as if searching for something, as if we had lost something. I followed Isabella inside. The ceiling was high; three men could easily have stood on each other's shoulders in there. Along the walls were racks full of wooden barrels, boxes, and jute sacks. In the middle was an immense machine. Cogs, tubes, glass flasks, pipes, and gauges made up a phenomenal mechanism that Mr. Booth no doubt used to brew his beer, and yet there was something curious about it, as if it did not fit, either inside the room or inside my mind.

Isabella walked around the machine, running her hand over the various parts.

"Why isn't anyone working?" I asked.

"Mr. Booth works mainly alone," she said. "It truly is his passion. I believe he only has help when loading and unloading the barrels. He likes to be alone."

"What's that?" In the corner of the room was a machine on a wide board with wheels, a makeshift hospital bed. The device was partly made from the same components as the larger machine, but here the tubes and the glass elements had been replaced by metal spirals and a number of dishes attached to pipes. There was also a tall cabinet containing various dials and meters with big handles below. Isabella stood in front of the strange machine. Her smile was gone. The light no longer penetrated to us. We saw only the outlines of something we did not understand.

WE WENT FOR a walk. I think we both wanted to be far from the house, from the brewery. That we could talk only when we no longer felt the walls around us, no longer saw the tall windows behind which anything might suddenly appear, no longer experienced Mr. Booth's uncommon hospitality, which both enticed and intimidated us. As if we knew this hospitality also desired something of us. Something we did not wish to surrender.

The path was cut through with tree roots and became narrower as we approached the fields. Poplars stood along both sides, casting their long shadows like giants at our feet.

"I hope it stays dry," I said, but my voice sounded thin, power-less, as if something were taking the breath out of my words.

Isabella stopped, grabbed my arm. She looked at me. "There is an explanation. There must be an explanation."

I nodded. "I've been having such strange dreams, Isabella. And last night . . . I was standing at the top of the staircase and there was something that wanted to push me down. And then there's still that evening."

She raised an eyebrow.

"That one evening," I said.

She nodded. "Are you afraid?"

I looked at her. I was searching for the right thing to say. I was looking for words that would indicate I needed her help, that it was becoming too dark inside my head, that I feared we had entered a place where we should not have come, but everything I came up with sounded silly and childish.

"I think we should keep a very close eye on Mr. Booth," I said eventually.

The afternoon light cast a golden glow on her face, making her look unreal; she was so beautiful that I feared she might burst apart if I touched her.

"I think he possesses powers that no other human has." And as soon as I had said it, I knew it was true, and when I saw her face, I knew that she knew. My heart beat a number of cold, fast beats. The golden glow had disappeared. We stood in the gray-blue colors of the afternoon, far away under the old poplars, on a path full of tree roots on a country estate that was alive everywhere, had eyes and ears everywhere. It allowed us to walk around and to play, to talk and to imagine, to do as we pleased, because ultimately none of it mattered. Because it was getting ready.

"We need to find out who he is," whispered Isabella.

I took her hand, gave it a squeeze. It felt damp and too warm. A drop of sweat slid down my temple.

THE MARE STILL had colic. Mr. Booth had come home at the end of the day and had rooms prepared for us. Then he had left again. He had an appointment in Dundee and would stop at Mr. Baxter's to let him know we were staying the night in Fife.

Although we had only a candle on the nightstand, I saw myself in the dressing-table mirror opposite my bed, lying with my cheek on Isabella's breast. The warmth of her body penetrated the thin fabric of her nightgown, and it occurred to me that there was a warmth in her that was not human and that the more I touched her, the better I understood her. She is leaving traces within me, I thought. Spores, spoors. Sometimes like an animal, sometimes like fungus. She attaches herself with tiny claws and makes deep riddles within me. She pins down an unbounded desire with me and I begin to yearn for the very darkest part of her, because that is where not only the unknown is located, but also all of the warmth.

She looked at me, in the mirror. "You make me better, Mary. Did you know that? Every day since you arrived, you have made me better. As if you leave traces within me. Light traces. Light with happiness and good cheer."

I knew it was not possible. No one could see inside another person's head, the world of my thoughts was hidden, belonged to me. No one could get in there. Mind readers existed only in stories. So it had to be a coincidence. Or was it possible that Isabella and I had a sort of connection that existed outside all bounds of logic? One that we ourselves had created by fantasizing until we arrived inside each other's thoughts?

"I have the feeling that something bad is going to happen, Mary." Her hand slid over the sheet towards me.

I met her gaze in the mirror, eyes in which I read fear and confusion. Her heartbeat pounded deep into my ear. The room around us seemed to become a shade darker.

"You are the only one." She stroked her index finger over my shoulder, along my throat. "You are the only one who can stop it. When I'm with you, it's far away. You keep it at a distance."

"What exactly?" I asked. I knew she would be unable to answer my question. Just as I knew she truly felt it. I felt it too. And I, too, had no name for it. I, too, knew no words for what was watching us from the shadows, what was waiting for us, until at some unguarded moment we would allow it into our midst. It had been waiting for weeks, maybe much longer, even before my time in Dundee, maybe since the day my mother had brought me to life, when I demanded so much life that it had to come from somewhere, or since the winters with Mary Jane, Fanny, and Claire in front of the fire that gave off no heat, while we drank warm milk, waiting for my father to come home and bind us together. And because it had no name, because it was invisible, I had dismissed it as my imagination. But now that Isabella felt it too, I feared that it existed. Existed just like she and I.

I sat up, my face close to hers. The agitation in her eyes was covered with something I could not quite place. I kissed her. Those lips, her tongue warm and wet, our tongues dancing around each other like electric eels, wanting to merge, become entangled, to go deeper into each other's mouth, deeper into each other. Isabella's scent, so sweet, so familiar yet unknown, floated around me, my fingers hooked behind the neck of her nightgown and clawed it down. I thought about our adventure, her pale breasts outside, just before we discovered the monster, how her nipples were the color of raspberries. Now, in the candlelight, they were dark, dark and hard, and when I pressed my lips to her nipple, took the firm bud into my mouth, that hardness drove itself into my body, through my entire self, downwards, downwards. My breathing stopped for a moment, just a raw moan coming from my throat. In a sudden movement, the room tilted, I saw Isabella above me, her sweet, insane face, until she disappeared from my field of vision, her head nestling between my legs, and it began to flow. And although I was young, I knew that this existed, that this happened, that this did not need to be punished or to have consequences, but the awareness of what we were doing, the image I saw when I raised my head and looked between my legs, filled me with a delicious sense of outrageousness, more and more intensely. And everything that I already knew myself, from those nights when I could not stop my own fingers, the moisture that seemed to be my body's approval, could not compare to this; her mouth, her tongue, her saliva joining, mingling itself with my wetness, sending sparks through my body, shivers, shots of pleasure that were almost painful, her head between my legs, her face, there, making me say things I had never said. Waves with foaming crests broke upon the rocks, a shell opened up, a quivering oyster waiting to be taken away by the creatures of the sea, so that they could do whatever they wanted to her; and that was what *she* wanted, she longed for it, she trembled so violently, so violently, until she burst, opening up, jolts of electricity sparking from her loins, seizing her body, making her shake, quietly curse. Until she lay there, cracked, wounded, sobbing. I kissed Isabella, who had crawled up and was lying beside me with her head on my pillow. I kissed her, she tasted salty, I kissed her.

IN THE NIGHT, I awoke. For a moment, I did not understand what had woken me. I had not had a dream, Isabella was sleeping quietly beside me, her hand on my stomach, because that was where it belonged. Then I heard once again the sound that had woken me. It was not a scream, more a muffled cry. A deep, pitiful sound. Gently, I slid out from under Isabella's hand and the sheet and walked to the window. The moon was captive behind thick veils. But down below, on the grass in front of the house, beyond the gravel path, there stood a figure. He was larger than a human being, coarser and wider. He stood differently too: like an animal, wide-legged, as if he might lose his balance. Even before I realized what he was, I felt my hands trembling on the window frame. He had come. Our monster was here. I could no longer move, I stood there, fearing that he would see me, recognize something within me that I myself did not even know existed. Who had he come for? But even before asking myself that question, I knew the answer. It was staring at me in the reflection in the windowpane, with wide, sensuous eyes.

July 1816
Chamonix-Mont-Blanc

Ice and tableau

"This is it." Percy slumps back in his chair, his elbows over the armrests.

Mary presses herself to his chest. She is sitting on his lap. Earlier this evening she thought that inappropriate, here, in this inn, which is not too luxurious but still respectable. But then wine came, lots of wine, and she kept looking at Percy, at how he ate his pie, how he dabbed his beautiful mouth with the napkin, how he laughed half-heartedly at a joke from Claire, how his gaze wandered to Mary, the look that is reserved for her, at least she really believes it is. It was that glance that made her succumb, that made her long for them together, that made her dream of this man, he who was allowed to know her innermost being, because she believed that in a certain, though not predestined, way they belonged together.

"That's it, then. Just look."

They are sitting in the bay window, which looks out onto Mont Blanc. It is the largest thing she has ever seen. Great in terms of size, yes, but also in terms of emotion. Albe and John have remained behind in Cologny; Albe was in a frenzy, writing and writing and scarcely leaving his room. John wanted to keep him company. William stayed with Elise; he was obviously too small for such a journey. Claire came along, although she was not feeling well. She had little appetite and was frequently so tired that you could see it in her eyes: a deep, hollow space in which she herself no longer seemed to be present. The donkey they hired to transport their luggage was used several times to carry Claire. So perhaps she was not just making a fuss. That said, it would not have been the first time she had feigned misery in order to get Percy's attention; and although he was giving it to her, in ample quantities, Mary felt happy here, on the road, in this world of ice. It was as if, with every mile they covered, with every new view of a misty, colorless valley, a high, white summit, each one whiter than the next, brilliantly, dazzlingly, unreally white, everything fell into place. She did not know what it was that seemed to be making more and more sense, but it unleashed an overwhelming excitement within her. The desolation of this piece of world, the cruel mountain ridges, the merciless ravines a few feet away from their footpath, no, perhaps not merciless. Indifferent. This nature did not care about them. The travelers left her just as cold as she already was. Whatever happened to one of them, it did not matter, and strangely enough that felt like a deep consolation. Nothing was the central point of the world. Not Mary herself, not Percy, not even little Willmouse. There was no center. Everything was the same; one thing worth no more than another, and loss was no more than a fact. Could she hold on to this feeling? This feeling of infinity, of invulnerability?

SHE COULD NOT hold on to it. The days went by. They had reached Chamonix: the end of their journey. In a day's time, they will leave:

back to Cologny and their little house on the lake. She hates becoming accustomed to things, how impressions wear out at the same rate as the soles of their shoes. Every night, the three of them share a room and Percy lies between them, usually facing Claire, his arm around her, offering comfort for her upset stomach, her nausea, her headache, or whatever it is this time. Mary lies on his other side, her body yearning for his touch, her mind angry, anticipating, and when he finally turns to take her in his arms, touching her in such a way that she knows she is the only one, after all, she cannot help but sullenly reject him. Somehow, she hopes this will result in a plea, but it never does. She pretends to have the power—yet loses. In the hour that follows, when the two bodies beside her are making sleeping noises, Mary stares at the window, thinks she can see the twinkling of light on snow, and tries to recall how it all works again with love and freedom, which she, in theory, agrees with. She attempts to reconcile the inherent logic of free love with her deep sense of injustice and sadness when he takes another woman (Claire!) in his arms. She tries to make rational thought weigh more heavily, to place it above those childish, primitive, tender feelings, to suffocate them with reason. But they do not wish to be covered completely; elements remain visible, fragments that sparkle so intensely with indignation and desire that they keep surfacing and seeming like truth.

And truly, she does see the irony. How she has to contain her feelings in order for the ideal of love to prevail. But damn it, she wants no one but Percy! Which means she has to start from scratch with her reasoning. She often lies awake.

CLAIRE IS SICK. They are staying an extra night. Percy is with her. All day in that room. He says he reads a lot. Fetches water for Claire.

Comforts her when she vomits. Mary does not wish to appear insensitive. She really does feel sorry for Claire. But that is the point when there is always something to be dramatic about: people lose interest, lose sympathy. Except for Percy. But, says a mean thought inside her, that is because he loves her. She is sitting in the small library, which has an impressive amount of literature for such a modest establishment. Earlier this morning, she went for a walk through the snowy forest behind the inn. The reflected light did something to her eyes and her mood; as if all the whiteness shone so brightly into her that it dissolved everything else. For a moment, it was all gone: the blue eyes of her little girl in the cradle, her father's tall back when he sat hunched over his desk, trying to block out the children's voices, Willmouse, whom she loved like no other, but who in that very love tugged on her so that she would never be free, Percy and Claire, Claire and Percy, Percy who brought her everything, and took it away, over and over and again, the empty space that represented her mother, who was always present, precisely by being so very absent, and then that other thing, the thing that lives inside her, that is there, even without words, that feeds her, that frees her, that fills her with fear. And in the emptiness that all of that left behind, she could feel complete joy.

Back at the inn, the joy seeps away like meltwater and she does not know how to summon it back. She goes to their room, but Percy warns her to be quiet, as Claire is finally asleep. Mary tries not to see how he looks at Claire's sleeping face, the lock of hair on her cheek, her bottom lip moist and sensual in complete repose. Mary turns tail, seeks out the quietest room in the inn, and sits down in a large armchair. She picks up her writing book, her ink and quill, and says quietly, "I'm back. Come to me." And it comes. It comes.

Cautiously, silently at first, but unmistakably. And now that she sees him, beholds him in all his amazing realness, he makes her shiver, even though she knows him, in fact because she knows him, he urges words into her, stories, letters, landscapes, people of blood and letters. And it becomes more real as her fury increases, and it becomes more furious as it becomes more real.

LATER—HOURS?—SHE IS STILL in that big chair, which conceals her presence in the library because the back is turned to the door. She has filled page after page, she, of course, but actually that thing inside her, which gave words to her, except words for itself. It has become dark. The glacier through the large window is only a shadow, a mass of future or past, or perhaps both, substantial and immutable. And yet, thinks Mary, and yet I am changing things. Writing is an act. And she thinks of her mother, her fearless mother, how her mother had fought against marriage as it was, against the subjugation of women. And Mary wonders, not for the first time, if she is subjugating herself, in a certain way. Is love not subjugation, after all? Is Percy not subjugating himself just as much to her? No, says accepted wisdom, not to the same extent.

CLAIRE FEELS A little better, but they take a carriage anyway, even though they cannot really spare the money. They sit with three strangers in a coach that smells of soup and sweat. Claire sits by the window, but the lady sitting opposite will not allow them to open it, as her daughter is pregnant and she fears she will catch a cold. The girl herself says nothing. She is very thin, so her large belly stands out strangely against the rest of her body. She looks younger than sixteen, thinks Mary. She was the same age when her first child was growing inside her, but her stomach had never become that large, not with her little girl. She sees that Claire is also looking at the girl, her eyes wide and angry. Does she have a fever? Percy is staring straight ahead, saying nothing. Sometimes she wants to get inside his head. Sometimes she is glad that she cannot.

They leave the narrower roads, leave the mountains behind. This is where the landscape begins that she has come to know well. A few more hours and they will be back at the lake. She will take William in her arms again, hold his warm body to her, his babbling sounds in her ear. Percy will leave for Diodati at once, for Albe, and he will take Claire with him. She will remain at Chapuis, with William. In the end, nothing changes. She only thinks it does when she writes.

"STOP." IT SOUNDS soft, yet urgent. Claire is hunched over, her arms around her stomach.

There is a moment when no one does anything. Then Percy stands up, opens the window, and calls something to the coachman. They come to a standstill. Claire quickly opens the door, almost falls out, runs, stooping forward, to the rear of the carriage. Mary wants to ask what on earth is going on, but Percy has already gone after Claire. The ladies opposite avoid her gaze. Mary climbs out of the coach, a leaden sky hangs over the valley, lending a strange shading effect to the things below, as if they have more depth, have been elevated some distance out of reality. Just behind the wheels of the carriage, Claire is kneeling on the ground. A gleaming thread hangs from her mouth. Percy is beside her, on his haunches, rubbing her back, quietly saying something to her. A new wave, Mary looks away. In the distance, she sees a flash of light in the clouds. It is strangely still. No birds, no bees, no crickets. As if everything is holding its breath. Percy's hand keeps rubbing Claire's back, in a perpetually repeating motion. The ladies in the carriage, the coachman, they have turned to stone. They will be waiting for them forever. They will not understand, but they will know that something is happening here that is making everything subservient to this moment. Mary does not understand it herself yet, but she knows it too: she has been waiting for this. Maybe she has long known this was coming, that this moment would become part of her life, was part of her life even before it happened. Even before it was set in motion, even before the seedbed was prepared and the mold was forged. They are a tableau, a work of art with a message that is not immediately apparent in the depiction, and it is not until later, when she gets home, lights a few candles, finds William in his cradle, sleeping, breathing, completely whole, when she loosens her tight-fitting garments and unlaces her boots, boils water for tea, and he takes her by the hand, leads her into the small drawing room, sits her down on the sofa, comes to sit beside her, looks at her, really looks at her for the first time in days, that it comes to her in its full, subtle yet sun-clear significance. Because she already knew.

He tells her, but she already knew.

Only one candle is lit in the drawing room. A little light in his eyes. It is far too late. She is so tired.

"How long?" she asks. And why has Claire not said anything to her?

"A couple of months, she thinks."

"When did she tell you? And what does she want from you?"

"A few days ago, before we left." Percy pulls her close. He smells floral, of Claire. "I'm sorry I didn't tell you sooner. Claire didn't want me to."

She has to ask. That is better, because it will surely come out. She had better just ask. She feels her eyes becoming thick and warm, but it is so dark that she does not need to conceal them. She swallows, audibly, there is something hard in her throat.

"She met Albe before, in London, of course." Percy is not looking at her. "She hasn't told him yet."

She did not have to ask him. He has spared her that. That is why she loves him. For that and for a thousand other things. But still. Are they going to pretend now there is no other possibility? Can she do that? She does not know the nature of the relationship between Percy and Claire. Not exactly. And she does not wish to. So perhaps she has no need to worry. Perhaps this has nothing to do with her at all.

But she notices. When the two of them are eating dinner that night at the kitchen table. The way he looks at her, smiles, sometimes puts his hand on hers. He knows that it is a possibility. And invisibly as she clears the table, invisibly as she puts on her nightgown, invisibly as she feeds William, invisibly as she nestles against Percy's warm, dear back, she falls apart.

September–October 1812
Dundee

September 18, 1812

Isabella believed me. Of course she did. We had seen each other's inner world last night. We did not speak about it. How could we have done so? But I knew she would believe me, no matter what. We tried to imagine what that monster had come for, under the window at Mr. Booth's house. Isabella thought there was no way he had come for us. How could he have known we were there? I did not know. It was all strange and illogical. Unlikely and unreal. And yet. Did Mr. Booth have something to do with him? The idea stirred up our feeling of tension. There was so much about Mr. Booth that was not to be trusted that even the most unlikely things took on a hint of indisputable logic, and we were determined to find out if our suspicions were correct.

A DAY AFTER we had returned from Fife, we were sitting at the table with the whole family. Mr. Baxter had said that afternoon that Mr. Booth had invited Isabella and me to go riding with him the next day. It was a good opportunity to find out more about him, so we accepted the invitation, but since then I thought Isabella seemed gloomy and distant. She sat beside me at the table, helped herself to food, and ate without looking at anyone, even me. Elsie had made a large pan of vegetable soup and duck liver pâté. I was glad that she had also baked bread. I sometimes walked up the hill past the duck farm, and the ducks had such soulful eyes that I could not bring myself to eat their meat. Johnny looked drowsily ahead. Maybe he was tired. It was not any later than usual, but I had heard from Grace that he had not been sleeping well lately; she often had to go to him in the night to comfort him after a bad dream. I felt sorry for him. He was pale and his eyes, normally full of zest and fire, seemed dull and dim. Mr. Baxter and Robert were talking about Margaret's grave, how Mr. Booth was having it looked after so well and how fine it was that she had had such a good life with him, even after her accident.

"How did the two of them actually get to know each other?" Isabella's question was prepared, but she asked it at exactly the right moment and her tone was just casual enough.

"You already know that, don't you?" said Mr. Baxter. He took a swig of wine and cut a slice of his pâté.

Johnny coughed a few times, barking like a dog.

"Don't cough over the table," said Robert.

"Margaret and Mr. Booth met at the fair. Four years ago?"

"Five," said Robert.

"Five years ago. They had met each other before, of course, but they really got talking for the first time at a show. Margaret said that she was completely indifferent to him at the beginning of the show, but that by the end she knew: I want to marry this man." Mr. Baxter smiled. "I believe it was true love. Margaret was not interested in love before she met him. You know that: she was a down-to-earth kind of girl. Dutiful, she always thought of others first."

"She never demanded anything for herself." Robert cut a few slices of bread and passed them around. "Mr. Booth was a fortunate man."

"But he was good to her, too," said Mr. Baxter. "She was happy. I really do believe that."

Robert nodded. "I can remember only one time when I wondered if they had had a disagreement when I saw her. That was around Christmas. Before her accident, a couple of years ago."

"She had her fall just after Christmas," said Mr. Baxter.

Isabella pinched my leg so hard that I gasped.

"I think it was the same year. That was also the Christmas when she and Mama were working on those quilts."

I wanted to look at Isabella, but her eyes were fixed firmly on her plate.

"Oh yes." Mr. Baxter chuckled. "They were using a stitch that kept going wrong. It used to make her furious, your mother. Do you remember?"

A fork clattered onto the table. Beside Robert, Johnny was shaking, his eyes big and tearful.

"Ah, Johnny." Robert took Johnny on his lap, rocked him, laid his head on his shoulder. "We miss Mama, don't we?"

Johnny did not reply, just sobbed even louder.

"Come on, lad. I'll put you to bed." Robert heaved himself up from his chair with Johnny in his arms and carried him up the stairs.

For a while, we said nothing, eating in silence. Then Mr. Baxter said, "You like him, don't you? Mr. Booth?"

Isabella looked up. She had a very strange expression in her eyes, as if she had just woken from a bad dream.

"Mr. Booth is going to want a new wife. He is not the kind of person to spend a long time alone." He looked at Isabella for a moment. "We shall see," he said.

I felt Isabella's hand clawing at me under the table.

WE LAY CLOSE together in Isabella's bed. She was shaking continuously.

"Are you cold?" I asked.

"What Robert said, about the disagreement between Margaret and Mr. Booth, a few days before her fall down the stairs, and their encounter at the fair, how he won her over. She wasn't like that, it's true, as my father said. And do you remember how secretive he was being at the fair when we were there a couple of months ago? That was a month before Margaret died."

I nodded. I put my arm over Isabella's warm belly. She took a very deep breath.

"What if it's really true?"

"What do you mean?"

"This. What we imagine. What we think we can see. What if it *is* real?"

"That's what we're trying to find out," I said.

"And then? What are we going to do then?"

It was strange that I had not thought about that before. What if we found out that something was wrong with Mr. Booth? That he practiced some sort of witchcraft? That such a thing might actually exist? That he might have used it to cause Margaret's death? Who would believe us?

"I don't know," I said. "But shouldn't we find out anyway?"

She closed her eyes. She was so beautiful. I planted a sweet, soft kiss on her mouth.

"I'm scared," she said.

"So am I," I replied.

September 29, 1812

I am not at the Baxters'. I had strange dreams. "I knew that you would return," said a voice without a mouth in the dead of the night. I believe the room said it. I know this room, but I do not know where from. Isabella has been to visit. She brought me books, my diary, which I always hide deep under my mattress. I sleep a lot. Across from me, there is a girl who is looking at me.

October 3, 1812

Isabella says I have concussion. When I sit up, it is as if the world tilts. Mr. Booth says I must stay lying down. He brings me tea and toast. Sometimes soup. The soup is delicious. It tastes of the past. My father used to cook before he married Mary Jane. Tomatoes, onions, carrots, bay leaf. Widower's soup.

THEY HAVE TOLD me what happened, but I keep forgetting. I hit my head. I have a vague throbbing, nagging pain on the side of my head. There is a lump, dried blood.

October 6, 1812

It is just a shadow. There is no one sitting beside my bed at night. There is no one sitting beside my bed.

October 8, 1812

There was a dream in which Margaret was alive. She lay here, in this bed, next to me. When I asked her what had happened, she began to cry. "It hurts so much," she said. She undid the buttons of her nightgown and in her chest was a deep hole into which I could look. There was no sign of blood, no innards, just a blackness like a night sky, sometimes with a flash of bright white, a forked shaft that made her gasp for breath. "Who is E.L.?" I asked her, but she said nothing, turned around, and the blackness in her chest ran out over the sheet, over the whole bed, and it was all my fault.

October 10, 1812

I went riding with Mr. Booth, alone. Isabella was ill. My horse bolted and I had an unfortunate fall, hitting my head on a stone. That was what Robert told me. He and Mr. Baxter came to visit. I asked for Isabella, but they said she had to help Mr. Booth.

THE LIGHT IS beginning to fade. Summer is over. It is becoming colder. I miss her.

October 11, 1812

After breakfast, Mr. Booth came to sit on the edge of my bed. There was a serious look in his eyes that I had never seen before.

"When can I go back to the Baxters'?" I asked, realizing how ungrateful I sounded.

"In a few days, I think," he said. "A bumpy ride could do you a great deal of harm. Your brain is not up to it yet."

"Where's Isabella?" I asked. How long was it since I had last seen her?

"Mary." Mr. Booth's expression was unemotional, almost stern.

Outside, it began to rain. The light grew weaker.

"Mary, did you leave your room last night?"

An image came into my mind of myself, or a woman who looked like me, in a white nightgown, wandering the hallway like a ghost. She had hollow, unseeing eyes. She was asleep.

"No," I said.

"It is very important that you are honest, Mary." He looked at me as if trying to open my mind with his gaze.

"I truly did not go out into the hallway." What I had seen had not happened. It was not real. I was certain I had not left my room that night. I never left my room.

"Good," he said. He stood up, walked to the window, and looked outside, at the gray clouds from which rain poured as if it would never stop. Or maybe he was looking at something in the distance.

"You don't remember much about the day of your accident," he said. It was not a question.

I shook my head. "Nothing. Maybe," I said, "I remember us riding together. I had a horse that was almost white."

Mr. Booth turned and came to the bed. With his long fingers, he stroked my head, my hair, which hung over my shoulders. "I shall have some soup sent up for you later," he said. "Now you must rest."

I did not feel tired, but when he left the room and I heard the click of the door, my eyes fell shut, like the heavy curtains on stage at the end of a performance.

October 14, 1812

Isabella has still not visited. I ask for her every day. I am beginning to remember more and more about my fall, but there are still white patches over certain events. I know Isabella had become ill and so could not go riding. I did not want to go on my own, but she said it was a good opportunity to find out more about Mr. Booth. I was given the most docile horse, as I had never ridden before. She was called Ivy. She was white and had deep, dark eyes and a long mane. The weather was calm, not too warm. First we rode for a while along the banks of the Tay. Mr. Booth asked me questions. About London, about my father, about my time at boarding school in Ramsgate. It was all perfectly normal. He was perfectly normal. I remember wondering what I could ask him that might help us, without alarming him. Then there is nothing more. A patch of white.

October 15, 1812

I dreamed that Isabella came to fetch me. I was lying in bed and she had to fight Mr. Booth, but she could not win, because he was too strong. Then she produced a snake, the same as Mr. Booth had shown us that evening. She released it, the snake moved across the floor, and for a moment I was afraid it was crawling towards the bed. But it went to Mr. Booth, slowly and surely, circling up around his leg and then darting to bite him in the groin.

I awoke, my heart pounding loudly, and I was afraid someone had seen my dream. As if the room, the swallows on the wallpaper, or the girl I sometimes saw in the mirror had been witnesses and would inform the owner of the house, prepare him for his unmasking.

THE WHITE PATCHES are starting to disappear. We rode at a walking pace, side by side, Mr. Booth and I. We were no longer riding beside the Tay, but farther inland, on a wild heath. The heather was blossoming; wherever I looked, I saw every shade of purple. It was making me slightly giddy. I wanted to ask him about his brewery. How long he had been a brewer, who had taught him. My heart was thumping so loudly that I feared Mr. Booth would hear it. How was I supposed to find out if something was not right about him without putting myself in danger? In the safety of her bedroom, Isabella and I could have come up with all manner of ideas, but here on my own, with this man beside me, everything was different. I hardly dared to look at him, afraid that my expression would give something away.

And then it happened. Mr. Booth made our horses stop, took my wrist, and looked at me, his face unfathomable. He said, "Is there something you and Isabella would like to know about me?"

From that point on, I remember nothing. I desperately try to recall what happened after that, but all I encounter is emptiness. I am so cold, and Isabella has still not come to see me.

October 16, 1812

I am trying not to cry. When he brings me soup, the soup I can barely get down my throat anymore, and strokes my head, not in a kind or concerned manner, but firmly, almost hard, to press me into the bed, into my place, where I belong and must stay, I fear him as never before. I remember everything. I want to get away from here. Away from the room where an unfortunate woman lived and died, away from the windows through which only rain and clouds and muddy paths can be seen, away from the swallows forever fleeing and never escaping, away from the girl in the mirror, who is supposed to be me, but whom I do not know. Away from this man's house. Away from the house of this maniac, this creature. This witch.

"IS THERE SOMETHING you and Isabella would like to know about me?"

The heath had given way to clay soil. Here and there, small shoots poked out of the ground, as if curious about this place, but now that they were here, had shown their heads, they were stuck in the soil of this desolate spot and could not go back.

"What do you mean?" I was not looking at him, my eyes were fixed on Ivy's long mane, my sweet, beautiful fairy, my angel.

"I thought we were friends, Mary."

I looked up at him, but his face gave nothing away. "Indeed we are," I said quietly.

Mr. Booth shook his head. "Friends," he said. It was silent for a moment. "Friends trust one another. Friends want the best for each other. Friends," he said with a smile, and it was actually a friendly smile, and for a second I thought Isabella and I had been horribly mistaken, "want to make one another happy. I want to make you happy, Mary."

I looked at him, this man with so many faces, who at one moment was a handsome, amiable gentleman and yet the next had a twisted bestiality in his gaze, compared to which the eyes of the creatures in *The Sacred Deep* seemed tame. If everything we had always imagined truly existed, then he might be anything.

"I should like to go home," I said. The sky became a shade darker, the heath grayer, Mr. Booth took on angular forms, as if shadows hung about him. I could not do it anymore. I could not stand up to this man, this thing. He was not only physically stronger. I was no match for him mentally either. He was old. So very much older than I, so very much older than everything around us. He possessed knowledge of which I was unaware. All I wanted to do was to go home, back to Isabella, to Robert and Johnny, back to Mr. Baxter at the table full of candles, with Elsie preparing the food, the smell of roasted lamb, of bread and coffee.

"Fine." Mr. Booth nodded. "As you wish." He let go of my wrist, urged his horse on. We set off. But he kept urging his horse onwards, Ivy trotted along too, and then galloped. Faster and faster we went, side by side, I gripped the reins so tightly that my hands were shaking. I could no longer see our surroundings clearly; the colors had disappeared, everything shook and I was doing my utmost to remain seated on Ivy's back, when a sudden blow behind me made her speed up even more, she took a sharp turn, the reins slipped from my hands, my feet shot out of the stirrups, I took a tumble and felt a dull thud in my head, so hard that I wished I was no longer there.

The next moment I was lying in Margaret's room, in her bed. Was it he who had caused me to fall, so that I would end up here?

I NO LONGER dare to sleep. Isabella, where are you?

October 17, 1812

I am home. The last night in Fife, I tried to remain awake. Sometimes, when I feared I would fall asleep, I would get out of bed for a while. I looked out the window; outside there was nothing but black gloom. I sat at the dressing table, looking at the girl, this young woman who was looking at me, and tried to find similarities. Maybe I no longer knew myself. Maybe I had simply changed. Maybe I was becoming an adult.

The next day, Mr. Booth sent me home in his carriage. He was not there but left a note for me, which I found beside my breakfast plate:

> *Mary, you can go home. The journey should no longer pose a danger to your health. We shall see each other again soon, I have no doubt. Yours, David Booth*

I felt relieved when the carriage drove away from the house. It felt lighter and lighter inside my head. As if there were a thread of spider silk between me and the house, which became thinner and thinner as the distance grew.

I FOUND ISABELLA in the garden. She was pruning the rosebushes along the fence at the back of the house. When she saw me, she snipped two more branches.

"Mary," she said. For a moment, she seemed surprised to see me. Then she smiled. She put her clippers down on the grass and embraced me. Her touch and scent, her hair tickling my cheek, I had so longed for this that now that I actually felt her, now that I was actually here, it barely felt real, like an imitation of my fantasy. I let go of her.

"How wonderful that you're back," she said. "How do you feel?"

"Fine," I said. "I had hoped to come home much sooner, but Mr. Booth wished to keep me there."

Isabella smiled. "He was taking care of you. I'm glad." She picked up the clippers again. "Come on, let's go inside, and I'll ask Elsie to make tea. She came back from market this morning with a currant loaf. I'm sure we can have a piece of that. Oh Mary, it's so good to have you home." She turned and walked briskly ahead of me to the house. On her wrist, a bracelet with dark blue stones was sparkling.

IN THE KITCHEN, it was warm and the steam from the kettle clouded the windows. There was no one there but the two of us. Isabella cut two slices of currant loaf for us.

"Where were you?" I asked. I had not intended to ask. Not like this. But there was something in her manner, something playful and lighthearted, that annoyed me.

She looked at me, smiled as if I did not know her. "I came to visit," she said. "At first. But sometimes I had to help David, Mr. Booth. And I had a lot to do at home. The garden. And Johnny needed me. He's not been well lately. And you were being well taken care of."

She had called him David. She never did that.

"How do you know that?" Only then did I realize just how angry I was with her. As if the fury could make itself known only when I saw her. "You left me there," I said. "With him."

Isabella's eyes grew large. "Oh Mary, I . . ."

Then Johnny came racing into the kitchen. "Mary!" He leaped onto my lap, and I could not help but laugh. "Are you better?"

"Yes, all better." I kissed his head. "I heard that you're poorly, though."

"No, I'm fine."

"You were in bed all day yesterday," said Isabella, cutting a slice of currant bread for Johnny.

"But not today," he said with a grin.

Isabella and I looked at each other over the top of his head. I did not know what I saw in her eyes. I did not recognize it.

I USED THE rest of the day to write to my father, to Claire and to Fanny. I went for a walk towards the hills, and I could see that autumn was on the way. The heath had finished blossoming, the bushes were becoming dry and brittle, and even though there was no wind, it was getting chilly. I pulled my coat more tightly around me and, for the first time since my arrival in Scotland, I felt alone. I realized that during my stay at Mr. Booth's I had believed there was a good reason Isabella had not come to see me. There had to be. But there was not. What had happened to her? Did she regret our closeness? Did she wish to distance herself from me?

AT DINNER, Mr. Baxter toasted my good health.

"To celebrate your recovery and return, we shall go to the theater tomorrow night."

Johnny clapped his hands, Isabella looked delighted, and Robert smiled.

"Have you ever seen *Macbeth*?" asked Mr. Baxter.

I shook my head.

"Wonderful. Mr. Booth will be our guest of honor. He took such good care of you that I should like to thank him."

I nodded. I tried to catch Isabella's eye, but she was looking at her father and smiling.

October 18, 1812

My father took me to see a play for the first time when I was seven. From that moment, the people who filled my books gained faces, like the people on the stage. They became made of flesh, breathing and supple. Blood flowed through their veins, propelled by their hearts, which, as with all humans, were complicated; disgust and desire, tenderness and brutality, courage and mortal terror all exist there, and sometimes simultaneously. Stories are a mirror. You see yourself, but not always as you had expected. A story like a mirror; not real, but still true.

The Theatre Royal is located at the highest point of Castle Street and was very similar to the London theaters I know, except it was very new. The streetlights cast patches of yellow on the cobblestones. Mr. Baxter did his best to keep an eye on all of us, often standing on tiptoe, shepherding us through the crowd to the large doors. Suddenly, Mr. Booth was there. Seemingly without effort, he guided us into the foyer. The ceiling must have been at least fifteen feet high. There were chandeliers and ornate candleholders on the walls. The carpet under our feet muffled the sounds of all those mouths to a pleasant hum. Mr. Baxter gave everyone a ticket. Johnny looked at his with big, wide eyes.

"Keep a tight hold on it, Johnny," I said.

It was Johnny's first visit to a theater. He did little jumps, trying to see as much of his surroundings as possible, but it was too busy and the adults around him were blocking his view. Robert lifted him onto his back and spun around slowly, so that Johnny could take it all in. Isabella had gone to stand with Mr. Booth. He pointed something out to her on a poster in a display case on the wall and she smiled. A bell rang and we started moving as a single organism. I had to take care not to lose sight of Robert, who I was following. I sat by the center aisle, with Isabella beside me. Next to Isabella sat Mr. Booth, who was talking to Mr. Baxter, but I could not hear what their conversation was about. Isabella turned to me.

"How do you feel?" she asked.

I shrugged and kept my eyes on the curtains, which were still closed in front of the stage.

Suddenly she took my hand and I looked at her. She breathed in, it seemed as if she were going to say something and then thought better of it. She smiled. "I'm glad you're here," she said.

The curtains opened and a set of heathland, purple as it was in our summer, appeared. The backdrop was a black sky with a flash of lightning. Three witches sat around a cauldron.

HALFWAY THROUGH the play, I became aware of a quiet voice beside me. I thought Isabella wanted to say something to me, but when I turned my head towards her, I saw that she was facing Mr. Booth. In the semi-darkness, I tried to make out their expressions, but it was impossible. Their words were also hidden from me in darkness, so softly were they spoken. And then I saw it: Isabella's hand was on the armrest between her seat and Mr. Booth's, and he, he had placed his hand upon hers, interlacing his fingers with hers. She let her hand lie there, as if it did not bother her at all that this creature who looked like a man but most definitely was not had taken possession of her hand.

I WAS NO longer angry. I was not even sad. I was afraid. Above all else, I was very, very afraid.

October 19, 1812

I sat beside Johnny's bed. I dabbed his burning forehead with a damp cloth. He had not opened his eyes since I had come to sit with him. There was a lamp on his bedside table, but I had turned it down low. I had not been in Johnny's room very often. I could not see much of it in the gloom, but above his bed was a cheerful picture of a white dog with a ball and there was a large toy box beside his bed.

Isabella had avoided me yesterday evening, from the moment we arrived home. It was as if she were afraid to look at me, scared of what she might see in my eyes, or maybe scared of what I saw in hers. I lay in bed that night with a fearful sort of loss pressing heavily on my chest, and with every sound I imagined her coming to me, knocking and asking if she might come in. Slipping into bed beside me, warming her cold feet on mine, the two of us laughing. Not having to say a word about what had happened in the theater, which, no matter how it had seemed, could not be of any particular significance because . . . look: us. Look at us caressing. Look at us kissing. Look at how our bodies fit around and into each other in a wonderfully logical, beautiful, sensuous way, a way I would never have believed possible. Look at our passion, look at our hands en-twined, look at how together, without the rest, without the whole world, just the two of us, precisely the two of us, are everything. But she did not come. My imagination was a cruel lover. I awoke many times that night, and each time I did, the new truth rushed towards me, hastening to press itself to my breast, to lean forward, calm and heavy, and whisper in my ear: you have lost her, in the end you lose everyone.

This morning I was awoken by Elsie's sharp voice and rapid

footsteps. The door to Johnny's room was open, and in the doorway was the shadow of Mr. Baxter.

"Shall we call for the doctor?" asked Elsie.

"Robert, ride to the doctor's house. Tell him about this sudden high fever. Tell him about the past few weeks too."

Robert looked at me with an almost wild, absent gaze and hurried past me down the stairs.

Johnny lay propped up by three pillows. His cheeks were deep red, but his forehead, nose, and chin looked pale, and his hands lay on the cover, fingers outspread like big white spiders. He had his eyes open, but his gaze was turned inward as if seeing his surroundings were too much effort. Mr. Baxter was sitting on the edge of the bed, his hand on Johnny's leg. He said nothing. He just looked at him, with an aggrieved expression; was it familiarity? Did this moment feel like those earlier times? Was this the moment when he realized it was not going to end well? Or did he only fear it?

I laid my hand on his shoulder. A shock went through him, and he looked up. "I've sent for the doctor," he said, and those words contained a despair that the words themselves did not possess.

THE DOCTOR HAD examined Johnny, but other than a high fever and general lethargy he could not find anything, nothing he could do anything to treat. We just had to wait. Perhaps, if there was no improvement within a few days, he could do a bloodletting.

We took it in turns to watch over him, Isabella, Robert, Mr. Baxter, and I. In between, Grace sometimes sat with him, speaking in a whisper, unintelligible, reassuring. I saw his pale skin, clammy and hot, his eyes restless under the lids, dreams in which he fought sea monsters, flew on the back of a ladybird or a dragonfly, in which he had a baby sister he could cuddle. I stroked his little white fingers. Johnny's eyes opened. He looked at me, wordlessly. Then he gave me a brief smile.

"How do you feel?" I asked.

He turned his head to the window, the shutters of which were closed.

"It's evening," I said.

"I had such a strange dream. A woman was chasing me. At first it was a game, but then I could feel that it became real. I called for help, but everyone thought we were playing." Johnny looked straight ahead again, as if seeing a world in which his dream still existed. "She was a witch, I think."

I gave him a sip of water. "Witches don't exist," I said.

He looked at me long and pensively. "Yes, they do," he said then. "You know that."

"Excuse me?"

"What is it?" Johnny looked at me as if suddenly waking up.

"You said, 'You know that.'"

"What do you know?"

"No, I said witches don't exist, and you said, 'Yes, they do. You know that.'"

He shook his head. "I'm tired." He yawned and sank deeper into the pillows. He closed his eyes. I watched him as his breathing slowed. All at once, he opened his mouth, like a fish gasping for air, but instead words came out, very quietly, almost unintelligible: "He did something to her, didn't he?"

"Who?" I leaned forward. "Who did something? To whom?"

Johnny's breath was very slow and heavy now. I thought he had fallen asleep, until he opened his mouth again and, as soft as a gasp, said: "Isabella." He breathed out deeply, and his face relaxed completely. I got up off the bed, smoothed his blanket, and was walking to the other side to plump his pillows when I saw something on the mattress: it was Fingal. Fingal the fish head. The white stranger.

"WHAT IS IT?" Isabella stood before me, in her bedroom doorway. There was something aloof about her demeanor.

"May I come in?"

I saw she was hesitating. Then she nodded.

I sat on the edge of the bed, as I had done with Johnny, and Isabella sat opposite me in the window seat. She was still dressed, and the curtains were still open. The gleam of the almost-full moon embraced her, lending a glow to her hair that was at once dark and light. I could not see her expression. The only lit candle was the one on her bedside table. Beside it, open, was a copy of *Zastrozzi: A Romance* by an author with the initials P.B.S.

"I am afraid," I said. I had thought about what I needed to say. What I *could* say. What was it that made her treat me with such coldness? How could I regain her love and friendship?

"What is the matter?" she asked formally.

My heart thumped as if someone were pursuing me. "Please," I said, "I don't understand. What has happened?"

I tried to see some kind of sign on her face, but it was too dark. I heard her breathing: calm, collected.

"Dear Mary, I don't know what you mean. Nothing has happened."

"You were holding his hand!" I believe I almost screamed. I wished I were as composed as she, had everything under control, just as she did. But I had nothing under control.

Isabella sighed. It was a sigh that came from afar. A sigh that she had held back, until she could do nothing other than say what she felt, what had happened. "David is not as you think. As we thought."

So that was it. He had her. Johnny had seen it too. I wanted to look into her eyes. I wanted to see that he had extinguished what had burned there. I picked up the candle and walked towards her, but she turned away.

"And what about Margaret? You also thought that somehow he had . . ."

She shook her head. "Childish nonsense. Of course he didn't do anything to hurt her."

I was trembling all over my body, and fear and fury were singing out in my belly. "We were going to find out, that's what you said to me. Before I fell off the horse, off *his* horse."

She turned to me. "You don't think David was responsible for that, do you? He took care of you. For weeks." In her eyes, I saw sheer horror.

"And now Johnny is sick. And I don't know how, but I think Mr. Booth has something to do with it. And with you, with how you are now. This is not you, Isabella." I put the candle in the window and took hold of her hands. I felt something press against my hand. It was the bracelet with the blue stones. Margaret's bracelet.

"Please," she said. For a moment, I thought she wanted to say something else. Something that she was trying to stop. Then she looked up at me. She did not look at me as a friend, not in an attempt to reach me. She looked at me with wonder, with amazement and horror. "Mary, you need to listen closely to me. There is nothing going on. There was never anything going on. We told each other stories, nothing more than that."

"But we said to each other, we swore that it was possible, that witches exist. That monsters exist. We knew it was possible. We saw one."

A quiet, disbelieving laugh. "A game. It was a game, Mary. You knew that, didn't you?"

"And what about us?" I could not help it anymore. My face was wet with tears. My hands clutched at the fabric of Isabella's sleeves.

She looked at me without the slightest spark of recognition. "We are friends, dear Mary. That is not going to end."

"And what about the kissing? And that time in the bath, in the lake? And in bed?"

A slight frown appeared on her face. She smiled and gently shook her head. "I think you had better go to bed. You still need a lot of rest. David said the same. A concussion can have unpleasant after-effects."

I was sobbing now. "Please," I said. "You were there. You were there for all of it."

Isabella soothed me. She stroked my hair, wiped the tears from my cheeks. "Come on," she said. She walked with me to my bedroom, sat me down on the bed. She unlaced my boots, unbuttoned my gown, my corset, peeled off my stockings. She turned down the cover, and I slid under it like a child. For a moment, she put her hands on my cheeks and looked at me. Concern and patience were all I saw. Then she kissed me on the forehead and left. The kiss hurt. It stung and it continued to sting for a whole hour after that, for as long as I lay awake.

October 25, 1812

The days were long and gloomy. Rain clattered constantly on the road in front of the house, and everyone who came past had spatters of mud up to their knees. I did not go outside. I missed Isabella so terribly that everything hurt: getting up, washing, dressing, eating. Even sitting in a chair at the window and looking out was painful. There was an agonizing fire inside me that sealed my lips and made my eyes burn. The fire burned around her, it burned around us. It burned around all we had seen, what we had felt, what we had recognized. I barely left my room, only when it was my turn to watch over Johnny. Then I sat beside him, for hours, and I watched the rain meandering down the windowpane, and Johnny's face, which grew thinner by the day. I fed him porridge whenever he woke up for a time. He did not say anything else. It was not going well. The doctor had taken some blood, but it did not appear to help. Elsie let the milk boil over. I had seen Mr. Baxter crying.

I imagined Isabella sitting in her room, just like me. I imagined her missing me. If not in the heart-engulfing way that I missed her, then at least with a mysterious turbulence, a vague and restless longing. I could not imagine anything else. The idea that she did not think about me in the same way as I thought about her, the idea that the feeling we shared had been unilaterally dissolved, cut off at her end, suddenly, and that I had to bear that feeling on my own, was unbearable and impossible.

AND THEN, all at once, Johnny was better. I came into the kitchen in the morning and there he sat at the table, grinning, his mouth full of bread and jam. He lugged his fish head around the house again, counted the slugs in the garden after it had rained, and leaned against me in front of the fire, while I read him the story of the bogle, which I knew better as the bogeyman. Maybe it had been the bloodletting. Maybe his own body had fought off the sickness.

Whatever the case, he was better, as if he had never been ill. As Johnny's health improved, so did my spirits. That day, I saw Isabella only briefly in the drawing room, when she came to choose a book. She smiled at me.

"Such good news about Johnny, isn't it?" she said.

I would have liked to embrace her. I nodded.

"All this family's troubles are over now." Isabella nodded decisively and smiled. Then she disappeared with the book under her arm.

WE ATE IN the dining room that night, for the first time since my arrival in Dundee. Grace had been busy all that afternoon, dusting, cleaning the windows, and polishing the wooden furniture. Twenty-one candles shone in the chandelier above us. Johnny was the sweet, delightful focal point. Mr. Baxter often had to calm him down, but he did it with a smile. The relief could be seen on everyone's faces. Even Mr. Booth seemed affected by Johnny's recovery; he was quieter than usual and looked at him many times, with a charming smile. Isabella was radiant. Sometimes her eyes met mine, and she seemed to be giving me a signal, but it was not clear enough. I decided that, after the meal, I would go to see her. I would enter her room and lay my hand on her back. I would kiss her cheek, whisper in her ear. She would listen to me.

The chocolate pudding was served, Johnny's favorite dessert, but before we could take a bite, Mr. Baxter stood up and raised his glass. The room fell silent.

"I should like to make a toast to my youngest son," he said. "My dear Johnny, who has turned out to be stronger than everyone expected. I cannot tell you how happy I am to have you back in our midst, Johnny."

We raised our glasses and drank to Johnny.

"But," said Mr. Baxter, "Johnny's miraculous recovery is not all that we are celebrating this evening."

I believe that, at that moment, I knew. It was as if the room started to spin, slowly but unmistakably, and something in my throat prevented me from breathing.

"Isabella and David. It gives me great pleasure to officially announce that my dear daughter has found the man with whom she wishes to spend her life and that the man in question is someone we all know and love so well. Yesterday he asked me for her hand in marriage, which I immediately and in full confidence granted to him, on the condition, of course, that Isabella agreed. I am delighted to tell you that she has done so. David and Isabella are to marry later this year. Congratulations!"

THE NIGHT WAS long and there did not seem to be enough oxygen in the room. I had lain down on the bed, still in my evening gown, in the dark, and I tried to breathe. My heart was hammering, my fingertips tingling. My legs and arms grew heavy. I sank. I drifted into the depths of the sea, where it is always night. Now and then I felt a fin skim past me, sometimes affectionate, at other times sharp as a knife. I had stopped breathing. The silence around me was complete. This was where the sadness was kept when you could no longer go on. This was where it sank to when it fell from your hands. It found its way out into the open sea, plunging into the waves, where it would wait for you, in the cold deep wetness. It could not disappear, but you had let it go, it would wait until you came in search of it, on the bottom, in the night. You would not be able to see your hand in front of your face, but that did not matter, because sadness has no color. And you would not be able to hear it, because sadness has no sound. But if you found it, then you could feel it: soft as the tenderest kiss on your cheek, but as painful as the wound it left. This was where your mother lay, this was where your child lay, this was where your words lay, softened in the darkness, detached from the paper. And you could cry, you could keep tugging at your mother, limp and heavy at the bottom of the ocean, but the seaweed was already growing on her face. You could try to take your child with you, but you soon found out that only the seawater was keeping her whole.

And would you dare to swim after your words? Would you dare to fish them up and deposit them on the beach? Would you dry them, letter by letter, so that everyone could read what was written there? Would you dare to re-create it all?

October 26, 1812

My eyes were rimmed with red, but I pretended I knew nothing. My heart pounded in a disturbing rhythm and my stomach clenched painfully, so I knew I would be unable to tolerate any food. I showed no sign. My deepest thoughts were chaotic and desperate, but I smiled with every step that I took outside my bedroom. I believed I had little time.

ISABELLA WAS STILL sleeping when I knocked on her door. Her voice croaking, she called me in. One shutter was half-open, and the morning sun shone through, its light reflected in the mirror opposite her bed. She sat up a little.

"What time is it?"

"We need to talk," I said.

She seemed to oscillate between resistance and genuine interest.

"You are getting married," I said. "To Mr. Booth." Did it sound as ridiculous to her as it did to me?

She gave a small sigh.

"Why?" I asked.

She slid over a little and patted the bed, as a sign that I should come and sit beside her.

I smelled her scent, her pure Isabella morning scent that the day had not yet crept into. My eyes began to fill with tears, and I closed them for a moment to hold them back.

"David is kind to me. That first and foremost. He is family. He is respected and wealthy." She seemed almost unemotional. She did not look at me, stared at the blanket and picked at it.

"Do you love him?"

She nodded firmly, and the strange thing was: it did not pain me. Because I did not believe her.

I shook my head. "I don't know what has happened," I said, "but this is not like you. Dear Isabella, you and I, we would never marry a man like him. Don't you remember?" My voice made a strange, sad crack.

"We have talked, David and I. Very long and often, after you had that fall. I came to know him. Really know him, I mean. He has a good heart, Mary. You have no need to worry."

I jerked to my feet. "Our friendship . . ." I searched for another word. I did not find one. "How is this possible?"

Isabella reached for me, but I pulled my arm away. She looked at me, her eyes large and bright—and, it seemed, sincere. "What did you think was going to happen? How did you think this would end?"

I took a deep breath. Then I turned around and walked to the door. With the handle in my fingers, I said, "Not like this." Then I left her on her own.

I FOUND ROBERT by the woodshed at the side of the house. He was wearing work trousers and a shirt, with the sleeves rolled up. It was properly autumn now. Under the eaves, new spiders were beginning new webs, and old leaves were beginning to let go of their trees. Robert stopped chopping wood when he saw me approaching. He was sweating and there was a deep frown line between his eyebrows. Hope swelled within me that he was as opposed to this intended marriage as I was. Then his frown disappeared.

"What news, eh? My big sister." He smiled. "Life can take strange turns."

"Yes," I said, "strange indeed."

It took me some time to decide how to proceed.

"Do you think he's good for her?" It was burning inside me. I swallowed a few times, held on to the woodshed.

Robert nodded. "Don't worry, Mary. We've known Mr. Booth so long. He's family. He was good to Margaret and now he'll be good to Isabella. I have seldom seen her like this. You know how she was: aloof, unreachable. Now I see that she's happy."

I thought about her. About her skin, her scent, her hair. About the wet warmth between her legs. Her mouth. A joke, a grin. For a moment it felt as if she were behind me, her touch featherlight laying her hand on my waist.

I nodded. "That's good," I said.

He was about to continue chopping wood, but then I said, "I don't believe that Margaret was very happy."

Robert looked at me for a time, not unfriendly, but cooler than before. Then he said, "Mrs. Thomson came to talk to me this morning as well. The news is spreading fast."

"Mrs. Thomson? From the church? Doesn't she want Isabella to marry?"

Robert looked at me, confused. "Of course she does. She is merely concerned. Isabella is intelligent, just as Margaret was. She said she hopes that Mr. Booth will give her every opportunity to flourish." He was silent for a moment. "He will do so, I'm sure of that. He loves her."

A slow shiver ran through me.

"Yes," I said, "of course." I turned around.

"Mary?" Robert took my hand. "You are a very good friend to her. Mr. Booth said the same. Isabella is lucky to have found such a fine friend in you."

I smiled and felt my eyes growing warm. I pulled my hand from his and began walking, down the garden path, through the gate, onto the street. Someone in town would know where Mrs. Thomson lived.

HER HOUSE WAS in a narrow side street off Arbroath Road, it was small, just one story. Rosebushes grew around the windows, here and there a withered rose could still be seen. I knocked and after a while Mrs. Thomson opened the door. She had a yellow checked shawl around her shoulders and a tea towel in her hands, which were covered in red jam.

"Mary! How wonderful to see you. Come on in." She stepped aside and I went in.

The house was packed to the eaves with everything from framed pictures to vases and brass figurines. There were two armchairs and she pointed me towards one of them.

"I'll just wash my hands," she said. "I'm making bramble jelly. Would you like some tea?"

I shook my head. "No, thank you. I just wanted to ask you something."

Mrs. Thomson nodded and went into the small kitchen. She soon returned with clean hands and collapsed into her armchair with a sigh.

"I've already heard," she said.

I must have given her a vacant look, because she smiled. "About Isabella and Mr. Booth. They're getting married, aren't they?"

It was hard for me to say yes. As if every time someone confirmed it, it became more likely. I nodded.

"Ah, you poor child." She slid forward in her seat and took hold of my hand. "That can't be easy for you. You have such a close friendship. I've often seen the two of you together."

I nodded again, using all my willpower not to start crying. "I don't understand," I said. "He . . . We . . . Do you know him?"

"Mr. Booth? Yes, I know him. Everyone around here knows him."

"What do you know about him?"

"What I know about him is not the same as what I think about him," said Mrs. Thomson. "He is a respected man. Wealthy, too. Very clever. Charming. Ah, but you know all that. A good match, one might say."

"But?" I was sure she knew something, at least that she felt something that I felt too. It was in the way she looked, the way she chose her words.

"I understand your concerns, Mary. I don't know much more than you, I'm afraid. But I see another side to him, as I imagine you do too. I cannot really explain to you what exactly it is, no more than you can. And that is our problem."

"Isabella felt it too," I said. "And now she wants to marry him."

Mrs. Thomson stood up and walked over to a cupboard in the corner. She removed the cloth that was over it to reveal a surface with several candles upon it, along with glass dishes with some sort of powder or ash in them.

"There's not much we can do," she said. "In my experience we have to put such things in God's hands. Pray with me. God's grace will be scattered over Isabella and the angels will guide her."

"Praying won't help," I said. "I want to know what he is."

"I can't tell you that." She started to light the candles with the lamp on the dresser.

"You don't know?" Maybe it was not a real question. I do not know why I thought Mrs. Thomson knew more about him. Because, like me, she saw the dark side in him?

"No one knows exactly," she said, her head turned away, busy with the candles, with rearranging the objects on the altar.

"I'm leaving." I had stood up and was walking towards the door.

"Come on, pray with me," she said. "You want to help your friend, don't you?"

I turned around and looked at her. There was a hint of irritation on her face. As if I were one of many people who had let her down, and her sadness had by now given way to indignation.

"I'm sorry," I said. "I'm sorry, Mrs. Thomson, but I don't believe in God." I opened the door and stepped outside.

"Why do you believe in Satan, but not God?" she called after me.

AS I WALKED back to the Baxters' house, I kept my arms wrapped around myself. I did not know what else I could do. I wanted to go and talk to Mr. Baxter. I had to find out if he had any doubts. If he truly, with all his heart, believed that Isabella had chosen Mr. Booth, and that he was the right man for her, would I be able to resign myself to it? Could I reduce the things I'd gradually come to believe since Isabella had entered my life to what they had once been: fantasies? The things that had emerged, become reality, that we had seen and felt, so real, could I simply forget their existence, as she had? That was not possible, was it? How could I deny the existence of something that had made me so happy?

MR. BAXTER WAS having tea and playing a board game with Johnny. It was a melancholy pleasure to see them like that; Johnny so lively, with a slight flush on his cheeks, Mr. Baxter laughing exuberantly, enjoying the game with his son, doom averted and almost forgotten. They sat on the rug in front of the big bay window, the sun laying a track of orange light across the board.

"Mary, will you play too?" Johnny immediately started putting out playing pieces for me.

I smiled and nodded, joined them on the rug. Johnny's fish head was by his feet. He occasionally stroked it with his fingertip.

"It's your turn," Mr. Baxter said to me.

I rolled the dice and moved my piece forward a couple of squares.

"Congratulations on Isabella's engagement," I said quietly. It still felt strange to say those words, as if they were a combination that did not exist.

A broad smile appeared on Mr. Baxter's face. "Thank you. Oh Mary, it feels like such a blessing. First Johnny makes a miraculous recovery and now my daughter is to marry the man we are all so fond of. It's what Margaret would have wanted, I'm sure of that."

I nodded. "I'm very happy for Isabella," I said, and at that moment I felt how much Mr. Baxter had longed for this, for the moment when Isabella would find peace with someone, would smile again, would be able to accept the death of her mother and the death of her sister and would live a life that would make her happy, and then, like a splash of cold water in my face, the question hit me: Was I right? Her family knew her, after all. They had known Mr. Booth for years. Maybe I had seen it wrong. Maybe I had seen everything wrong. Maybe I just wanted so badly to believe that it was all true.

I KNEELED AT her graveside. There was a layer of autumn leaves on the moss now, which I brushed away. What was I doing here? I had thought it was important, that this was the last thing I could try, but now that I was here, I had no idea what to do. Then I began to talk, and it all loosened up. "Hello, Grissel," I said, and I started telling her everything. I told her about Mr. Booth, about his parents, who were buried a few yards away and had both died in the same year. I spoke about Margaret, about her accident, about her sickness and her death. I told her about the fair, about the strange sensation in the tent, which both Isabella and I had experienced, but in different ways, about that evening with Mr. Booth when he showed us his snake, about his laboratory. I told her about the monster, how big it was, how hairy and how terrible yet pitiful its face had been. I told her about Isabella. About what she was like, how we were together, about how terribly I missed her, about how I was no longer entirely sure what was true and what was not, but that I loved her, that I loved her so much. How scared I was that Mr. Booth would hurt her and that I loved her. That I did not want to lose her, that I missed her, that I loved her. That I wanted to save her, but that she did not want to be saved and that I did not know how. That I loved her. I placed two shillings by Grissel's stone, covered them with leaves.

ON THE WAY home, I knew it was over. Isabella would marry Mr. Booth. And at that moment I longed so terribly, for the first time in months, for Papa's arms. For his thoughtful, stern voice. I longed for his smell, the scent of cigarettes and books, and for his big, soft hands. His eyes which, although ever critical, would always have a certain love in them. I longed for Claire, for her whining and utterly trivial gossip, I longed for Fanny's rare, fleeting smiles, when she sat in a corner, secretly listening to us. I even longed for Mary Jane, for her clumsy attempts at closeness, for her loving devotion to the cake she was baking, the dedication she could put into that, but not into us, not into me, but that was simply how she was, and how she kept on trying, with us, with my father, while the portrait of his first wife, his great love, still hung above his desk.

I DO NOT know how, but when I held the letter in my hands, I knew it would say that it was time to go home. The family seemed to sense it too, because they came to stand with me, Robert with his hand on my shoulder. My father had heard that my skin condition had been under control for some weeks now. He said that Claire and Fanny were missing me. And he had met a young, very talented poet, whom he wished to introduce to me. Percy Bysshe Shelley was his name. My boat would leave in three days' time.

October 29, 1812

I filled those last days with long walks. I roamed the harbor, saw the whaling boats being cleaned and readied for winter. They would not sail out again until the spring. I walked inland, along the paths I knew so well, sometimes striking out along a path I had not taken before. The heath was parched out, finished for this year, and the sparse trees were losing their brown foliage. Of course I thought about her. I thought about nothing else. I had not spoken to her again. As always, she spent a lot of time in her room, but she also went out often. She would take a carriage, to go to Mr. Booth's, I think. I dreamed that I had only been dreaming the past few weeks, that I told Isabella about it and she was horrified and laughed out loud at my dream, my ridiculous dream in which she was going to marry Mr. Booth, called him David. It was so real. It was really her. Then I awoke and was back in a world that was even more real, as that was what had been decided. I cried softly.

I AM SITTING on a low rock. In three hours, the boat will leave, and I will go back to London, back home. Isabella and I were here. We saw a monster. We were the only ones who saw it. Now nothing is there. Not a trace. Did we want to see him? Did we want to see him so much that it happened? Did we think him into existence? And am I now the only one who still wants that? Keep looking. I must keep looking. Keep writing. Because once there was a monster. He lived beside a rock, and he lived inside my head. He lived.

August 1816
Cologny

He lives, she keeps him warm

She gives Percy a telescope for his twenty-fourth birthday. They make a special day of it. They travel by stagecoach to Geneva, eat sponge cake at a small bakery, and walk around the town for more than an hour until they find the shop Albe recommended. They are given a tour of the shop by the owner, who wants to sell them not only a telescope, but also, if possible, a grandfather clock, a barometer, and a diving bell. This sends them into fits of giggles, and when they are back outside, with only the telescope, Percy kisses her so fiercely and unexpectedly that she is startled and almost bursts into tears.

They eat pies in a park, dark clouds swell in the distance, and she is happy.

BACK AT DIODATI. Claire is in tears. Tongue-tied. Mary takes her upstairs. She sits Claire down on the bed, gives her water.

"He says it's not his."

Mary's heart skips a beat. "Who?"

"Albe. He says it can't be his." Claire falls back onto the bed. She has closed her eyes. Her chest is going furiously up and down. Her breasts have grown, become fuller. There will be a baby who will long for them, who will cry for them. A baby who is soothed by her nipple in its mouth.

"But the two of you . . . You and Albe, in London, in the spring?" Much depends on Claire's answer. Much, everything.

Claire nods frantically. "Yes, it's his. I'm certain. It has to be."

There is a slight relief, but nothing more than that. She will have to make do with it.

"Percy will talk to him. Albe is just shocked. It will all be fine."

"Do you think he wants to marry me?"

Her sister. Is it a fantasy? Should she play along? Albe will never marry her. There are many stories, and many of them are true. About him and his half sister, about him and the affairs with married women, about him and his relationships with men at Cambridge and Harrow.

"If the child is his, he will take care of it," says Mary.

"It's his. It's his, Mary." Claire looks at her insistently.

Mary wishes she would shut up.

"Go to sleep," she says. "Just go to sleep and don't worry. We'll talk to Albe."

AT THE TOP of the stairs, Mary wonders if it will ever end. She can think of only one thing, one thing that is completely, entirely her own. One thing she must never lose.

◆ ◆ ◆

Percy and Albe have been out on the lake in their boat all evening; the weather is mild, almost summery, and now she hears Percy coming home. Mary was asleep. She was finally asleep, but now she is awake, strangely convinced of a change, a rupture.

He comes to lie beside her, his skin cool and taut next to hers. On her other side, she hears William cough. A dark strand inside her chest.

"Are you awake?"

She nods, strokes his arm, feels his muscles tense.

"Albe has agreed. He will accept the child."

"How did you manage that?" But Percy can do whatever he sets his mind to, she thinks.

"He does not want to support her. Not Claire, and not the child. He will acknowledge the child, but he won't include it in his will."

Something else is coming. Percy's words are faltering in an ominous way. She knows how he speaks. She knows what is coming. Not exactly but still she knows.

"I have promised him that I will change my will. Claire will receive a sum of money, as, when it is born, will her child."

She cannot speak. Percy is generous. He has lent her father money. And Claire is his friend, his sister-in-law. More than that. It is good of him. Noble. Foaming fury rises within her. She turns around with a jerk, tries to calm down as she listens to William's breathing.

"Don't be angry. What is she supposed to do?"

She does not want to say anything. She wants to grit her teeth, swallow her anger. But the poison seeks a way out. The poison wants a vessel to flow into.

"You know what people will think, don't you?"

"Mary . . ."

"You know. Now you're going to say that it doesn't matter, that no one will think anything, because it is going to be a secret. But such things do not remain secret. Because it's Claire."

"I'll take care of it, Mary. You have my word."

"And no one will know that you're doing this for her?"

"No one."

Percy's hand bridges the gap between their bodies. His fingers draw over the curvature of her back.

"You can't promise that."

"I just promised you."

She shakes her head. He does not see. He is drawing, drawing fiery lines of love and loss in her.

"Don't you understand?" she says. "You've already broken your promise. Because I know. I know, Percy."

The drawing has stopped. Percy turns around. It is quiet. "This has nothing to do with you, Mary."

It must be intended to reassure her. But it dissolves her words.

A FINAL WALK along the shore of the lake. Tomorrow morning, Percy, Claire, William, and she will travel through France to Le Havre, from where the boat to Portsmouth departs. None of them want to go back, but the money is running out and Percy's father will only help if he returns to England. The lake is glorious. Above the Jura, gray clouds hang, full and heavy as silver, and in the lake they swing under the pointed summits of the mountains, gently swaying in their mirror, edges shifting, like a dream.

She fears she will have to leave him behind. She fears he will not want to come with her across the Channel, to that other country. Maybe he belongs here. What if that is true? What if he remains here, among the pine trees, at the foot of the Jura, alone? Maybe he will think she has left him, but it is he who has left her, because everything leaves her in the end. Come with me, she says inside her head, come with me across the water, I cannot be without you. The story is not finished yet. Nothing responds to her, because he is inside her, she knows that. Does that mean that it is she who decides if he stays? If she awakened him, feeds him when he is hungry, leaves him alone to scream and cry, will he want to stay with her? Will he follow her as if she were his master? Mary smiles. Often enough it feels as though *he* is *her* master. It is he who decides what is to come, which words, which images. She bends her fingers, closes them around the quill, dips it in ink, makes letters, combines words until they are right. And afterwards she is empty. Empty and happy. Then she holds William tight and forgets for a moment that she had forgotten she is his mother. Then she is everything at once: a woman, a mother, a creator. Then she believes it is possible. Then she believes everything can exist, all at the same time.

AT DIODATI, the candles are already lit. Albe has asked Adeline to prepare a farewell meal. He and Claire have made peace, more or less. Albe will acknowledge the child if Claire demands nothing from him. Claire has agreed. In England, she will stay with them, with Percy and William and Mary. They will think of something. It is not forever.

Claire takes a sip of wine, gazes dreamily ahead, seems half-asleep. Percy and Albe talk about their work. John eats in silence, sometimes looks at her. Maybe she should smile at him; he looks so unhappy. Is she still angry? Does that matter?

BY THE FIRESIDE, they read aloud. Not their ghost stories, no, Albe had soon returned to his poems, Percy could not put his mind to it either. They seem to have forgotten about it. Mary has told them, by now, that she is working on her story. Percy said he was proud. Albe smiled. Now they are sitting together, as they did weeks ago, but differently. Claire is trapped in her impending motherhood. No one can do anything for her. John is also trapped, but only Mary will be able to free him. Percy is years older. He is sober; traveling tomorrow. He is reading Coleridge again. He is reading about the girl and the seductive woman who turned out to be a witch. Only Albe is unchanged, unaffected. And Mary? She is listening to Percy's voice, the voice she knows as well as her own breathing. The sonorous vibration when he pronounces the *o*, his hoarse *r*. She looks at him, her beautiful elf, and as he reads he looks at her. He looks at her. Every few sentences, as if he is reading for her, as if every sentence is for her. That witch, that witch in the poem changed shape, but why? Was that necessary because she could not be a witch otherwise? Is wickedness visible? Or is its very invisibility an indication that one will never know it, never entirely, never fully understand it? Does it show how each of them also has evil within? Selfishness, arrogance, pride?

And now she understands what it is about. Two women, they loved each other. Is one a witch? Does she cast a spell on her lover? Perhaps they were simply in love. And that was the only enchantment that mattered. And as Mary listens to the voice of her life, the voice that will always be there, she sees it.

◆ ◆ ◆

He was alive, she was sure of that. It was the end of the afternoon and she was walking back, all the way along the path, across the faded heath, beneath the gray sky of the last day. She held her diary beneath her arm, she was keeping it warm. She did not see him approach, although the hill was only a gentle slope. If she had seen him approaching, would it have turned out differently? Mary had not seen him for days, it felt like weeks, months even. He seemed to have become older. His dark hair graying at the temples, silver hairs in his sideburns. Mr. Booth walked towards her with a gait of certainty. Her heart stood still. Her arm twitched and her diary fell to the ground.

"Come, I shall walk back with you," he said. He picked up her diary from the path, brushed the earth from its pages. He held it for her.

There was no one else. The world was without people. She heard no birds, no animals rustling in the bushes. She held her breath.

After a time, he began to speak. "I know what you think about me."

How did his voice sound? How could she know for sure what lay behind it?

"I tried to warn you. What you are doing is not good, Mary. You are upsetting Isabella, yourself. Me."

She looked at him. His eyes, the exact same gray as the sky, were calmly waiting for her. She was no match for him.

"I do not believe that Isabella wants to marry you." She knew there was no point. She knew this would change nothing. That this conversation might just as well not happen.

"Mary, I want you to stop this. You have ideas in your head that are not healthy. Today you are returning home." Mr. Booth looked straight ahead, towards the harbor, which was still just a dot on their retinas, but within a few minutes would become reality.

"Leave everything here," he said. "And let her go. They were dreams, stories. Now it is time to forget them."

A wind arose within her. A flame flickered. "I can't," she said. And it was true.

"They are lies. It never happened. No one will believe you," said Mr. Booth. His voice pressed upon her, as opaque as dense fog.

She began to walk faster, but Mr. Booth was tall and easily kept up with her.

"This is the diary of a child. A child with no understanding. Do you know what they do to girls who write such things?" He held her diary in the air.

Mary raised her hand, stretching for the book, fully aware that she would be unable to reach it.

"What you have written is not without danger. You know that, don't you?" He stood still and looked at her for a long time. She saw a warmth in his eyes that she had never seen before.

"I just want to help you," he said. "It is time for you to grow up."

They started walking again. The path became firmer, they passed small houses with meadows full of goats and horses. People were walking on the streets. The harbor was ahead of them, just a few hundred yards. Clouds like blankets hung over the sea.

On the quayside, they stopped. The wind tugged at her hair, pulling it down, up, out of the grasp of her hairpins.

"What do you think?" asked Mr. Booth.

Mary looked at the water in front of her feet, glinting and splashing against the quay below. Her eyes felt dry and warm. They stung.

"Here." He held out the diary. She took hold of it and at that precise moment the last bit of humanity seeped out of him. The creature no longer had a body, no form; he was all forms at once. He was a mirage of ever-changing guises, from snake to fish to water horse, to something so unspeakably terrifying that she knew it must be the Draulameth.

"It is time," he said.

Mary held her diary with both hands, against her chest, to feel the words against her, to give them her warmth. She gazed up, into Mr. Booth's face. She could not look at it, he was looking at her so seriously but gently. Her gaze sank down into the water. She reached out, her words above the waves, opened her hand and they slipped through her fingers, and with the fall, which was uncompromising, the book landing flat on the surface of the water, instantly sucking itself full of sea, because pages are always thirsty, she knew that it was over. Then it sank, becoming a patch of light, increasingly hazy, until it could no longer be seen, far below her, among everything that was invisible and unimaginable, among everything that could not exist.

SHE CRIED AT the scent of Mr. Baxter's pomade. He hugged her so tightly that her rib cage hurt. Robert embraced her too, with, she noticed, tears in his eyes. He promised to write and she promised him the same. Johnny pushed his wet face into her skirt. She crouched down and had to hold him firmly by his shoulders, kissed his sweet head, wiped away his tears. His head lay on her shoulder. It was heavy and full of dreams.

Isabella took her hand. It felt as if an opaque layer between them fell away. Mary stood there, she missed her so much, and Isabella held her tightly. The scent that Mary knew was mixed with another, unfamiliar one. The skin of her throat was just as soft as she remembered, but it was no longer hers to caress, to kiss. Mary kissed her cheek, and when she looked up, freed herself from Isabella's embrace, she saw a strange expression on her face. An enchantment that, for a fraction of a moment, had been broken.

ON THE QUAY full of people, only one family caught her attention. One young man, one older, a boy, and a young woman, looking up at her, waving silently but constantly. She went on waving too and looking at them and looking and waving and waving, until long after the ship had sailed. Even when they had almost left the harbor and she could feel the swell of the sea on the deck under her feet. Until Dundee disappeared into the horizon. Only then did she turn around, look forward, out to sea, and beyond, to the land that still lay invisible ahead of her.

◆ ◆ ◆

On their return journey through France, they visit the castles of Fontainebleau and Versailles, and the immense cathedral of Rouen. And in spite of the beauty, that overwhelming and wondrous world, in her mind she is already at sea. In Le Havre, Claire whines that she already feels sick, and they search for an easy chair for her on board, into which Claire collapses, staring ahead at the horizon with dull eyes. They set sail and have no one to wave at, so they stay with Claire; Percy caresses her cheek, strokes her arm. His other arm is around William, who is sitting on his lap and keeps dozing off.

"I'm just going to go up on deck," says Mary.

The sun is so low that the sea becomes invisible, a surface of brilliant, pure light. Beneath which anything might exist.

Yes, she will write. It is her story. She brought it into the world. She gave it life, fed it. She will care for it, her sweet, true imagination, her monster, her growling, snarling, unyielding beast. He is back. In the twilit world under all that light she sees the things she had forgotten. There is a world of spirits and marshes, of water beasts, snakes, monsters, and witches, a world of gold filigree bracelets with stones glittering as deep and dark as the sea, a world of mirror images, of sheet lightning and birth. She holds on tight, her hands like claws on the rail, leans forward to look, to see, she makes no concessions, she is a woman, and her gaze falls down, into the water, and there she sees herself, it is her, in the midst of all those other things, all that she brought into the world. She stays there for a while, watching, wondering, remembering.

She comes back up. Her head is pounding gently. She blinks at the sun, cannot see anything for a moment. Then everything is there once more.

"Never leave again," she whispers so quietly that the words remain in her head. They would never leave again.

Acknowledgments

It was wonderful to write this story, and I have Mary Shelley to thank for much of it. I learned about Mary at the Keats-Shelley House in Rome, from Mary's letters, diaries, and biographies, not to mention the many helpful websites, including the Shelley-Godwin Archive. In those places, I found the slivers of a life from which stories can grow. Deep within, I hope Mary would have appreciated what I have done with the story of her life.

In addition to all my fabrications, many of the things in this book actually happened. I have tried to create an authentic story with a life as its starting point. That life has become dear to me. And the nice thing is, so have the fabrications about it, just as much.

I would like to thank the following people for their time, attention, love, and knowledge, which I experienced while writing *Mary and the Birth of Frankenstein* (and in many cases, in the rest of my life as well):

My dear family: Alba and Magnus, Pappa and Mamma, Judith
    My dear husband: Bertram Koeleman
    My dear Bees: Nienke Beeking, Katrijn van Hauwermeiren, Anne van den Heuvel, Merijn Hollestelle, Suzanne Holtzer, Jessie

Kuup, Uta Matten, Marijke Nagtegaal, Romy van den Nieuwenhof, and Soesja Schijven

Dear writers, dear friends: Ineke Riem, Inge van der Krabben, and Gean Ockels

Dear wise people: Willem Bisseling, Niek van Sas, and Bart Gielen

Texts to which I am indebted:

The Life and Letters of Mary Wollstonecraft Shelley, compiled by
    Florence A. Marshall, 1889
Mary Shelley, Miranda Seymour, 2000
Romantic Outlaws, Charlotte Gordon, 2015
In Search of Mary Shelley, Fiona Sampson, 2018
The Castle of Otranto, Horace Walpole, 1764
"Christabel," Samuel Coleridge, 1800
Frankenstein, Mary Shelley, 1818
At Home, Bill Bryson, 2010
An Illustrated Treasury of Scottish Mythical Creatures, Theresa
    Breslin, 2015

A Note from the Translator

Where does Mary stop, and where does Anne begin? Clearly, one of the perils of translating a richly detailed book about such an iconic figure in literary history is becoming sidetracked, both by the volume of fascinating background and research material and by one's own questions and pondering. My parents-in-law, Jane and David, live in St. Andrews, less than half an hour by car from Dundee, the setting for young Mary's stay. I have my own experiences of how the landscape there looks and feels today; Mary Shelley, however, spent her time in Scotland over two centuries ago. Dundee and its surroundings have clearly changed since then, but given my personal connection to the region and because I knew so little about the young Mary's stay in Dundee, I was particularly drawn to the parts of Anne's book that dealt with this particular locale.

How then does Anne Eekhout's vision compare to the reality of Mary Shelley's life?

Which facts did the author choose to employ in her account of Mary Shelley's life and literary creation, and which did she embroider upon or decide to let go? I found myself wondering how what I pictured when I read Anne's descriptions matched up with what she herself envisaged, then in turn how closely this reflected historical fact.

As Anne's book was written in Dutch but based on the lives and experiences of English speakers, much of the background material involved English-language sources. The background reading and fact-finding was a wonderfully engrossing process, often frustratingly so. As I translated Anne Eekhout's words, I followed her, treading along paths she had taken, while also dashing off along other tracks and taking detours that turned out to be only tangentially helpful to the translation even though they proved so engrossing to this translator.

For instance, if the author had written in the Dutch about beans and fish being served for a meal, what kinds of beans and fish does she picture then? How would the food have been cooked and presented? Is the meal that the author writes about based on a historical account, which might contain helpful information for the translator, or was it inspired more by the author's imagination? Are the author and the translator picturing the same kinds of beans and fish? Almost certainly not. How much freedom does a translator have?

Although beans and fish might be rather unremarkable subjects, they still sent me on long and winding paths. Other parts of the book proved even more rewarding and absorbing sources of fascination and distraction: those involving the history and the legends of the area. What tales of monsters would have been told in the city and surroundings of Dundee at the time Mary Shelley lived there? Which of the local tales had the Dutch author read and incorporated into her book? Which characters in the book were historical? Which fabrications? Why had I never come across the Draulameth before? Had I spotted a reference to Thomas the Rhymer?

Research helped me to answer many of the questions, and the

author was kind and patient, providing useful support and answers, not only through the sources she lists in her book but also through personal responses when it came to questions of the imagination. These are just some of the many questions that occupied me while translating this wonderfully atmospheric tale. There is only so much that history books can tell us. Our imagination must do the rest.